ACKNOWLEDGMENTS

"A big Thank you to my Port Moody Writers Group for their patience and good advice every week."

A Score To Settle

Gisela Woldenga

A Black Opal Books Publication

GENRE: MUSIC/SUSPENSE/SMUGGLING/MYSTERY-DETECTIVE

A SCORE TO SETTLE
Copyright ©2022 by Gisela Woldenga
Cover Design by Transformational Concepts
All cover art copyright ©2022
All Rights Reserved
Print ISBN: 9781953434708

First Publication: APRIL 2022

Published by Black Opal Books **http://www.blackopalbooks.com**

Chapter 1

Crash, thump! An angry outcry! Daniel jumped up from his desk. His mind had been far away. He pushed his chair back. *Julian again, so impatient.* Daniel opened the door to the music room. His son sat dejected on the piano bench.

"What's happening, Julian?"

"I'll never learn this, never," the boy hissed through his teeth.

Daniel picked up the music book from the floor. "It's not the book's fault. Don't smash it around." He sat down beside the boy. "What part can't you get?"

Julian shook his head. "I don't want to see it."

"Okay, take a break."

Julian looked at his father hopefully. "For the rest of the day?"

Daniel got up and sighed. "If that's what you need, all right, but…" he pointed a finger at him, "only if I see your essay for tomorrow finished and done well."

Julian slipped off the piano bench. "I promise." He looked up at Daniel again. "I want Mama to help me."

Don't we all, Daniel thought. "I know, buddy, I do and Mia does, too. But Mama is somewhere else now. We have to try and work through it." He put his arm around Julian's skinny shoulders. *He needs to eat more.* "Talk to Mama tonight."

Julian nodded and climbed up the stairs to his room.

Daniel went back to his studio, sat down at the desk, and looked at the score of Brahms' Fourth Symphony in front of him. How thoughtful this work was, the composer's last one. Daniel leaned back in his chair. After five years as their music director, the San Francisco Symphony had asked him to stay on. With his other duties at the Seattle Chamber Orchestra and various jobs as a guest conductor in different cities, everything was just going perfectly. Too perfectly, as it turned out. He missed his wife Elvira beyond anything he had ever lived through. Elvira had started to complain about tiredness, pain, and bruises at the slightest bumps. The result of the tests showed leukemia. After the usual uncomfortable treatments of chemotherapy the cancer had gone into remission. However, everyone's hopes were dashed the next year. Even more treatments could not slow down the inevitable end.

Young, beautiful, the love of his life, a wonderful mother, talented cellist—gone. Erased from this world. Like a zombie, Daniel had floated through his work to stay upright and functioning. Then he'd wanted to leave, to be anywhere but here. But what about Mia and Julian? To tear them out of their schools, away from their friends, would only add more pain to their grief. In the end, Daniel's job, the beauty of the music he performed, brought him back to some normality. That was two years ago.

"Dad," came a call from upstairs. "Where is the dictionary?"

"Probably in Mia's room," Daniel called back.

Then there was Mia, Elvira's first child, he had adopted. She had been amazing. Fourteen when Elvira died, now sixteen, she had turned into a beautiful girl with great strength and determination. Even though heartbroken by the loss of her mother, she had taken over household duties, almost like an extension of Elvira. Although trying to be tough, Daniel often saw tears running down her cheeks while she was doing the dishes.

She also was a great help for Julian, who was only ten now. To make things a bit easier she had suggested, "Pretend to have a conversation with Mama every night before you go to sleep."

Julian had told him, "Girls write diaries, I'm talking to Mama."

Daniel had to admit, he talked to Elvira often enough standing in front of her picture on the mantelpiece. But he had to be careful. If he did it too often or too long, his heart started to break into pieces all over again.

The dingle of the telephone interrupted his reverie. My agent, he thought. She must know when I need a break from thinking. "Portland Opera needs help with *Aida*," Gwen Curtis told him. "The conductor has to go through chemotherapy and is not feeling up to it. He will assist but can't do the performances. Can you help?"

Chemotherapy! I know what that means. How many people have to go through this? "When is the opera planned?" Daniel asked.

"Next month. It's in rehearsal now."

Daniel ran dates through his mind for his own performances here—two nights for an international composers' concert, new rehearsals for *Carmina Burana,* and two nights at Seattle's Chamber Orchestra. "I'll call you back, Gwen. Let me check my dates." He got up and looked at his plan tacked up on the wall. It would be a tight fit between rehearsals and performances. Maybe the assistant conductor could take over some of them. People had helped Daniel during Elvira's problems, so the least he could do is to try to do the same. He would be in Portland for five days, a bit long for the kids to be alone. Babysitter time.

Daniel called Gwen Curtis back to confirm his help and asked for more detailed information. He heard the back door and Mia's voice, "Hi, I'm home."

Good, Daniel could talk to her about this right away. He met her in the kitchen and gave her a hug. "How is my favorite daughter?"

Mia groaned. "Your only one, you mean."

He chuckled. "Yeah, at least I think so. Nobody has said otherwise yet."

Mia gave him a poke in his side. "Were you such a Casanova?"

He knew she liked to banter. "Only when I was overwhelmed by the beauty of you women. But listen, next month I'm going to be away." He told her about his appointment.

Mia filled a glass with juice. "We don't need a babysitter, Papa. I'm sixteen, I'm babysitting others myself."

Daniel knew this was coming. "It's a five-day stretch, night and day. You and Julian go to school, need food. Somebody has to be here to keep you guys in check." He had to make it sound a bit funny. "I think Mrs. Gantrey next door would love to stay here and look after you. She used to before."

Mia sighed. "Okay, as long as she lets me go to my friends after school without flipping out. She actually makes a good pizza. Julian likes her."

"Good, that's done. What's for supper?"

Mia laughed out loud. "Left-overs."

Daniel rubbed his chin. "My artistic nature needs something inspiring. Let's go out tonight." He got no complaints from his kids about that.

Chapter 2

On his way to rehearsal the next morning Daniel's thoughts returned to *Aida*. From Gwen Curtis' descriptions, he remembered working with the two main sopranos for Aida and Amneris before. The tenor Radames' name also sounded familiar. It had been a few years since Daniel had conducted the opera. I better look into the details again, he thought Even though the music was so well known, the details between the big choruses and arias were just as important to him. *Back to the score.*

Just then he noticed the car beside him speeding up and trying to get in front of him. Daniel had barely time to slam his foot on the brakes and blast the horn. "You darn fool!" he yelled. "Are you crazy?" He tried to take note of the make of the car and the license plate number. A blue Lexus sedan. But the numbers registered only partly in his brain: 951something, VL something. By that time the offending car had sped back into the other lane and raced ahead. Daniel looked into his rearview mirror. Luckily the car behind him had been far enough back to be able to slow down safely. Lord knows how many times this guy has done it before and is going to do it again, Daniel thought. He took a deep breath. *Onto the rehearsal.*

At the Symphony Hall, Daniel heard the sounds of practice. He smiled. *My loyal band:* his favorite name for the musicians. Without their enthusiasm and hard work, he wouldn't have a job. This morning was the last rehearsal for two nights of French composers: Saint-Saens' Bacchanal from *Samson and Dalilah*, Bizet's *L'arlesienne Suite,* and then Caesar Franck's one and only symphony. Daniel liked the variety, light and serious.

On his way to the podium thoughts of the offending driver came back into his mind. I should call the police and make them aware of it, he thought. He could already be on their list.

Except for a few timing corrections, the playing of the first part went smoothly. It would be a good concert tonight. During lunch and before the symphony Daniel got a phone call from Mia.

"I'll be a bit late after school. My singing teacher is in hospital for observation. A car knocked her over and drove away. I want to visit her."

A big, red flag popped into Daniel's mind. "Would she remember what kind of car it was?"

"I can find out, why?"

"I had a close encounter with a speeder this morning. Now you be careful, okay? See you later." Could it have been the same crazy driver from before? Even if not, Daniel was going to alert the police. *Another coincidence like so many in my life? First back to work with Franck's masterpiece, powerful, mysterious, and sometimes ominous in character. Like for me this morning.*

For the next hour, he kept his mind on the symphony. As usual, he got so taken over by the music that he forgot the time. When he heard a few sighs from his musicians after another repeat, he knew he had to wrap it up. "Good work," he called, "see you tonight."

The manager came up to him. "You won't forget the meeting tomorrow morning, will you? It's important, we need your input."

"Oh yeah, thanks for reminding me." *And there I*

thought I could sleep in. "Money again?" *Wasn't it always?*

The manager gave him a lopsided smile. "And other things." He waved and wandered off.

Daniel's phone rang. Mia. "Miss Lewis said it was a blue car. But she doesn't know which kind."

"Aha," Daniel said. "I know what I have to do. Thanks, Mia." On his way home he drove to the nearest police station. It had to be the same driver. He needed to be taken off the street.

The policewoman looked up from her paperwork. "What can I do for you, Sir?"

"My name is Daniel Abogado…"

The woman's eyes lit up. "Oh, you are the conductor of our symphony. I'm glad to meet you. I go as often as I can."

"I want to report two incidents involving the same car," Daniel continued. He explained the first one on the road and his suspicion about the hit-and-run later.

She took a breath. "You're a big help with the description of the car, even if it's not complete. We might contact you later if that's okay with you. I mean, you're a busy person." She gave Daniel a big smile and a piece of paper. "Keep this number. Now you're in the system."

Daniel handed her his phone number and address. "That driver is a menace. I want him to be caught."

The woman nodded. "I'll pass your info on right away."

On his way home, Daniel had to smile. Another music lover, how good to know. It made him feel better that he had reported the driver of that blue Lexus, even if he wasn't involved in the hit-and-run.

Mia had just arrived when Daniel got home. "How is your teacher doing?" he asked.

"She has to stay one night in hospital because she might have a concussion." Mia grabbed two cookies from the cookie jar. "She feels okay, though."

"Where is Julian?" Daniel hadn't heard any piano practice.

"Upstairs, working on some math."

"Okay." He headed toward his studio. "I'll be working on *Aida*." He knew Mia would be coming up with something for supper—or not. It didn't matter to him. He would have to leave for the performance tonight anyway. He only needed something light. It amazed him again and again how he could rely on his daughter to keep the house running smoothly. It also worried him that it would be too much for her. She had school and singing lessons. Since Mia had a good, strong mezzo-soprano voice, Daniel and Elvira had encouraged her to be serious about it. After Elvira's death, he had asked her to think about playing the cello like her mom. But Mia had shaken her head. "Definitely not. I would never be as good as Mama. It's too late to start. I'll stick to singing." *What a logical girl.*

Daniel dug out the score of *Aida* from amongst stacks of other scores and shut out any other thoughts. Soon the notes in front of him resonated in his mind and turned into the love of his life: music. "No better job in the world," he mumbled.

When Daniel was interrupted in the middle of Aida's and Radames' death scene, he got annoyed. "What is it?" he called rather sharply.

"It's me, Papa," he heard Julian's quiet voice.

"Oh, okay, come in." *I should have known.*

Julian opened the door. "Sorry, but I have to talk to you."

"That sounds rather serious." Daniel turned around and looked at his son.

Julian showed him a piece of paper. "From school. You have to sign that it's okay with you. Some of our class are supposed to go to an old people's home and do something for them."

Daniel took the sheet of paper. "What are you supposed to do?"

Julian shuffled his feet. "Play the piano."

"That's great. Show them what you can do. That's an opportunity."

"But what should I play? What if I'm flubbing it and can't remember?" Julian's dark eyes were worried.

Daniel sat up. "Listen, Julian. Take the music with you, never mind memory. Play something you have learned before, not the hard stuff. Don't panic over a wrong note. Nobody knows the piece like you, they won't notice. It's your choice what to play."

Julian wasn't quite sure yet. "How much should I play?"

"I think two pieces or one of your sonatinas. Don't worry so much. You have to start sometime to play for people."

With a small sigh, Julian took the paper back. "I'd better get working then. But I don't want you to come and listen."

Daniel laughed. "No chance. I don't have time. When do you have to go?"

"Day after tomorrow."

"Okay, review the pieces you want to play. You'll do great."

"Thanks, Papa." Julian went and closed the door behind him.

Daniel put away the score of *Aida*. He remembered how he felt the first time he played in a concert in church. *I figured I knew my music but alone up there on the podium was scary. I wasn't so sure anymore. It had gone well and it gave me enough confidence not to worry so much. Julian is a good player for his age and likes the piano. He just needs a bit of success.*

Daniel looked at his watch. *Time to get ready for the concert.*

✂✂

On his way to the dressing room, the assistant concert-master called to him. "Maestro, the concertmaster is in hospital. I'll take over today."

Daniel stopped. "What? He was fine this morning."

"He already didn't feel right, and it got worse–high fever."

That's all I need. "Good Lord. I hope nobody else gets it, whatever it is." Daniel clapped the musician on the shoulder. "Have fun being numero uno."

"Will do my best." The assistant jogged away.

Daniel changed into what he called his monkey suit—spats, black bowtie, and shiny shoes. Even though many conductors now wore casual clothes, even turtlenecks, he still liked to dress the old-fashioned way. He thought back to his concertmaster. With a big orchestra like this Daniel had to expect sick people now and then. A concertmaster was trickier, being the second in command. Daniel could only hope that his sickness was not serious.

The audience greeted him with applause when he strode to the podium. Soon Saint-Saens's Bacchanal filled the symphony hall.

The performance went well. Caesar Frank's symphony at the end got a standing ovation. It surprised Daniel and made him happy. *Maybe because it is not performed too often, they appreciate it,* he thought. *One more time tomorrow.* The assistant concertmaster did well too and Daniel told him so. But he wanted to know how his number one was doing.

"Can you find out if Gary is still in the hospital?" he asked.

The violinist nodded. "I'm going over to find out. See you tomorrow."

On his drive home, Daniel turned on the radio. Was there any news about the driver of the blue car? Did they find him? He hoped the police would call him if they had. He would probably have to identify the car. Maybe it wasn't important to contact him. After all, their forensic team would take care of everything. *Well, more time to dig into the music of our next concert, Carmina Burana.*

For a long time, he had wanted to perform this work again. With its medieval text, choir, soloists, and its interesting rhythms, he had loved it the first time he heard it as a child. He was sure Mia and Julian would like to finally hear the whole thing. They had only listened to bits and pieces of it. Both of them were already singing along with them whenever they caught them on the radio. Mia should be in this choir. Daniel would suggest it to her.

Wouldn't it be wonderful to come home to Elvira and discuss all of this with her? Daniel sighed, drove into the garage, closed the door, and went upstairs. He still had the habit of looking into the living room, expecting Elvira to be sitting there waiting for him. *How can life be so unfair?*

He checked on Julian who slept peacefully. Mia's door was closed with a *Don't Disturb* sign hanging on it. Daniel chuckled. *One already grown child.* She would leave a note if he had to know something important. *Okay, I'm ready for bed—after my customary brandy. Better get used to drinking it by myself.*

Chapter 3

The soft chime of the alarm clock woke Daniel. He grunted. *Already?* He opened one eye. Yes, eight o'clock. *Why do they plan meetings in the morning? Why not in the afternoon?* Daniel untangled his legs from the cover and yawned. *Okay, I am the music director, meetings are part of the job. A shower might put me in a better mood.*

Finally dressed, Daniel looked into the mirror. He avoided it as much as possible, but then—he was fifty years old. Not too bad for that. His hair was still dark, curling around his ears, with only one or two white hairs which he could still conceal. And so what? He could look distinguished with marbled hair. *Oh, vanity.*

Mia and Julian were already in the kitchen: Julian spooning up his beloved Cheerios, Mia toasting a slice of whole-grain bread. The sun-painted colored spots around the walls from a prism in the window.

"Why are you up?" Mia asked.

"A meeting at ten." Daniel cracked two eggs into a bowl and added some canned milk.

"What about?"

Daniel sighed. "Money, selection of music, money, selection of singers and soloists and—money." He poured the eggs into a frying pan.

"I thought the symphony was rich with all the people

coming." Mia drank some orange juice.

Daniel scooped the scrambled eggs into a bowl. "The soloists are asking stiff prices these days. Then the upkeep, wages, managers, director—no end to it."

Mia turned to go. "I have a singing lesson after school. My teacher is okay."

"And what about Julian here alone if I'm not home?"

"Mrs. Gantrey is coming," Julian piped up. "I have to practice piano for tomorrow."

Daniel got up. "I have to say, you guys are organized. See you at supper. Be safe." He looked at the dishes in the sink. *I'll take care of them later. Might as well help out.* The phone rang. *What now?*

"Mr. Abogado?" an official-sounding voice asked.

"Yes, speaking."

"This is Inspector Lankin, police headquarters. Would you be able to come in for an interview this morning? You are a witness of the blue Lexus from yesterday, is that correct?"

"Correct. But I have to be at a meeting in half an hour. Can I come after lunch?" *It never fails, all at the same time.*

After a pause, the inspector answered, "Okay, let's say one o'clock?"

"Good. I'll try and make it on time." The inspector hung up. That was fast, Daniel thought. Aren't there other witnesses to the accident? Maybe they didn't get the license plate number. Daniel grabbed the car keys and made his way to his car.

As usual, Daniel was the last one to arrive for the meeting. Director, managers, librarian, and some from the first chairs of various orchestra sections were already into discussions. He braced himself for a long session. After the first hour, they agreed on which two sopranos, two tenors, and one baritone to approach for next year's B-minor Mass by Bach and Massenet's opera *Werther*. Daniel had to outline his program of symphonies and concerts as well as tell them the times when he had to be in Seattle for the Chamber Orchestra and Portland for *Aida*.

At a little after noon Daniel said, "I have to leave for an appointment with the police."

"What? What did you do now?" The director's eyebrows rose in surprise.

"Not what I did but what someone else did. Just a witness," Daniel said.

"Well, good luck," came the chorus around the table.

When Daniel arrived at his car he found a note under the windshield wipers. "You are a witness and you are dead!!!" was written on it in capital letters. Daniel held his breath. A cold shiver ran down his spine. *Not again.* He had experienced criminal revenge ten years ago when he had prevented a beating on a street in Vancouver, Canada. Was he now getting himself involved again in something bigger than a crazy driver? He placed the note carefully on the seat in his car. *The inspector can try for fingerprints. How convenient that I'm going there.*

At the police station, a sergeant ushered Daniel into the inspector's office. After the introduction Inspector Lankin waved to the chair opposite him. "You might as well sit down, Maestro."

Daniel looked up in surprise. "It seems I'm famous around here. I also have a surprise for you, Inspector." He pushed the note across the polished table. "This appeared on my windshield today."

Lankin whistled. "Really? Not good. So, he's going to the next level." He retrieved a bag out of a box on a shelf and gingerly deposited the note into it. "Usually someone who runs over people doesn't go that far. Just tell me about your encounter with this speed demon."

Daniel repeated what had occurred yesterday morning,

pulled out his notebook with the partial license number, and read them out. The inspector nodded.

"We located the car after the accident, abandoned. We're testing for drugs. The owner had several outstanding fines and probably thought he needed a different car. He doesn't live at his old address anymore." He drummed his fingers on the desk. "Now we have to find his new one—and him." He turned to Daniel. "You didn't get a glimpse of him in the car, did you? Young, older, dark hair, blond?"

Daniel shook his head. "I had a hard time keeping on the road and out of his way. But—it looked like a younger man with dark hair if that helps."

"That's what the witnesses at the accident told us. According to our computers, the owner looks older. It's possible he wasn't driving. However, since it's his car that's involved in the hit-and-run we'll bring him in." Lankin got up. "Thank you for coming by. We'll try and find fingerprints on the note. Be careful. Any more threats, let us know."

They shook hands and Daniel made his way back to his car. Do I have to look over my shoulder again? he thought. How would this man have known who reported him and where I was this morning? Not only that but what about Mia and Julian? Could they be in danger? Daniel didn't want to scare them and tell them about the note, at least not yet. It might just be a bluff or this man was involved in more than crazy driving.

Daniel started the car. He needed coffee and lunch. At a restaurant? Better not, he had work to do on *Aida* and start on *Carmina Burana*, aside from the performance tonight. And the dishes in the sink. It had to be lunch at home.

☙❧

After a quick look through the *Carmina Burana* score, it occurred to Daniel that there was no need for Mrs. Gantrey to come over. He would be here working. He called her and apologized for the change of plans. Now he needed to treat himself to a short nap.

It was a rare occasion for Daniel to take that time but it gave him the opportunity to collect his thoughts. So much went on around him through his job that often plans and ideas for the children and the future fell by the wayside. Now he had to prepare for two weeks of *Aida* in Portland and before that four days in Seattle with the Chamber Orchestra. The life of a conductor often turned into a traveling one. In the quiet of the house stretched out on the burgundy couch with the velvet cushion under his head, he was able to assemble those things in his mind and maybe even fall asleep.

A *bang* woke him up. He listened. *Okay, Julian coming home from school through the back door.* Elvira used to bring Daniel a cup of tea whenever he woke up. That was then. *I will never forget the caring touches of her hand, however slight, and small actions like a cup of tea.* He ambled into the kitchen and put the kettle on.

"Isn't Mrs. Gantrey here?" Julian asked and threw his school bag on a chair.

"Hey, I'm here. Isn't that better?"

Julian frowned. "I guess, but I have to practice."

Daniel rinsed the mug. "Be my guest, practice. I won't listen."

"Okay. We had two guys snooping around on our schoolyard today. Principal chased them off."

Daniel's ears perked up. "Who were they?"

Julian shrugged. "Don't know. We are supposed to be careful and report stuff like that."

"I hope so." *Am I getting paranoid again? The threatening note and maybe going after my kids?* "Make sure you'll get a good look at any strange acting people around you. Are they young, old, fat, thin, what hair color, how tall?"

"Okay, okay, I didn't see them. Can I have a strudel?"

"Right. Go on and then to the ivories." *No use getting him anxious.* Daniel sat down with his mug of steaming tea. After a few minutes, he heard Julian running his fingers up and down the keyboard on scales and arpeggios. He was getting good. *Would Inspector Lankin get fingerprints from the note? Probably not. People like that wear gloves. Maybe the* lettering *will give something away.* Daniel just had to wait until he got an answer. He got up. Back to *Aida.*

❧❧❧

Mia came home shortly before Daniel had to leave for the evening performance. He could always depend on her. She brought some Chinese food which delighted Julian. "I've practiced hard, now I can eat," he announced.

What a character, Daniel thought, and he is *my* son. During his previous marriage, he had given up hope to ever be a real father. Julian had the dark eyes of Elvira but the face and figure of Daniel. Yrina, the Russian pianist he had worked with, had predicted at his birth, "He will be a heart breaker." Thank Heaven, that's in the future, Daniel thought.

On his way to the Symphony Hall, Daniel wondered whether Gary, his concertmaster, was back. The assistant had done a great job yesterday, but Daniel would be happy to see his first one in place. As it turned out, Gary was still at home recuperating.

The audience filled the hall quickly and, after the

oboe's A, the usual expectant quiet settled over them. Saint-Saëns, Bizet, and Franck soon filled Daniel's head, the whole space around him and—with his hope—the listeners. *My escape*, he thought, *carried away on the wings of music.*

During intermission, the stage manager called Daniel. "Telephone for you, Maestro."

"Who is it?" *It better not be a crank call.*

"Didn't leave a name, just said it was urgent."

Daniel's hackles rose. "I'm not talking to anyone without a name. Tell him to leave a message." It reminded him again of incidents years ago with taunting phone calls and messages. He wasn't going to fall for it again. Unless it was an emergency or a call from the kids he never answered the phone during a performance. Then a thought occurred to him. Did anyone call his house? To make sure all was okay he dialed his home number.

Mia answered right away. "What's up, Papa?"

"Is everything all right? Did you get any phone calls?"

"Just one where nobody answered, like so often."

I'm getting rid of the landline. "Just don't answer unless I call your cell phone, okay?" He could almost see Mia's questioning look.

"What are you worried about, Papa?"

Daniel took a breath. "Nothing, just a stupid call for me here. See you later." It would be better to tell her and Julian about the note, however disturbing it might be. They should be old enough to understand that not every person can be trusted. Elvira had drilled that into Mia already from an early age. Now it was up to him to relay the same message to Julian with carefully chosen words. Not good to give him nightmares. He needed to play for his recital tomorrow which had made him anxious. Right now his own thoughts needed to be expelled and drowned in the music of Caesar Franck's symphony.

The performance went smoothly with enthusiastic applause at the end. No matter how many performances Daniel had done, it felt so gratifying to hear that they were appreciated and enjoyed. It was worth the hard work and—sometimes—worry and small mishaps like differences of musical opinions between soloists and conductor.

As Daniel walked towards his car in the parking garage he saw a scruffy-looking young man leaning against the barrier to the elevator. *Is he waiting for someone? Breaking into cars?* Only a few people from the audience had trickled back into the garage. Daniel tried to ignore the man. He didn't want to give him a reason to come nearer. But the man did. He ambled towards Daniel with a big smile. "I'm waiting for a lady in the violin section. Are they still upstairs? And—eh—would you have a lighter?" He came closer.

"I don't smoke and I'm on my way home." Daniel made himself sound as short and snappy as possible. The man's smile turned into a frown. *Dark, cold eyes.* At that moment the elevator door opened and three of the musicians came out talking and laughing. The man looked at them, smiled again at Daniel, and walked quickly away.

Daniel let out a breath. Was he being saved by the appearance of his musicians? He trotted around the corner where the man had disappeared, but he had vanished. This person had not been waiting for any lady. An icy shudder went down Daniel's spine. Memories from years ago flashed through his mind when he had been kidnapped by an unsavory group of criminals he had unwittingly disturbed in their dealings.

"Who was that guy?" the oboist asked. "He looked sneaky."

Daniel opened his car door. "He most likely was up to no good. Good night. See you Monday morning."

On his way home he realized that reporting the bad

driver had not been a good idea. But finding out that the same man had run down a woman had been the turning point for him. Would he now have to carry a weapon with him? Or was his imagination running away with him again, and this creepy snooper had not looked for him but for an easy car to break into? Daniel was still hoping to hear from Inspector Lankin. Despite all of Daniel's negative thoughts his stomach growled. He looked forward to some left-over Chinese food and the sanctity of his bed.

Chapter 4

Daniel woke to a sunny Saturday morning. Nothing moved yet in the house. This was one of the rare weekends without a performance for him. Someone else took over for a more operetta-style evening. It gave Daniel time to organize his schedule for the next few months until the end of June. For *Carmina Burana* he needed an inflated percussion section with glockenspiel, bells, ratchet, castanets, tambourine, sleigh bells, xylophone, gong, and two pianos. The German composer Karl Orff used his music very effectively, even doubling some of the instruments. Daniel decided that one of each percussion instrument was enough. He preferred a clear sound over massive volume. The chorus could be left to the choirmaster, he would check it at the last rehearsals. Bach's B-minor Mass had to wait until Christmas, but Daniel had planned an international concert with Brahms, Tchaikovsky, and Debussy as well as Schumann's piano concerto sometime later. He already had an amazing, young pianist for it, Mark Hamel. Hearing him might give Julian a reason to go on working hard with his studies.

Daniel's cell phone hummed on the table beside him. *On a Saturday morning?* His agent Gwen Curtis' voice made him sit up.

"I have some good news for you," she said. "You are going to London, England, the first two weeks in July."

Daniel swung his legs over the edge of his bed and stood up. "Hold on a minute. The end of their season is June like ours."

"They're planning a summer festival with international composers and, of course, their own like Elgar and Britten. They want you to do it." She sounded excited.

Daniel raked his fingers through his hair. "What do you know. I've never conducted in London before. Why do they want me?"

"Daniel, why not? You're well-known for great work. Do you remember the English Youth Orchestra you saved years ago when their conductor was called away? The kids promised to get you to London. Don't be so humble."

Daniel sat down on the bed again. "You're right. What an experience that was. They're probably full-fledged musicians by now. Well, thank you for telling me. When do we get the details?"

Gwen chuckled. "As soon as you say, yes."

"Of course I do, who wouldn't? It will give the kids a holiday too. Let me know as soon as you get an answer." He put the phone down and took a breath. Wow, what an opportunity. As long as London didn't put in too much twenty-century music he hadn't worked on before, it would be exciting. Of course, with a bit of score revision ahead of time.

Daniel got dressed. Today was his pancake-making morning, he'd better get organized. Mia sat already at the kitchen table, sleepy-eyed. *My Lord, she looks so much like her mother with her curly dark hair around her shoulders. How many boys will fight over her?* "You're up early, why? Want to help with the pancakes?"

Mia smiled. "That's your job, Papa. I'll just eat."

"This afternoon I have to talk to you and Julian about two different things. But he has to do his recital first." Daniel put the strawberries on the table.

"But I want to go out to Sigmund Stern Grove with Cherryl. Can we talk after supper?" Mia gave Daniel a worried look and snatched a strawberry.

"What do you want to do? Swim, walk?"

"It's nice there for jogging and maybe some tennis. No swimming today."

Daniel plopped two pancakes on her plate. "Okay, as long as you're here for supper. And…"

"What, Papa?"

"Never mind, you know how to be careful, yes?" *No use talking about it now.*

Mia just rolled her eyes.

Julian padded down the stairs. "The smell woke me up."

Daniel set the whipping cream on the table. "Do you need a ride to the Old People's Residence, Julian?"

"No, we meet at the school, they take us from there at two o'clock." He sat down and cut his pancake into pieces.

All organized again, Daniel thought. Gives me time to do some quick walking around the neighborhood myself. The only exercise I like.

After Mia and Julian had left, Daniel got his walking shoes out of the closet. A half an hour's march would be good. What was the goal, 10,000 steps a day? *I'm way behind that by taking the car everywhere.* He just opened the front door to go out when a man with a toolbox came up the driveway.

"I am working my way through the neighborhood," he called. "Checking TV and computer cables. Can I come in?"

A twinge of suspicion traveled through Daniel's stomach. The man didn't look like the scruffy one in the car park, but these people didn't work on Saturdays, did they? "Sorry, I'm on my way out. You'll have to come some other time."

"Oh dear, that breaks up my route. Are you sure you can't spare fifteen minutes?" The man's eyes narrowed as he looked at Daniel.

"No, I'm leaving. And by the way, the house is alarmed." Daniel locked the door and stared right back into the man's eyes.

The stranger turned around. "Okay, okay, it's Saturday after all. Monday all right?"

Daniel started walking. "You can try." Shouldn't there be at least a small truck nearby with tools or whatever they use? he thought. *The real workers have logos on their jack-ets. This did not feel right.* He saw the man walking down the street to the next house. *I'm going to call my neighbor this evening and see if he actually has checked anything. If not what would the guy be looking for anyway? Something to steal at another time? Maybe even me?*

Daniel broke into a fast trot. The light breeze on his face felt good and the colorful flowers in people's front yards lifted his spirit. *If I could run away from my problems, I would do this more often.*

Daniel rounded a corner and spotted a small park with some benches. *Good, I'll sit for a while.* He had marched for twenty minutes and welcomed a minute's rest. The thought of going to London came back into his mind. *I wonder whether they have picked the music already or if I have some choices.* Why hadn't he conducted there before? Too busy elsewhere. He also wanted to go back to Vancouver as a guest conductor where he had started years ago. He smiled to himself. *Maybe I should clone myself.* He looked at his watch. *Time to make my way home.*

Close to home Daniel heard a police siren. *Strange for this neighborhood.* He sped up to a jog. People were standing in front of his house milling around a flashing police car. *What is going on?* He tried to swallow down a tightness in his throat. *Not us again, is it?* Daniel's neighbor came running up to him.

"Someone tried to break into your house, Daniel, through the back door. When the alarm went off, we called the police." The man was clearly upset. "I guess the guy ran."

Daniel's heart pounded. *What did they do to the house?* "Let me talk to the officer."

The officer held the phone against his ear. "Send them over now." He turned to Daniel. "Another Saturday break-in. We seem to have a few of them. Don't touch the door handle, we're checking for fingerprints. Can you check if anything was taken?"

"Right away." Daniel ran around the house. *What would have happened if the kids had been home? They wouldn't have had the alarm on.* He pushed the door open with his foot and walked into the laundry room. There wasn't anything of interest for anyone to take. Upstairs he found some dirty footprints. Maybe they should be preserved? His studio? The door stood open, but nothing seemed to be disturbed. *He must have bolted before he got any further.* Daniel went back outside through the front door. "Nothing taken as far as I can see. But there are footprints you could look at." He still shook and had to take some deep breaths.

The policeman nodded. "Very good. Here come the forensics team." He pointed to two female officers, went over, and spoke to them. They smiled at Daniel and went to the back door. Some of the neighbors wandered back to their own houses. Daniel went to talk to the people living next to him.

"I have a question, Greg." He explained about the person with the toolbox. "Did he come to your house?"

Greg shook his head. "We weren't home until later."

"Okay, another of those fakes." Daniel did not want to scare Greg anymore. But he knew what it meant—trying to upset and scare him and it would go on. He had to inform Inspector Lankin. But on a Saturday? Someone must be at the station.

Daniel went back into the house and called the inspector's number. A detective answered.

"Is Inspector Lankin in?" Daniel asked

"No, he's out on a case. What is it about?"

Daniel explained about the threatening note, the encounter at the parking lot, and the break-in. "Can I come in on Monday and talk to the Inspector?"

"You can try, Mr. Abogado, no guaranty. But I'll give him the message," the detective answered.

Daniel went into the kitchen and filled a glass with cold water.

The front door slammed, and Julian stormed in with a huge smile on his face. "I did really good. I only had one slip at the end. Nobody noticed and they clapped."

Daniel made sure he acted like his usual self and gave his son a big hug. "Didn't I say you could do it? Your first concert. But you did well, not good, right?"

"Sorry, *good* is faster." Then he frowned. "Some of the old people sat and slept, why? Were they bored?"

Daniel sat down. "Maybe they are quite sick and can't stay awake for the whole performance. Did your classmates do a good job?"

"Yeah, they danced and sang. And then we got cake and ice cream." Julian still paced around the kitchen. "I don't have to practice today, do I?"

Daniel laughed. "You already did. Any homework?"

Julian shrugged. "Ah—I'll go and have a look." With that, he skipped up the stairs to his room.

Daniel felt sad. As soon as Mia got home he had to dash their happy Saturday with the criminal intentions of other people. And all because he felt that lawlessness should be reported. In the meantime, he had to look into the freezer for some supper ideas. Stir fry? Soup? Wieners? Stir fry it would be. He heard Mia's voice.

"Why is the back door open?" She came into the kitchen with a worried face. "Anything wrong?"

Daniel turned on the microwave. "There was but not now. I'll tell you in a minute. Did you have a good afternoon?"

"Yeah, I won in tennis, for the first time. But tell me before supper."

"It's a long story, Julian has to hear it too." After Daniel called him, his son came ambling down the stairs. "Is it supper already?"

"No, and I want you two to sit down and listen carefully. I have some bad news and some good news. Bad news first. Mia, do you remember the driver who almost ran me off the road and then ran over your singing teacher? Well, I reported him to the police." Daniel told them of the threatening note, the strange man in the garage, the guy with the toolbox, and the break-in.

Both children stared at him. "Are they after you like they did in Vancouver?" Mia asked. "I remember how scared Mama was." Her hands were folded tightly, her knuckles white.

"Well, it's something like that. Somebody doesn't like the police to be involved and keeps trying to scare me. But the inspector has the note and Monday I'll tell him about the other things." He bent forward. "I don't want you to panic. I only want you to be extra observant and careful. Report anything strange, anyone following you, that sort of thing. And put on the alarm when you are in the house in the evening. Any questions?"

"Do we have to buy a gun, Papa?" Julian's eyes were big and serious.

"No guns in our house, Julian. Just locked doors and windows, and the alarm. The driver will be caught, he can't help himself driving too fast again."

Mia looked up. "What happens when you're gone to Seattle and Portland?"

"Mrs. Gantrey needs to be told. I'll talk to her." *She'll only hear about the break-in, which she already knows. The rest is too complicated.* Daniel took a breath. "Now to the good parts. Mia, would you like to sing in the choir for *Carmina Burana*?"

Mia's mouth dropped. "What? Really? Am I good enough?"

"With your singing lessons probably better than some of the other singers. You almost know the score already. You have to be at rehearsals. Would that work with school?"

Mia beamed. "I'll make it work. Yess! Yess! Thank you." She ran around the table and hugged Daniel.

"Can I sing too?" Julian asked.

Daniel shook his head. "Not yet. You're too young, this time there are no children in it. Besides, you had your debut today." Daniel got up. "Guess where we are going on our holiday?"

The kids looked at each other. "Somewhere on a beach?" Julian asked.

"No beaches, but exciting anyway, London, England. I have been invited to conduct there for two weeks."

"Wow!" two voices yelled. "Our famous Papa," Mia added.

"So, all is not lost. But think about being more careful than usual. Now, how about supper?"

"We should celebrate. With pizza." Julian was ready to go.

Daniel and Mia looked at each other. "Can we? Just this once? At least we can celebrate going to London," Mia said. Quietly she added, "The rest has to wait. Okay, Papa? I'll order." She was ready too.

Daniel nodded. What else could he do? May my guardian angel be as ready in the future as those two, Daniel thought.

Chapter 5

On Monday morning Daniel debated with himself whether he should try and see Inspector Lankin before ten o'clock rehearsals or after. He looked at his watch. Eight-thirty, Mia and Julian had just left for school. Daniel would have time to see the inspector first, that is, if he was in his office that early. *I'm going now.*

Traffic was heavy at this hour. Daniel checked his rear way mirror constantly, looking for another attack from the blue Lexus. The driver would have changed cars by now, he thought. However, everything went smoothly.

At the police station, Daniel got a big smile from the woman he had talked to the first time. "You are early, Maestro. I'm not sure if the Inspector is in already."

Another detective opened the door and looked at Daniel. "I think we talked on the phone the other day. It's Mr. Abogado, right?"

"Yes, I'm getting a little worried right now. Is the Inspector in?"

"He is now," came a voice from behind the detective. "Come on in." Lankin motioned to Daniel to follow him.

He closed the door of his office and sighed. "I heard you had more trouble. What's going on?"

Daniel explained about the man in the parking garage, the worker with the toolbox, who didn't go to the neighbors as he had told Daniel, and the break-in. "Someone doesn't want the police involved, and my reports put a kink into his plan, whatever that is. Have you found the driver?" *You should've found something by now.*

The inspector shook his head. "We know the owner now. We are checking everybody he hangs out with or is connected to, wife, girlfriend, whatever. He certainly wouldn't drive the Lexus anymore. He doesn't have a steady address either. What else is new. But we'll keep after him."

Daniel sat up straight. He couldn't suppress his impatience. "I have a suspicion that he's involved in more than bad driving. Since he didn't kill the lady on the street he would have been better off to come forward and pay up. Why make it worse by hiding? Maybe someone told him to lie low. By the way, the man in the garage had dark, long curly hair and a baseball cap. Could that help?"

Lankin tapped his pen on the table. "Could be. Are you turning into a detective now? Is music doing that to you?"

Daniel had to smile. "Well, everything is in the details, Inspector. But I ran into bad guys years ago. Their thinking can be devious. Did you find anything interesting on the note I left you?"

"The prints we found had grooves on them like from gloves, no fingerprints. Everything else is ordinary: paper, glue, colors. Not much to go on." He looked at Daniel. "Do you want police protection?"

Daniel stared at him in surprise. "How would that work? A policeman in my house and a bodyguard? I appreciate that thought but mostly I'm worried about my kids when I'm out of town. Someone might take that opportunity to get to me through them. They have a babysitter but they're also in school and with their friends, not always at home."

Inspector Lankin sighed again. "Kids are a worry, aren't they? Let me know when you are away, and I'll have a car cruising by your house at night. How's that?"

Daniel got up. "If that is possible I would be much obliged. Thank you. I'll leave you to your work and I'll tend to my rehearsals." He shook Lankin's hand and closed the door on his way out. He felt a bit lighter and pleased with the inspector's willingness to help. *Maybe I'm overblowing everything. But I don't believe in coincidences.* For now, he had to get his thoughts back to the rehearsals and organization of *Carmina Burana*.

❧❧❧

At the Symphony Hall, Daniel was happy to see his concertmaster back again. He shook his hand. "Welcome back. All recovered now? What was the problem? You still look a bit pale."

"Oh, I'm as fit as a fiddle now, pardon my pun," the violinist answered. "I had a severe kind of a bug. Too many around."

"Just to let you know, I'm in Seattle for three days this week. The assistant conductor will take over until next Monday. Now we better get started."

After everyone had settled down, Daniel looked over to the percussion section. "You'll have a great time with all your toys. I hope you appreciate what I did for you."

"Thank you, Maestro," came a deep voice amongst laughter.

Daniel opened the score. "We don't have the choir, so it will be a bit empty, music-wise. Our faithful pianist will fill in. Let's give it a go." With the strong chords showing the Wheel of Fortune his mind dove into the sounds of Karl Orff's mind Daniel wanted to recreate.

After two hours of repeats and corrections, the work sounded close to his ideas of how it should be. "After lunch, we have to work on some of the music for the international performance coming up. I'm going to be in Seattle Friday, Saturday, and Sunday. That leaves us a few days to put a finish on it." Daniel had Brahms' Fourth Symphony in mind, one of the four composers on the program and the longest piece. Right now his stomach grumbled and he was looking forward to a much-needed cup of coffee.

☙☙☙

Starting Brahms after Karl Orff needed some adjustments for Daniel as well as for the musicians. Daniel had the feeling that Brahms knew that this was his last symphony. At that time he was already sick and died shortly after the symphony's performance. Written in e-minor the emotions in the music wavered from tragic to thoughtful, then in the third movement to happy but back to sad at the end. Despite this Daniel didn't want it to sound like despair or a funeral. During rehearsal, he tried to give it a feeling of a life well lived by Brahms. It was almost three o'clock in the afternoon when he dismissed the musicians.

Daniel's phone rang on his way to the car. Julian's piano teacher. "Sorry to disturb you, but Julian didn't show up for his lesson after school. Is he sick?"

A hard fist punched into Daniel's stomach. *No! Not Julian.* He tried to steady his voice. "No, he's fine. If not, the school would have called me. Could he just be a bit late?"

"Julian got out of school earlier and wanted to come right after," the teacher answered.

"Okay, I'll call the school and phone you right back." Daniel's hand shook as he dialed the school's number. *He wouldn't go with anyone except Mia or myself. Not after what I told him.* Daniel paced around until he heard a woman answering.

He couldn't keep his voice from shaking. "Is Julian still

there?"

"Let me find out, Mr. Abogado."

Daniel heard her calling someone, then she came back to the phone.

"Yes, he's still here. He had a detention."

Daniel let out a long breath of air. "A detention? What did he do?"

The woman chuckled. "He got into a fight with another boy who apparently bullied him. They're being sent home soon. It was a surprise. Julian is usually pretty quiet."

Daniel leaned against the car. "Thank you so much. I got worried." He called the piano teacher back and arranged another time for Julian's lesson. In his car he sat and closed his eyes. He had to laugh. Julian fighting? What could that have been about? *I will soon find out. At least he's safe. Time to get home.*

When he arrived at his house he had to tell himself not to smile. After all, a detention was serious business. Mia and Julian were sitting at the kitchen table. Julian jumped up.

"Papa, I didn't…"

Daniel held both hands up. "You scared the heck out of me when your piano teacher called me. Especially right now with all the threats. But I want to hear your side of it. Just sit down and tell me."

Julian wiggled back onto the chair. "Jason is a bully. He bullies everyone. Since I play the piano he called me a wimpy-climpy and yesterday he called me an ivory-thumper. He doesn't even know what ivory is." Julian took a breath. "I yelled back at him and he pushed me against the wall and then…and then he put his fist into my stomach. It hurt. I stomped on his foot and he howled, 'You broke my foot.' Then the principal came out and took us into his office."

Daniel sat down. "You had all the right to defend

yourself against Jason. Don't the teachers know that he bullies other kids too? Why is he doing that?"

Julian shrugged. "Maybe for fun. And nobody fights against him." His hands clamped into fists. "I told him not to come near me again."

Daniel couldn't suppress the smile anymore. "Okay, easy there. Did the Principal give you two a good talking to? Did he listen to you?"

Julian nodded. "I'm sorry, Papa. But I couldn't take it anymore."

How dramatic. Daniel got up. "Come, here Buddy. You need a hug. Your piano lesson is tomorrow after school. So go and practice. I'm home tonight. I'll make supper."

After Julian went into the music room Mia started to giggle. "I guess, when he gets mad he really gets mad. I never thought Julian would fight with anyone."

"He had to defend his honor if it involved his piano and music. I was worried that something had happened to him."

Mia got up. "I have to go for *Carmina Burana* choir practice after supper. I'm excited."

"You can't be late so let's investigate the fridge." Daniel hoped that he could find some pork chops. After a day like today, he needed something solid. Parenting was full of surprises, and Julian wasn't even a teenager yet.

⁂

After supper, Daniel had just settled in his study when Gwen Curtis called. He had been waiting for an answer from London. "What kind of music do they want?" he asked.

"London has four concerts in mind: two nights indoors and two singles in a park. Since it's supposed to be international they want German, French, Russian, and of course Mozart. Because it's summer not too heavy or too long. There you have it. It's more or less up to you."

"All right, I'd better make up a list and dive into my scores. I'm sure management wants to know ahead of time. I'll make the park music a bit shorter than the indoor ones. Hopefully the weather plays along with us. Thanks, Gwen. Tell them I'll send my choices soon. Right now I have to think about Seattle and *Aida* in Portland."

In the back of his mind, Daniel had already been thinking of various composers who would be fitting for summer music. After the upcoming performances here and this busy weekend, he would have more time to select the compositions. Right now he needed to work through his own international performances. That included Rimsky Korsakov, Bizet, and Gershwin besides Brahms. He sat down with Gershwin's score of *An American in Paris* and hoped nobody would interrupt him.

After two hours Daniel got up. *What is Julian up to?* He walked up to his room and peeked into the door. Julian was reading in bed. "What are you reading? Homework?"

Julian sat up. "Papa, not this late. This book is great, all about some composers, like the Bach family."

Daniel was surprised. "You're really into music. It's good to know some of the differences between the composers, like their life and how they got started. But go to sleep soon. Don't forget your lesson tomorrow."

"But Mia isn't home yet."

At that moment Daniel's cell phone buzzed. Mia's voice. "Can you pick me up, Papa? Someone has been following me here and is still outside."

An icy lump formed in Daniel's throat. *Now Mia?* "I'll be there in ten minutes. Hang in there." *Another thing to tell the inspector.* He turned to Julian. "Hurry, put on your jacket. You're coming with me. Now!"

Julian jumped out of bed. "Now? Like this in my PJs?"

"I'll explain in the car." Daniel was already down the stairs when Julian stumbled after him. Daniel was out on the road in minutes. He screeched to a halt at the entrance to the rehearsal hall. He didn't see anyone in the front. "Julian, stay in the car, put on the alarm, and lock the doors."

He jogged around to the side. A figure stood under a tree. Daniel walked towards it. It didn't move. He called. "Are you waiting for someone?" No answer. *Dare I walk closer?* He stood right in front of the person when suddenly two arms shot out and shoved him backward with amazing force. When he tried to regain his balance Daniel saw whoever it was running through the trees.

In his anger Daniel had a good mind to follow but he knew he wouldn't catch him or her. *Darn it all! What are they trying to do?* In the dark, he could not recall the colors of what the person wore, except black. The head had been covered, slim figure could have been a man or woman. Only one thing stood out: the shoes. The stranger wore sneakers in neon pink with shiny shoelaces. Would a man wear those colors? Probably not.

Daniel ran back to the front door. The singers drifted out now and Mia stood on the steps by the door. Daniel waved and she ran down.

"Thanks, Papa. Did you see anyone?" She looked worried.

Daniel told her about his encounter with the mystery person by the trees. "Could you see anything about her or him, Mia? The clothes, a face, short, tall? I noticed some colorful shoes, shiny pink. It's the only thing I could see."

Mia shifted her shoulder bag. "What do they want with me? Am I now a target too?" She took a breath and continued. "The person looked shortish, dark hoodie or hooded jacket could be dark blue or black. I think it was a woman."

"She had a powerful punch, probably trained. Let's get home. I'll tell the inspector tomorrow. Too late now." *If I don't keep calm the kids will fall apart.* Although his chest still felt tight he changed the topic. "How was rehearsing?"

Mia smiled. "Awesome. Pretty tricky rhythms. We just did a few songs. The choirmaster is quite specific."

Daniel nodded. "He'd better be. I would be too."

In the car, Julian sat in the back seat huddled in his jacket. "You okay, Mia?" His face looked white in the streetlight. Mia threw her bag on the seat beside him and put on her seatbelts.

"I'm fine, just—careful. Right, Papa?"

All through the night, Daniel's thoughts drifted from one explanation to another why his actions of reporting a bad driver had caused such aggression toward himself and now Mia. Julian might be next. Daniel was now convinced that erratic driving alone was not the only reason. More seemed to be at stake here. What was he going to do? What was going to happen when he had to leave for Seattle and Portland? He truly needed the police to keep an eye on the house, at least at night. Daniel could only hope that no one else would know that he was away, except Mrs. Gantrey and the police inspector. *Oh, Elvira, why can't you be here to help me to look after things, to talk to me, so I can listen to your good sense and not feel so alone.*

☙❧

When the alarm went off at eight o'clock Daniel opened his eyes and closed them again. *I need more sleep.* But the ten o'clock rehearsal did not wait, and if anyone was late it could not be him. He scrambled out of bed, padded into the bathroom, and looked into the mirror. *I don't deserve this. The Lord help you if I catch you, whoever you are.* With a sigh, he went ahead with his daily routine and finally went down into the kitchen. As usual Mia and Julian were already having breakfast.

"It might be a good idea not to walk by yourself wherever you have to go," Daniel said and plopped two sugar cubes into his coffee.

"But nobody goes with me to piano lessons," Julian objected.

"Then stick with the crowd. It doesn't have to be a friend. All I'm saying, be extra careful. Promise?"

Julian nodded and stirred thoughtfully in his cereal. "As long as they don't beat *you* up."

Daniel had to smile. "Thanks for worrying about me. Just concentrate on yourself."

"Julian is right," Mia added. "You got kidnapped once."

"Not going to happen again." Daniel got up and dropped two slices of bread into the toaster. *Even though I might have to rely on my Guardian Angel.*

❧❧❧

Daniel's first destination needed to be the inspector's office. This time an officer sat at the front desk. "No secretary today?" Daniel tried to push his frustration down. *No use showing my anger.*

The officer leaned back. "Called in sick. Probably back tomorrow. You want to talk to the inspector again?"

"Yes, if possible. My daughter was followed yesterday evening by someone who stood and waited for her. When I approached I got a strong push into my stomach. The person ran away. The inspector needs to know."

"I agree." The officer nodded. "What's going on?"

Daniel shrugged. "I'd like to find out too."

After a call to Lankin's office, Daniel walked down the corridor and knocked on his door. The inspector looked up from a stack of folders. "I hear you had more trouble?"

Daniel told him what had happened. Again he tried to stay calm but couldn't help pacing around.

"This is getting serious." Lankin paused. "Well, one good news. We found the owner of the car who claims he wasn't driving, his friend was. Naturally. He hasn't seen his friend and all the rest. However, the fingerprints show that he was in the car. Still, no proof that he was the racer. And no proof yet that he's the troublemaker."

Daniel took a breath in. "At least you have a starting point. My daughter thinks that the person yesterday was a woman. By the size of her, I would agree. But she has a hefty punch. There should be some shoe prints under that tree. The ground was moist. And she wore some way-out shoes—bright pink with metallic laces. I wonder how many stores sell them." *Your job to find out, Lankin.*

The inspector rubbed his nose. "Being a detective again? But yes. Draw up exactly where she or he was standing. Maybe that person thought you wanted to attack her."

"Why? I called out to her. She was already there when my daughter arrived. She must have felt she was discovered." Daniel drew a map and got the promise that someone would go and check it out. One baby step at a time, he thought as he made his way to the rehearsal hall. *If I could just live my life without constantly worrying. At least I have music to rescue me for a few hours.*

Chapter 6

Before starting rehearsals Daniel got himself coffee from the restaurant. After his restless night, he really needed it. He sat down in the lounge and savored the taste. He remembered that the orchestra had to give a concert in the park on Saturday, this time without him. The assistant conductor had taken over, as well as Friday's rehearsal. It worked out well since Daniel was in Seattle. Half the glamor of being a conductor was organization and score studies, aside from dealing with management. But what incredible satisfaction came out of that work, the sounds of the orchestra, and the fact that he had the control to present them as close to the composers' ideas as possible. It's the only job I ever wanted, he thought. On his way to the podium, he hummed the beginning bars of *An American in Paris. This will be fun for a change. Away from the troubles that might await me.*

And it was. The musicians enjoyed the lively music interlaced with car horns and bells as well as the off-beat rhythms. They had a few laughs when the horns came in too early and Daniel called, "You are running over the pedestrians!"

At lunchtime, he wondered if he should call Mia and make sure she had no other encounters with unwanted watchers. Then he decided not to. She would phone if there was a problem. He didn't want her to feel hovered over.

She needed to feel that Daniel trusted her. Would the police ever get to the bottom of the real reason for the threats? Daniel sighed, finished his sandwich, and went back to the rehearsal hall. He wanted to do work on Rimsky Korsakov's *Russian Easter*. His colorful description of the Russian Orthodox festival needed precision in rhythms and a variety of instruments.

It took some starts and stops until Daniel thought the music sounded good enough to let rehearsals go for today. "Tomorrow Bizet and Brahms again," he called before closing the score. That way he wouldn't have to worry about being in Seattle.

On his way to his car, Daniel's phone hummed. He heard the precise voice of the police officer. "The inspector wants you to come in to identify a suspect, if possible."

Daniel thought for a moment. "But I never saw anyone close enough that I could identify."

"Come by anyway. We'll explain," came the answer.

Wouldn't it be wonderful to find the culprit, Daniel thought. Too much to hope for?

At the station, Inspector Lankin took Daniel to a viewing room. "We finally got a witness who recognized the person who drove the car at the accident. She stood on the other side of the street and saw the driver. I want you to look if he resembles any of the men who approached you."

Daniel's heart started pumping. *Another baby step.* "Fine, I'll try."

Four men walked into the room opposite the glass wall. Daniel tried to remember the man in the car garage: black cap, curly hair hanging from under it, unsavory.

"Take your time, Maestro," Lankin said.

Daniel focused on number three: long curly hair. "Can number three put on a baseball cap? I think that's the man in the garage."

From somewhere a cap appeared and number three stepped forward.

Daniel was sure now. "Yes, that's the guy who approached me at my car."

Lankin nodded and talked into his phone. Then he turned to Daniel. "Great, the witness identified him as the driver because of his long, curly hair. At least he's one of them, one we can put away for some time for injuring a pedestrian and not stopping. But I have a feeling there are more in the basket."

Daniel chuckled. "Funny way of putting it. But I agree. There is the so-called inspector of cables and the woman under the tree. Have you looked for footprints?" He couldn't help himself, he had to ask.

"Yeah, they're out there now. We'll see."

Daniel felt that Inspector Lankin didn't want to waste any more time. "Thanks for calling me, Inspector. Let me know what you find, please? I have my kids to think of."

"Will do." The inspector waved and disappeared upstairs.

ℰↃℰↃ

The empty house felt lifeless when Daniel arrived home. Mia and Julian were both at lessons—one for singing and the other for piano. As Daniel stood in the middle of the living room it seemed to be devoid of any feelings, thoughts, or human emotions that used to swirl around. Elvira would fill the house with her personality and laughter. *Here I go again, feeling sorry for myself. I'm the only string now that ties my little family together. Will I ever get used to it?* He turned around and saw the phone's voicemail button blinking. He had forgotten to cancel the landline. He pushed the button and heard a deep, threatening voice, "Now you've done it."

Daniel froze for a few seconds. A shiver ran down his back. *So, another attempt to scare me.* The voice sounded like the one on the first phone call. He got his digital recorder and transferred the call onto it. He was good at recognizing voices, this might come in handy. Many times the police had solved a case by comparing voices. Then he made a call to the telephone company and finally canceled the landline. To get his cellphone number would take a while longer.

He walked to the side table and Elvira's picture. *This might be strange to some people, but to me it's necessary.* Out loud he said, "Elvira, my love, are you listening? I'm coping all right but I miss you terribly, your common sense in any situation. If you can do anything, please, keep an eye on the kids. Sometimes I feel you close by and then again so far away. Be happy at where you are. I love you." Daniel's tears welled up and he turned away from the picture. *You are listening, I know it.*

The back door opened and closed with a bang. Julian. "Papa, are you home?"

"The door was open, where else could I be?"

"Well, maybe burglars?" Julian plunked his school bag on the floor and placed piano books on the table. "I got a new piece."

Daniel bent over the book. "Show me."

"A Mozart sonata. Boy, is that tricky." Julian wrinkled his brows.

"I'm proud of you. Your teacher must be convinced that you can do it. Get to it and don't be impatient with yourself." Daniel was surprised. *I hope the teacher isn't too ambitious.* "Look after your homework first. I have work to do too."

Julian nodded, poured himself a glass of milk, and grabbed a cookie out of the jar. Then he muttered, "I'll have to work hard. And Jason doesn't talk about anything else but baseball. Jeeze."

Daniel suppressed a chuckle. Apparently their feud was over. As long as Julian was proud of what he was doing, all would be well. Daniel went into his study, bent over the score of *Aida,* and tried to bring Verdi's music back into his mind.

∽∾∽

The next morning's rehearsal dragged on a bit longer than usual. Daniel wanted the assistant conductor, William Brown, to listen since he would take over on Friday. He selected Brahms and Rimski-Korsakov, music as different from each other as possible. William took notes and, during lunch, Daniel discussed a few sections with him that he thought were important. Finally he was ready to dismiss the musicians.

"I wish you luck for tomorrow and the weekend concerts," Daniel said and shook William's hand. "I appreciate you filling in for me."

William smiled. "Great opportunity for me, Maestro. Have a good time in Seattle."

Yeah, if it wasn't for the constant threats. Daniel had called the police and told them about the phone call. They had promised to keep an eye on the house. Now he needed to prepare for the flight to Seattle tomorrow morning. It was important to get one day's rehearsal in before the concert.

Mia and Julian were already home when Daniel arrived. He wanted to talk to Mrs. Gantrey about staying with them. Despite Mia's age he wanted to have an adult in the house, especially now. He called and asked her to come over for a few minutes.

Mrs. Gantrey looked like a happy grandmother with grey hair in a short ponytail, round light-blue eyes in a round face but with a determined-looking mouth. She had shown previously that she didn't care for nonsense from anyone. She came over right away.

"So, you're off again to entertain another city. Is there something special you want me to look after?"

Daniel hesitated. *How much do I tell her?* "As you remember, Mrs. Gantrey, someone tried to break into the house a while ago and left a few threats behind. I just want to be sure that the kids are okay during the nights I'm away. If anything isn't right, call nine-one-one. The police know about this and will keep an eye on the house. I have even considered that the kids could stay at your house. But how would that work?"

Mrs. Gantrey's eyes got even rounder than before. "Oh dear," she said. "All this is just plain awful. Darn right I'll keep my eyes and ears open. I just wonder, my house is small. The children probably feel better in their own beds and with Julian and his piano. They already have enough to go through without a mother. Daniel, I'll try and keep them as safe as possible, you can count on me."

Yes, as much as an old lady can. "Wonderful." He shook her hand. "What would I do without someone like you. I'll be gone by tomorrow morning."

Mia and Julian had come into the kitchen. Mrs. Gantrey turned to them. "We'll get along, won't we? I'll make a nice pizza again."

"Yaiii!" Julian squealed. Mia just smiled and poked him in the side. "Glutton," she chided.

After Mrs. Gantrey left Daniel went into his study to organize the scores for Seattle's concert. He had selected Dvorak's *Serenade for Strings*, Boccherini's *Symphony in D-minor,* and Mozart's *Divertimento*. Packing clothes for three days was no problem, as long as his performance suit didn't wrinkle too much.

The rest of the afternoon and evening went quickly

between Julian's questions about his new piano piece, Mia's report on *Carmina Burana,* and deciding on supper. Daniel called Inspector Lankin once more.

"Any news on our case, Inspector?" he asked.

"Not much," he answered. "The driver we identified didn't give up his friend. Hang onto the phone call you taped. Maybe we can do a voice comparison with them and whoever we get next."

"I'm gone for three days," Daniel reminded him. "Can someone go by the house once in a while?"

"Yeah, we'll do that. Good trip." The inspector hung up.

The inspector must be busy, Daniel thought. He's rather short. As long as he works on our case.

Before both children went up to their rooms to sleep, Daniel talked to them again about safety. "Remember, house alarm, windows, and doors locked, have your cell phones handy. Mrs. Gantrey has a key to get in. She'll be here after school and stay during the night. Tell her where you are if you go out. All clear?"

Both kids nodded. "Clear."

"I'll be out before you get up tomorrow. So, hugs and goodbyes now."

Mia and Julian made sure to get a big bear hug from their dad.

Daniel checked his luggage once more, stretched, and yawned. *Good, now to bed and as much sleep as I can get.* Which was always a problem before going out of town. Especially now. But he had to do his job and he needed to trust the alertness of the police.

❧❧❧

After getting out of Seattle's airport Daniel took the taxi to the hotel. As always, Miss Curtis had made sure it was close to the theater, with no further need for transportation. He had gotten into the habit of looking around him more, searching for faces that seemed to give him more attention than necessary. But he couldn't detect anyone who reminded him of previous encounters. In his hotel room, Daniel took a deep breath, turned on the coffee machine, and sat down on the bed. He checked his watch, nine o'clock. He had almost an hour to get organized before the rehearsal.

After a strong mug of coffee, he looked at his watch again. Nine-thirty. *It might be a good idea to walk over to the theater.* He liked to be there ahead of time even though he had conducted the Chamber Orchestra for many years now and knew the acoustics of the theater. But he needed to do what he called *sniff out the atmosphere* around him.

The foyer was empty except for the doorman. "Hey, nice to see you again." He shook Daniel's hand. During their small talk, the first of the musicians drifted in with waves and hellos. Soon Daniel heard the customary warm-up practices of violins, flutes, oboes, and trumpets. At ten o'clock he ambled up to the podium and spread out the first score. He waited until all eyes were on him.

"Hello again. It's been a few months," he said. "We'll have one more concert before the end of June. I'll tell you what music I have in mind for it. Right now let's get into the first piece by Dvorak. It's easy-going and mostly happy." Daniel never expected a perfect first run-through, so it didn't bother him to start and stop a few times. After some corrections, he finally went through the whole piece without interruption. *Not quite right yet.* "I need to hear it again. Imagine where Dvorak lived, in a village, greens and trees around, birds, shepherd's flute, sunshine, his daily walk, in a good mood. Try to bring that out a bit more." And they did. Daniel knew it would sound good for the performance. From there he went on with the program.

The small symphony of *Boccherini in D-minor*, only twenty minutes long, didn't take much to go through. They took a break for lunch after that. Daniel was ready for something other than sandwiches. He chose an omelet with bacon and spinach. After his first cup of coffee, he called Mia. It went to her voicemail. He left a message that she didn't have to call back if everything was okay. Sonja Cruise, the first player in the viola section, came to Daniel's table.

"Any room for me?" she asked.

"Of course, Sonja, please sit. How are you doing?" Daniel had noticed that she had looked at him a lot today. What was on her mind?

She stirred her coffee. "I'm just fine. But what about you? It's only two years since your wife passed away. How are you coping and the kids?" Sonja looked at Daniel with sad blue eyes.

"Thanks for asking. We have a routine that seems to work well. Of course, the house is a lot emptier."

She nodded. "My husband and I have separated, unfortunately no future there. But it doesn't feel good. You never think it could happen to you."

Why is she telling me this? And she is wearing false eyelashes. "I'm sorry to hear that."

She looked up at him. "I'm curious what you have chosen for our next concert. Just in another month."

"I'll tell you all about it after we are finished for today." He got up. "I need another coffee."

Sonja hesitated then pushed her chair back too. "See you for Mozart later." She smiled and went back to her colleagues.

After chatting with his concertmaster John and one of the trumpet players, Daniel felt ready to go on with rehearsals. He still wondered what Sonja's real reason was to talk to him. *Oh no, not a crush on me. I don't need that at this time and not from her*. Daniel shook his head. She was pretty and lively but...*I'd better be careful*.

Chapter 7

Mozart's *Divertimento* went well. His music always sounded so easy, so natural. That's why Daniel took special care not to miss any of its nuances. He picked various sections for repeats but let the rest of it go. It would work well for tomorrow's concert.

After closing his scores Daniel called out, "This is what I have in mind for our June performance: Bach's *Brandenburg Concerto Number Two*, Respighi's *Ancient Airs and Dances,* and Tchaikovsky's *Serenade*." He heard "interesting" and "oh, good" from the musicians. "So, no complaints?"

"Do we have a choice?" John, the concertmaster, said and grinned.

Daniel laughed. "No, just being polite. See you tomorrow." *Good thing I'm the conductor.*

On his way out, Sonja approached him again. "A whole bunch of us are going for supper later. Please, come along." She brushed a strand of hair behind her ear.

Oh, oh. "Kind of you to ask me but…"

Sonja continued. "It's right around the corner from here with a funny name, Café Yumm, not too expensive. You're only here for three days." She looked at him with pleading eyes.

Eating alone was not a good option and there would be other musicians around. "All right, I'll come. Around seven?"

Sonja beamed. "Great, see you later." With a wave she turned the corner and walked on.

Good thing I don't live in Seattle, Daniel thought and scolded himself right after. Why did he feel so threatened by Sonja? He should be flattered. She was at least fifteen years younger. But she just wasn't a person he would like to spend a lot of time with. He shook his head at himself. *I need a nap. My hotel room beckons.*

The desk clerk at the hotel called to him. "There was a phone call for you."

Daniel's heart jumped. "Who was it?"

"He didn't leave a name, just said he would call again."

Daniel leaned on the counter. "If he doesn't leave a name, tell him the next time he calls, that I have moved out. Someone has been leaving strange messages lately. Was it a male voice?"

The clerk nodded. "Yes, very friendly."

"Yeah, he would be. Thanks." Daniel went upstairs and stood by the window. Had someone already found out that he was in Seattle? How? Was it someone Daniel knew? How far would anyone go to trace his every move? Daniel dialed Mia's cell phone. She answered after three rings. "Is everything okay?" Daniel asked.

"Yes, just fine. I just got home," Mia answered. "Why? Are you worried?"

Daniel kept his voice level. "Oh, someone tried to call me at the hotel without leaving a name. I'm just wondering. Is Mrs. Gantrey already there?"

"She came a minute ago. You want to talk to her?"

"No, it's okay. Call me any time you need to, okay? Even in the middle of the night." After hanging up Daniel still couldn't swallow the anger of being tailed. How would, whoever it was, know of his trip here? Why such an effort? He took off his shoes and stretched out on the bed. All of this had taken a chunk out of his energy. "You're not going to wear me out," he grumbled. "Sooner than later, you'll get caught."

The ringing of the telephone woke Daniel. *Mia would call my cell phone.* The voice of the desk clerk put Daniel on edge again. "The man from before called back. I told him you moved to another hotel."

"Thank you. I appreciate that. This should discourage whoever he was." Daniel paced around again. *I cannot let this rattle me. I have work to do. I have music to perform.* He took the score of *Aida* out of his suitcase. To take the opportunity of a quiet hotel room he had decided to work through it again. He sat down, closed his eyes, and tried to quieten his mind. Soon he heard Verdi's music and with it, he was able to push back thoughts of more unwelcome surprises.

After some time he straightened up and checked his watch. Seven o'clock? The supper date with the musicians. He covered up the score and put on his jacket. His stomach was ready for a good meal. A thought occurred to him. What if the caller was still waiting outside and would see him stepping out of the hotel's door? *I'm getting paranoid again. Stop it. I'm not hiding.*

The restaurant was just two blocks from Daniel's hotel. The musicians had already assembled at a large table and greeted him with raised wine and beer glasses. "Glad you could make it, Maestro," the concertmaster called. Sonja's smile lit up her face. Daniel decided that he would not pay too much attention to her. *Can't give her any wrong ideas.*

During the next two hours with good food and red wine, Daniel enjoyed himself. He was glad he had come. Sonja looked at him more often he had wanted her to so he made sure to spread his attention around the table.

Finally Sonja directed a question at Daniel. "What are you working on in San Francisco now and in the future?"

"A big question, Sonja." *I'll make it as short as I can.* "Right now it's *Carmina Burana* and an international concert coming up."

Sonja's eyes widened. "I'll come down for the international concert. I'd love to meet your children."

Hold on, lady. No, you don't! But I better stay polite. "Well, we need as many in the audience as possible, always appreciated." Daniel looked at his watch. "Time to call it a night. It has been fun." He got up. "We'll run through the program tomorrow morning, then to the performance."

On his way out, Daniel's uneasy feeling came back. *What am I going to do with that woman? Hopefully, she'll get over her crush when I'm gone.*

Almost back at his hotel he heard screeching car brakes behind him. He turned and saw two headlights heading straight for him on the sidewalk. He sprinted toward a shop entrance up the steps. The car raced past him just missing the steps Daniel was crouching on. He slumped forward, his heart pounding in his throat. His head spun and he had a hard time catching his breath. *This can't be happening. Can't I be safe anywhere?* He staggered up on shaky legs when three of his musicians came around the corner.

An oboe player came up to Daniel. "Maestro, what's wrong? You don't look so good."

Daniel had steadied himself and came down. "Someone tried to run me down."

The musicians gasped. "What? On the sidewalk? Did you see what kind of car?"

Daniel shook his head. "Too dark and too sudden. I barely had time to save myself."

"But why you?" The oboist grabbed Daniel's arm. "Who has it in for you?" The musicians exchanged glances of disbelieve. "We'll get you home. Can't lose our famous leader."

Daniel appreciated the lighter tone the musician tried to put on it, even though it could have been a disaster. At the hotel entrance the flautist said, "You have to call the police."

Daniel shook his head. "Not tonight, maybe tomorrow. I've had enough for now. Thank you. Good night." All he wanted now was his room, quiet and getting his thoughts together. I can't deal with another police officer, he thought. I'll call Inspector Lankin tomorrow. He sat down in a chair then got up again. Brandy, he just needed to relax. His hand still shook when he poured the brandy into a glass. He sat down and closed his eyes. *Do I need a bodyguard? I would feel ridiculous.* He would have loved to call Mia but she was in bed now. With the brandy's warmth spreading through his body Daniel's eyes finally grew heavy. Maybe he should try for bed and sleep, if possible.

❧❦❧

After tossing and turning for what seemed hours Daniel finally sank into a dreamless sleep. At least he couldn't recall any images floating through it. If it hadn't been for his alarm clock he would have probably slept through the day. Now, in the light of the day, he had his doubts again about the previous night's attack by the car. What if it had just been a drunk driver out of control and not aiming for him? *Am I making too much of everything?* But then he considered the two phone calls at the hotel. Anyone who wanted to talk to him would have left a name for a callback.

Daniel shook his head. It was better to inform Inspector Lankin. He had to leave a message with the sergeant. All he could hope for was that the children were okay.

At rehearsals, the word had gotten around about Daniel's near miss with the car. As he expected, Sonja came running up to him, eyes wide with concern.

"Are you okay, Maestro? I just found out about your close call."

Daniel brushed it off with a slight wave of his hand. "Probably drunk out of his mind or a case of mistaken identity. Don't be concerned."

But Sonja wasn't quite finished. "Next time I'll walk with you."

"And get run over too? No, I don't need a bodyguard." He turned away. "Let's get to work, there is an audience waiting tonight." *Heavens, woman, don't you get the message?*

Rehearsals went well and Daniel was deep into the music all the way through. Since all three pieces showed a relaxed, happy atmosphere, it had rubbed off on him. As usual, the music had pushed away the dark clouds over Daniel's head.

During lunch, he called Mia. It went to her voicemail. Where was she? She could be out with her friends. After all, it was Saturday afternoon. Daniel tried to reason and fought down the tightening of his stomach. After his second cup of coffee, his phone buzzed. Mia.

"Hi Papa. Sorry I didn't answer your call. I was talking to my singing teacher."

Daniel let out a deep breath. "Are you two all right? Did a police car come by in the evening?"

"Yeah, but it was a ghost car. I guess they didn't want anyone to know. How's Seattle?"

Daniel didn't want to tell her about his close encounter with the car, at least not now. "Fine, first performance tonight. Is Julian practicing?"

"Every day, don't worry." After some more small talk,

Daniel hung up and finally ordered a cheese and bacon sandwich.

After the rest of the rehearsal, Daniel got a message to come by the manager's office. Daniel had been the conductor of this forty-six-piece Chamber Orchestra for ten years now. *Maybe they get tired of me?* But so far he had heard only good reports about his and the orchestra's work.

Mr. Manning's door was open. Daniel knocked on the door frame. "Come in, Daniel. Good to see you again." He shook Daniel's hand. "Sit down. How are things with you? Are your kids okay?"

Daniel sat down in one of the cushioned chairs. "We are doing fine. Life is different now but—we have a routine. And the orchestra is doing great, as you will hear tonight." *You don't need to know about my personal adventures.*

Mr. Manning bent forward and slid his folded hands over the polished table. "I have been wondering if you could find the time to give a concert with our symphony orchestra at the end of the season in June. Maybe two nights of a varied program."

Daniel stared at him in surprise. "Is your present conductor not able to do it? Is he all right?" *How am I going to fit that in?*

"Oh, he is fine but he wants an early holiday. It would be good to have a guest conductor once in a while." The manager looked expectantly at Daniel.

Thoughts of all his other commitments whirled through Daniel's mind. "I really would have to think about that, Mr. Manning. I have concerts in San Francisco, an opera in Portland, and at the beginning of July I'm in London."

The manager nodded. "I know you're busy. But you're also very good. So far you conducted our Chamber

Orchestra. We would like to hear you with our symphony orchestra."

Daniel leaned back in his chair. "I thank you for the offer and the pat on the back. I will think it through. What music do you have in mind?"

"Oh, something exciting, not too long or too deep?"

Daniel couldn't help chuckling. "Even small musical creations are important and should be treated with utmost care. If I conduct music, it has to stir the audience in more than momentary excitement. I'll select something when I check to see if I have any spare time."

Mr. Manning smiled. "I understand. Just thought I would try and snag you."

Daniel pushed his chair back. "Thank you, I appreciate that. You will hear from me before I leave." They shook hands and Daniel made his way out of the theater.

On his way back to his hotel his head already buzzed with thoughts of a possible date to come back here and the music he could perform. Then he had an idea. After the last performance of the season at home, he would pack up the kids, do two nights in Seattle and fly from there to London. He could also use some of the pieces he had performed in San Francisco. Perfect. He hummed to himself and took the elevator up.

He had just opened the door to his room when he heard the phone ring. *What now?* The desk clerk's voice asked, "Do you want to take this call, Sir? It's an Inspector Lankin."

"Of course, put him through. Thank you." Daniel's heart pumped right up into his throat. "Hello, Inspector. What kind of news do you have for me?"

"It seems you're right in one thing. All the guys we have in custody have a connection with each other. They're either working in construction or real estate. They're not giving us much to go on but we'll find out."

"I'll bet there are drugs involved. Why else would they try so hard to kill me?" Daniel drummed his fingers on the table. "I just don't know if they're afraid that I want to dig deeper or if it's plain revenge for me telling you and identifying one of them." He heard voices in the background.

"I've got to go, always something. Stay safe." Inspector Lankin hung up.

Again, baby steps, Daniel thought. But every small thing helps. Like a picture puzzle it will come together. He looked at his watch. Now he needed to fill the time until the performance. A dip in the pool could be a good idea. He abhorred exercising but a few lengths of swimming didn't count as such.

Just two people, a man and a woman, were using the pool. They nodded to him and continued swimming.

Daniel swam with easy strokes. It felt good to just concentrate on the water around him. *I should do this more often.* After a few laps, Daniel got out and headed towards the showers. The man he had seen before came out and called to him. "Hey, nice to see you like the pool." He stretched out his hand. "Arnie Willows. You're the conductor for this evening. Looking forward to it."

Daniel hesitated but then shook his hand. "I'm surprised you recognized me."

Mr. Willows smiled. "We never miss the Chamber Orchestra concerts. See you tonight." He waved and left.

Daniel stared after him. He had to fight down his almost permanent paranoia. But that man had a clear look in his eyes and a strong handshake. *I can't mistrust every single person. It has become a bad habit. Shower and get ready for the performance. Maybe a bit to eat.* He never ate a full meal before a concert, but an empty stomach wasn't a good idea either.

Chapter 8

The parking garage was already filling up when Daniel drove in. A good sign, he thought, even though people are listening to a smaller orchestra than the full symphony. He wondered if he would see Mr. Willows from the pool again.

The musicians drifted in laughing and chatting. Daniel went to his dressing room to change. He felt good about Mr. Manning's offer to conduct a performance in June. Since he, Mia, and Julian would take off right after that for London, he would have the kids with him and didn't have to worry about them. He still needed to send London the list of his musical ideas. *Next on my list between now and Aida in Portland.*

When Daniel left his dressing room the concertmaster came up to him. "Maestro, Sonja hasn't shown up yet."

"Do you have her phone number? Call her. She might be sick." *Or another of her tricks?*

"I did. She doesn't answer." The violinist looked worried.

"Well, I can't do anything about it. Let number two take over. Get ready to go now." *What does he expect me to do? I conduct, not send out a search party. Just another of those hitches I cope with at times.* Daniel heard the oboe's A and made his way to the podium. *Music now, not people's sicknesses or whatever else.*

The audience applauded. He noticed a good turn-out. When all eyes of the musicians were on him, he raised his arms, and with a down-beat Dvorak's description of his wanderings through his beloved landscape filled the hall.

The first half of the performance went well, as he had anticipated. At intermission, he went out into the musician's lounge to get some water. In one of the chairs, he noticed Sonja, hunched over. He stopped. *What the...* "Sonja? What's going on?"

She lifted her head. On her face, partially hidden by dark glasses, Daniel saw bruises and some blood. "Good Lord, Sonja. What happened to you?"

She took off her glasses and uncovered a black eye. "My ex-to-be husband busted into my apartment, drunk as so often. He still had a key. He started yelling about how I had deserted him, not keeping to our deal, whatever that was." She stopped.

"And he did this to you? You should be in the hospital." Daniel had a hard time believing so much violence.

Sonja nodded. "I'm coming from there. Just wanted to show up here because I missed the performance."

"Where is your husband now?"

She got up. "At the police station being charged. Neighbors called the police. I'll be back tomorrow."

Daniel touched her arm. "Are you sure? You need some rest."

She shook her head. "No way. Just don't say anything yet to my co-musicians. See you tomorrow. Thanks for listening to me." She turned and walked out of the door.

Daniel stood still for a minute. *Unbelievable. What is going on in marriages? What kind of a man would beat up his wife like that? Even if he's mad about their break-up.* He shook his head. *And I thought I had problems.* Right now he needed to get back to the other half of the concert.

If Sonja was coming back tomorrow it would give the rest of the orchestra a lot to talk about.

Mozart got a standing ovation from the audience. The musicians beamed. Daniel was happy, no extra rehearsals tomorrow, just another performance. On his way out he heard someone call, "Maestro!" Daniel turned. Mr. Willows waved to him.

"I'm glad I caught you." He pointed to the woman beside him. "This is my wife Laura, all excited to be able to meet you." She came forward and Daniel shook her hand. "We enjoyed the concert so much, we might come again tomorrow. You should be here more often."

Daniel smiled. "I'm happy to have such big fans. You might see me again in June with the symphony orchestra."

Mr. Willows beamed. "Looking forward to it. We best be on our way." They both waved and went in the opposite direction.

They seem to be genuine, Daniel thought. Now his stomach growled. He was ready for a meal. As he had expected, a few other hungry musicians had gathered at the "Yummy" restaurant. The concertmaster came up to him again.

"Have you heard from Sonja?"

Daniel sat down. "She'll be here tomorrow. She is okay." *That's all I'll say.* "Why are you so concerned, John?"

John's face had a sheepish look. "Oh, just—we don't want to lose a good musician." He poured beer into his glass.

Daniel chuckled. There was more than just being a concerned colleague. But he let it go.

After Daniel had ordered his food he called Mia. He knew it was late but she stayed up late on Saturday nights. When she didn't answer, his stomach twisted again. Was she out with friends? *Wait a minute. She might be at another Carmina Burana rehearsal. She'll phone back. These things always take longer than expected.* But he didn't feel at ease until her return call and his second glass of wine.

"Everything is fine, Papa," Mia told him. "I would have called you otherwise. We had an extra *Carmina Burana* rehearsal. The choirmaster wants it to be perfect when you get home." Daniel heard her giggle.

"Good for him." Daniel laughed too. Now he could enjoy his meal. One more day, then he could stop worrying. *I might just take them with me to Portland. I'll be away for a whole week. That's too long for me to be on edge.*

On his way home that night Sonja's dilemma came back into his mind. No wonder she wanted to split up with her husband. What kind of deal had he been talking about? That word stuck out. No, that was her concern. She will have to sort it out. At least he might cool his heels in jail for now.

⁊ᕲ⁊

Sunday morning Daniel took a walk through the neighborhood of his hotel. He needed to move and later do a few laps in the pool. It also gave him time to think about the music for Mr. Manning's June performance. Wagner's *Meistersinger Ouverture* to begin with, Schubert's Sixth Symphony would be good to follow, light and pleasant, and then maybe Richard Strauss's *Don Juan*. That would be enough variety.

Daniel strolled through the side streets. Trees and bushes showed their fresh spring greens. San Francisco flowered most of the time, with hardly any seasons except for the occasional rain. Sometimes he missed the feeling of spring, new beginnings, new energy. Just like starting music again that he hadn't played for a long time.

Once in a while Daniel looked around him. Was anyone watching or following him? But nothing seemed to be suspicious. Maybe even bad guys needed a Sunday morning sleep-in. How good would it be to have Elvira walking beside him, exchanging ideas, commenting on the surroundings? He sighed. *Get used to it already. That part of my life will stay lonely.*

On his way back to the hotel he saw a familiar face, Mr. Willows. He seemed to be everywhere. "Maestro," he called. "Out for a morning stroll?"

Daniel laughed. "We have to stop meeting like this. I get the feeling you're checking up on me."

Mr. Willow's face got serious. He cleared his throat. "As a matter of fact, I am. After you nearly got run over, your inspector called me to keep an eye on you. I'm a police investigator. Lankin and I have known each other for a long time."

Daniel looked at him. He had to think for a few seconds. Then he shook his head. "Will surprises never end? That was good of the inspector to care so much. He's also keeping watch over my kids and the house. We'll probably never find out who the driver was."

Mr. Willows grunted. "Sometimes there is more to it than at first glance. I'll better let you go. Stay safe. I'll keep watching you."

Daniel shook the man's hand. "Thank you. I'll be out of here after tonight."

"Safe trip home." Willows waved and walked on.

Daniel decided to go for lunch. He needed to get his head around this new development about the private investigator. He had expected that Inspector Lankin would wave the car incident off as a drunken driver thing. Maybe now he had come to the same conclusion as Willows, that there was more at stake. Daniel felt protected. *Thanks, my Guardian Angel. This time in human form.*

Back in his hotel, Daniel worked on *Aida* again to fill the time until the performance. Operas had so many parts—the orchestra, soloists, chorus, here even dancers. He hoped that the scenery would be somewhat traditional. In his mind, the music had to fit the stage. Verdi in twenty-first-century costumes and settings felt alien to him. Since he was not the regular conductor he couldn't do much about it except throw out a few ideas. He would get to it once he got there.

Shortly before leaving for Symphony Hall he called Mia. "Everything is normal," she assured him. "Julian wants to talk to you."

"When are you coming home, Papa?" Julian asked

"I'll leave after the performance," Daniel said. "I'll see you at breakfast."

Julian sounded relieved. "I'm glad. I miss you. Bye."

Daniel grabbed his suitcase. *That strengthens my idea of taking the kids with me to Portland.* He stopped by at Mr. Manning's office. "I'll conduct in June," Daniel told him. "Here is a list of what I have in mind for it. Let me know if you agree."

Mr. Manning beamed. "That's wonderful, Daniel." He glanced at the piece of paper. "Couldn't be better, thank you." He shook Daniel's hand. "Keep in touch until then."

That's out of the way, now back to work.

The performance went well again to Daniel's satisfaction and strong applause. Sonja had appeared, as she had promised. She looked better. Probably covered up the bruises with makeup, Daniel thought. During the intermission, she had been surrounded by her colleagues. *That should give her enough sympathy, I'll stay away.* But he couldn't avoid saying goodbye to her and his musicians.

"As you see, I survived," Sonja said. "And I'll listen to your international concert in San Francisco."

Daniel shook his head. "No need, I'll be here in June with your symphony orchestra."

Sonja's eyes widened. "Finally!" She gave him a coy look. "I'll be much better by then."

Daniel just laughed and turned away. "See you all later. Practice your new pieces."

He was not surprised to see Mr. Willows outside the building, this time without his wife. "As always, my lookout. Anything suspicious?"

Willows chuckled. "Not as far as I could see. I ordered a taxi for you. I knew you wanted to leave right away."

Daniel grabbed his hand. "Want to come with me? I could use you at home."

Willows' face was serious. "I'm glad I could help and finally meet you in the process. Take good care of yourself and your kids. If you find out more about the threats let me know. Safe trip home."

During the drive to the airport, Daniel had to check himself. *Can I trust the driver? What if*—but he threw the thought out immediately. *I'll give myself a heart attack if I go on that way.*

The airport seemed to be quieter than usual. Maybe red-eye flights were not everyone's favorite. It didn't take long for Daniel to board the plane and settle into his seat, he was ready for a nap.

Chapter 9

Daniel woke up with a start. *Where am I? Oh, yes, I'm on an airplane going home.* But he felt disoriented and couldn't shake off a weight sitting on him. He took a slow breath. It was just a dream, he told himself. Daniel closed his eyes again to remember it. There had been smoke, people running, coughing, young people. Students? He saw a face, not a good face, distorted but well enough to draw it. *That's what I'm going to do to keep it in my memory.*

Daniel rubbed his forehead. In his dream he had been powerless to help. Was it a fire he saw? He couldn't remember witnessing a real one in the past. Television? He seldom watched the news. He tried to calm down a bit. Was the dream telling him something? It had been so solid, he almost smelled the smoke. He would keep his ears and eyes open, just in case. *Lord, what a dream. And that on an airplane. I'm glad I'm almost home.*

During the taxi ride from the airport, Daniel still couldn't shake off the unease the dream had created. Since he hadn't heard from Mia, Mrs. Gantrey, or Inspector Lankin he assumed that everything was in order. But anything could happen in a few hours. The dream had involved a lot of people but not his family or his home. So why was he still worried?

The house was dark and quiet. Only the security lights

came on when he ran up the front steps. He unlocked the door, disarmed the alarm, and took off his shoes. The less noise the less chance of waking up the kids. After all, it was 2:15 am. With a sigh of relief, he crept up the stairs to his bedroom. *Good, all is well.* Then he had to laugh. There, on his pillow, he spotted a paper heart and a piece of chocolate. It again reminded him of Elvira. She used to have small surprises for him after a trip out of town. Now the kids. Daniel popped the chocolate into his mouth and went into the bathroom. *I better get some sleep. Rehearsals start at ten o'clock.*

⁊⁊

The aroma of coffee and frying bacon woke Daniel the next morning. He grunted and rubbed his eyes. It had been a short night, but the promise of a good breakfast brightened his mood.

As quietly as he could he waited at the kitchen door. Mrs. Gantrey stood at the stove turning over slices of bacon. Mia and Julian already ate scrambled eggs.

"Good morning, everybody," Daniel called. He savored the kids' screams of, "Papa, you're up!" Of course, they needed hugs and asked so many questions that Daniel had to stop them and point to their unfinished breakfast. Mrs. Gantrey waved a spatula as a greeting.

"How many slices of bacon, Daniel? Eggs over easy?"

Daniel chuckled. "How did you know?"

Mrs. Gantrey smiled and turned back to the frying pan. "You're an un-messy person, not one for sunny side up." She slid two eggs onto a plate and topped them with three slices of bacon. "It's good to have you back. But we all got along, didn't we?" She looked at Mia and Julian.

They both nodded with mouthfuls of toasts. Daniel plopped two sugar cubes into his mug of coffee and sat back with a contented sigh. *Better than any restaurant.*

"Get ready for school," Mrs. Gantrey reminded the children, then she looked at Daniel. "Sorry to take over now that you're here. I got so used to it."

Daniel nodded and bit into one of the crispy slices of bacon. "I appreciate you taking over. It has given me peace of mind. But for Portland, I want to take them with me. I still worry too much." *No use telling her about the car incident.*

She filled the sink with soapy water. "Whatever you decide, Daniel. The kids might like that."

Daniel took out his wallet. "Let me pay you right now."

Mrs. Gantrey gasped when she looked at the check. "This is too much, Daniel."

He shook her hand. "You're worth every penny of it."

Mia and Julian both giggled and grabbed their backpacks. "Now you can buy the lamp you wanted, Mrs. Gantrey."

"Oh, hush, maybe I change my mind." She turned back to the dishes.

"Are you here when I get home, Papa?" Julian asked.

Daniel nodded. "Yes, the master is back and in full power."

With a "yaiii!" Julian slammed the door behind him.

Daniel looked at his watch. "I'll better get going too. *Carmina Burana* is calling." Today's rehearsal still needed to be without the choir. Tomorrow he would work on the international concert, then *Carmina* again with the choir. *I better get my mind together.*

On his way to the theater, the images of his dream came back to him. The more he thought of it, the more he convinced himself that it had shown him a school with students or a similar venue where young people would be. Maybe he should listen to the news and check the newspaper more often. *Maybe I'll ask Mia. She might have heard something like that.*

The assistant conductor greeted Daniel at the stage door. "Happy to see you back," he said. "I hope you're okay with the outcome of the rehearsals."

Daniel winked at him. "We'll see, won't we? How did the outside concerts go?"

"Quite well but lots of distractions. Noises from airplanes, trucks, people yelling."

Daniel nodded. "I know. I'm used to them, I tune them out. You have to work on that. Let's start with our daily work."

The rehearsal went well. Daniel only had to adjust the sounds of various instruments that came on too strong. "Remember, you're only the accompaniment of the choir," he told the musicians. "We'll have them all here the next time."

At lunchtime he got a call from Mia." I'll be home early, Papa. A fire broke out in the gym. We were practicing for the year-end sports day. Someone threw something into the gym and it exploded."

Daniel's throat closed. He could hardly speak. Finally, he asked, "Are you and the other girls okay?"

"Yes, we got out. One girl broke her wrist when she fell. But the thing, whatever it was, spread fire all over the floor."

Oh, Lord, my dream. "Did the fire alarm and sprinkler system come on?"

"Yes, and the firemen came. It's just very smoky everywhere." Mia sounded a bit breathless.

Daniel closed his eyes. "Mia, let the nurse check you out. If you feel okay get home, if not let them take you to the hospital." *Was this aimed at her?*

"I'll go home," Mia said. "I'm all right. Don't worry, see you later."

Daniel sat back and tried his usual deep breathing. By now this would be in the hands of the police. Maybe they already found the culprit. And maybe it had been a disgruntled student who didn't get the marks he wanted or someone whose girlfriend had spurned him. How else could that person get into the school? Nowadays everybody kept an eye out for unauthorized people, didn't they?.

Daniel got himself another cup of coffee. All of this was out of his hands. One thing he still had to do—draw the face of the person in his dream, at least as well as he was able to remember it.

Before going on with more rehearsals Daniel called Inspector Lankin. *He might not be in the office, but maybe I'm lucky.* As usual, an officer answered. He recognized Daniel's voice.

"I guess, you want to know about the fire in the school," the officer said.

"Because my daughter Mia was in the gym. She could have been targeted with all the other things that have been going on lately." Daniel knew he could be wrong. He wanted to remind the police of the threats against him.

"We have some idea who the arsonist could be. Someone was seen leaving carrying a blue backpack."

Daniel paced around. "I'm sure he got rid of it by now. But thank you. Let me know of any development, please."

"Will do, Maestro." The officer hung up.

Am I now a prophet who dreams of coming disasters? Then, please, show me the evil mind behind all this. For now back to music, then home.

❧❦❧

On his way home, Daniel drove by Mia's school. A police car still stood in front of the main entrance. An officer inside the car was talking on the phone. Daniel approached and knocked on the window. The man rolled it down and gave him a stern look. "Yes?"

"My daughter was in the gym when the fire started. Is there any news?"

The sergeant relaxed. "Sorry about that. Is she all right?"

"Yes, as luck would have it." Daniel asked again, "Any news?"

The officer shrugged. "I haven't heard anything. I'm just staying here for security reasons."

Daniel waved at him and walked back to his car. Some students still stood around chatting. One boy in a black hoody kept himself apart from them. He leaned against a signpost and stared at the school. Daniel wondered, who was he? Curious, but not every boy wearing a hoody was setting fires. He couldn't see a blue backpack. Daniel shook his head. That's what the police were here for. But the officer in the car didn't seem to look at the students or the boy standing by himself. Shouldn't he keep his eyes open for them? His phone was more important to him. Daniel went back to the police car.

The officer looked up. "Can I do anything else for you, Sir?" he asked.

"Yes, I have been curious about the boy over there. He doesn't join the others. Wouldn't you think it could be worthwhile to ask him some questions?" Daniel prepared himself for a sharp answer. But the policeman didn't look at him.

"Not my job to question anyone. And neither is it yours. Leave it to the right people. You worry too much."

Daniel's hackles rose. "Do you have children, officer? It seems you don't know my history. But I leave it to you. You get paid for this." He turned and went back to his car. *This guy turns me off on the efficiency of the police. I guess, his job description is to sit and do nothing.* It was time to get home.

෧෨෧෨

Mia was sitting at the kitchen table reading the text of *Carmina Burana* when Daniel came home. He noticed her pale face. "Are you all right? You look a bit washed out."

Mia put the book down. "I'm not sick, just still nervous. What was going on with the boy who threw the firebomb? How angry can anyone be."

Daniel plucked some grapes from a bowl. "Either he had a deep grudge, or he did it for someone else."

"You mean for someone who is behind all the threats?"

Daniel shrugged. "That's one possibility. But no proof as yet."

The backdoor slammed. Julian's voice, "I'm home."

Mia rolled her eyes. "We can hear that loud and clear."

Daniel added, "Will you ever learn to close doors quietly?"

Julian slunk into the kitchen. "Sorry, the door slipped out of my hands." Then he looked at Mia. "What's wrong, Mia?"

Daniel was amazed at the bond between his children. Just by looking at her, Julian knew that something was not right. Mia told him a shortened version of the fire in the gym. Julian's eyes now had the dark, angry look.

"That new guy in your class, you have to ask him why he did that. He's the bad one."

Mia put her hand on Julian's shoulder. "What evidence do you have, Mr. District Attorney? I can't just accuse him like that."

Julian turned to Daniel. "What do you think, Papa? Mia said he was rude."

Daniel held up his hand. "Number one, that doesn't

make him an arsonist. Number two, finding the real one is the police's business. Let them do the detective work. Even though they seem to be overworked."

Julian's head drooped. "Okay, I better go practice." Then he looked up. "Later I'll show you that I got better at my new piece."

Daniel smiled. "Great. I'll be all ears." *Anything to get their minds on other things.*

As Julian disappeared, Daniel turned to Mia again. "Tomorrow see if the boy in your class shows up. If he doesn't, let me know. In the meantime concentrate on *Carmina.* After tomorrow your choir will rehearse with me."

Mia's eyes lit up. "Finally! Just before that, I'll have my singing lesson. Perfect."

Daniel was glad to see Mia happy again, even if it didn't quieten his own fears. "What's for supper?"

Mia rubbed her nose. "How about Italian at Giovanni's?"

"Right after Julian's private recital. After a day like this, we have to feed our nerves, right?"

Mia giggled. "You're the best, Papa."

I wish I could protect you two with a bubble around you. Impenetrable to any hurt of any kind.

Chapter 10

On the ride home from supper Daniel said, "I want to tell you about my plan for Portland."

Mia frowned. "You're going to be there for a week, right?"

Daniel stopped at a red light. "Yes, but I'll take you with me."

Both children shouted, "What?"

Julian leaned over. "For a whole week? What about my piano lessons?"

Mia stared at Daniel. "I can't do that, Papa. I have exams coming up. There are quite a few until June. I can't miss them if I want good grades."

Daniel eased into his garage. "Let's talk about it inside." He had expected some resistance to his plan, only not quite as strong. On the way to the kitchen, he heard the kids talking quietly to each other. *I'll have to convince them.*

Settled at the kitchen table Daniel tried again. "I'm constantly worried about you when I'm away even with Mrs. Gantrey here. Just like the fire in your school, it doesn't have to be in the house. I'll be gone for a whole week and I have to concentrate on my work. I'm taking over someone else's opera. I want you close by."

The children looked downcast. "I can't miss my exams, Papa," Mia said. "They won't allow me to take them later."

"Fair enough." Daniel thought for a moment. "Julian, you can miss one lesson and some practice. From what I heard you're doing just fine. At least one of you can come with me."

Julian looked up. "Okay, maybe it'll be fun to see you at work with all those different people. But what about Mia?"

Daniel turned to her. "What if you stayed with Mrs. Gantrey? At least overnight and for meals? If you need anything from the house, you can get it during the day."

Mia's face lit up. "Do you think she would be all right with that?"

"Since it's only you she might even like it. I'll call her right now to make sure."

Mrs. Gantrey sounded happy with Daniel's suggestion. "That suits me just fine," she said. "Mia is a steady girl. I'll make a bed for her in the study."

Daniel felt relieved. "Mia, I don't want you in our house after dark, okay? I anyone breaks in, the police will look after it." *Hopefully.*

Mia let out a big breath. "I'm so relieved, Papa. That can work." She circled the table and hugged him. "If it had been a holiday, I would've loved to come along."

Daniel understood her worries about grades. Less than an A would never do for her.

After both disappeared into their rooms, he poured himself a brandy and sat down in his easy chair. Another problem solved, at least mostly. He looked over to Elvira's picture. "Life is complicated without you, but somehow we manage," he mumbled. "I could never replace you with anyone. I miss your advice. But the kids are developing well. You were a great part of that." Daniel leaned back.

Yes, she was still around, he had no doubts about it.

His thought drifted to his work for tomorrow: Brahms and Rimsky-Korsakov probably needed work. Also, he had to finally send a list of his musical ideas to London. They might be wondering why it took him so long. He yawned. *First on my list is sleep.*

☙❧

Before rehearsal the next morning Daniel called Inspector Lankin.

"So, you're home again," the inspector said. "I'm glad you've survived."

"I wanted to thank you for looking after me, Inspector. Mr. Willows is a great friend now," Daniel answered.

The inspector chuckled. "Yeah, we go way back. After your incident with the car, I knew you needed a bodyguard."

"Did you find anything out about the school fire? Mia was in it, right in the gym." Is there some good news? Daniel thought

"Actually, yes. We found the boy. Listen. Come by after work."

"Great. See you then." Daniel again felt the need to listen to his inner voice. What if the boy had been recruited by someone to create this fire with the promise of payment? It would have been easy to find out about the girls' gym routine. Even easier if the boy was in Mia's class.

Daniel remembered Jason, a young man from ten years ago in Vancouver. He had been used by crooks as a pickpocket and go-between. If Daniel had not interfered, Jason would have been beaten to death. The aftermath had not been pleasant for Daniel. He shook himself. *Do I have to live through that again, this time with two children at risk?*

But there was hope and a visit to the inspector. *Right*

now, get your mind on Brahms and Rimsky Korsakov.

As Daniel walked up to the stage he found the assistant conductor waiting for him. "I might just stay and listen and learn." Mark already carried the scores for the concert with him.

Daniel was surprised. *How dedicated!* "You did the work for two days. Any questions?"

Mark shook his head. "No, not really. I just want to watch you and listen again."

"Okay, let's start." Daniel turned his score to Rimsky Korsakov's *Russian Easter*. The percussion section with its bells and triangles needed to be exactly right. This was a good way to start.

After two run-throughs Daniel stopped for lunch. He was happy with the progress and told Mark about it. The assistant conductor beamed.

The rest of the rehearsal with Brahms went smoothly with only small changes in timing and musical inflections needed. "Tomorrow we have the choir here for *Carmina Burana*," Daniel reminded the musicians. He also talked to the manager responsible for the scenery about placing the risers for the singers. "We have forty-five singers," he told him. "Make sure the benches are steady." He still remembered an incident years ago where one tier broke and a bassist cracked his ankle. Not a happy occasion.

Now Daniel could make his way to the police station and listen to what the inspector would have to tell him.

On his way to Inspector Lankin's office, Daniel thought about how and why all the attacks and threats started. *How* he knew but *why* he could only guess. He was surprised that the school arsonist had been caught already.

The inspector's office was empty. Daniel looked around. *He knew I was coming. I hope he didn't skip out.* Then he heard Mr. Lankin's voice, "Get on it, man," as he came around the corner.

"Bad day, Inspector?" Daniel tried to sound sympathetic.

Mr. Lankin grunted. "More a case of a not so capable officer. Come in." He sat down and leaned back. "You want to know about the delinquent who likes to set fires. Well, he was recruited."

"Aha!" Daniel smacked his hands together. "I knew it. All the threats are organized by someone who hides real crime."

Inspector Lankin nodded. "You have a good nose for things." He shuffled some papers. "The race driver claimed he was in a hurry, nothing else. The one who broke into your house also said he was alone, the one in the garage did not threaten you, but he was the driver of the accident car. So, only minor felonies."

"What about the boy?" *Tell me something new.*

The inspector tapped his pen. "He's young and scared. Apparently, he never met the man who promised him money, just texted him where to get the bomb and when to do it."

"Where did you nab him?" Daniel asked.

"He hung around the school too much, maybe waiting for the money. We found the blue backpack in the bushes."

Daniel wasn't done yet. "Did you find anything out about the bomb?"

Mr. Lankin nodded. "Whatever got left of it was analyzed. We hope to trace its origin and—its maker." He looked at Daniel. "It's a long process without guarantees. You're all at risk. Maybe the boy's cell phone can tell us something. That is beyond me." He threw up his hands. "Do you still have the voicemail you taped before?"

"Oh yes. With all my work I forgot about it. Can you do a voice comparison with the men you're holding?" *It has worked before.*

"Yeah, bring it in. It doesn't hurt to try." Mr. Lankin

paused, then went on. "Another thing. All the men, except the boy, work on construction. They claim they don't know each other, which is baloney. And before you ask, the shoe prints by the tree are size seven. Remember them?"

This was the longest speech Daniel had ever heard from the inspector. "Yes, I do. I knew it was a woman. Thank you for telling me. I opened up a can of worms, so to speak. Someone wants to scare us enough to give up the investigation, which is too late. If I could help, I would."

The inspector flipped the pen between his fingers. "You stuck your nose already too deep into the business. Leave it to us." His phone chirped. Daniel waved and closed the door behind him. *Time to go home and be a father.*

♥♥♥

Nobody was home when Daniel arrived. Mia's voice lesson and Julian's piano would still take some time. It suited Daniel. He would finish the list of music for London. The indoor evening concerts needed a different selection than the ones outdoors. For the first ones, he thought Tchaikovsky's *Polonaise of Eugen Onegin* would make a good, strong entrance. After that Liszt's *Hungarian Rapsody* and Brahm's *Second Symphony*. In the afternoons a Rossini *Ouverture* would sound bright and happy. To keep the audience's attention, he chose Mozart's *German Dances* and, of course, something by Edward Elgar or Benjamin Britten. After all, he was in England. He still had Schumann's piano concerto in mind with Mark Hamels. But Daniel didn't know if they wanted a soloist this time. There was always time for some short pieces or waltzes. He hoped that London agreed with his ideas.

When his cell phone chimed he saw the number of the piano teacher, Mr. Crohn. *What now?* His voice sounded calm but Daniel heard the tension in it. "Someone is here claiming that you told him to bring Julian home."

Daniel jumped up. "No way! Call the police. Is he in your house?"

"No, I told him to wait outside, the lesson wasn't over yet."

That was clever. Daniel ran to his car. "Keep Julian playing. I'll be there in a few seconds." He was on the road before he could think any further. Stay calm, slow down, he told himself. As long as the man stays outside, he can't harm anyone. Maybe the police will be there before me.

To stay out of sight Daniel parked the car in the back of the house. He looked around. He saw someone close to the front door pacing and smoking a cigarette. He looked like a businessman, dressed in a blue suit and tie. Daniel took out his cell phone and snapped a picture. Not a good one because his hands shook and he didn't dare go closer and alert the man. Should he confront him? Daniel might look into the barrel of a gun or feel the point of a knife. Through a half-open window he could hear Julian playing.

When the man moved towards the front door, Daniel's fury bubbled over. *You bastard.* He knew he had to act. With his heart on fire, he strode into the garden. "Are you waiting for someone?" he asked.

The man jumped. He recovered quickly and crunched his cigarette stub into the ground. "Yes, but I can't wait any longer. I'm going." While he turned, his hand moved into his coat pocket. Daniel caught his breath. A gun? At that moment a police car screeched to a halt. The man tried to run but two officers pushed him against the car. The man struggled and tried to hit one of the officers. The handcuffs came out quickly to subdue him.

Daniel ran over to the officers. "This man tried to kidnap my son from his piano teacher and told him he was sent to bring him home. Mr. Crohn is my witness, he had the sense to call me first."

"You put yourself in danger too. Approaching this man was not the best idea," the officer said.

Daniel nodded. "I'm a father. I had to do something. But I think the man has a gun."

"We'll find it." The policeman turned to the offender. "You better come and make a statement."

After they drove off Daniel leaned against the fence and closed his eyes. *Too close for comfort.* Daniel tried to slow down his pumping heart. Finally, he walked up to Julian and Mr. Crohn at the front door. "Thank you for not believing that crook. Always, always call me if there is anything suspicious." He shook the teacher's hand.

Mr. Crohn wiped his forehead with his handkerchief. "I'll be your witness if it comes to court. This was brazen." He turned to Julian. "Good work, keep it up," then walked back into the house.

"You have to tell me what was going on, Papa," Julian said on their way home. "Mr. Crohn had me play the long piece twice. I'm exhausted."

Daniel shook his head. "That should be the least of your worries. But your teacher didn't want to scare you, so he made you work instead. I'll tell you the details at home." He needed to find the right words for that.

Julian kept bombarding Daniel with questions about what happened during his lesson. Daniel told him to wait until they were home. Mia would also be there to listen.

Finally, sitting around the kitchen table, Julian complained, "Papa, why do you always make me wait. If this concerns me you could have told me everything in the car."

Daniel pointed his finger at him. "You forget that you would miss my usual lecture on safety that goes with it. Mia would also miss it."

"Oh, not again," came out of both their mouths.

But Mia's face was pale when Daniel had finished. With her hands folded tightly, she said, "This man could have broken the door down, hurt or even killed Mr. Crohn, and taken Julian."

Julian's eyes blazed. "I would have screamed and screamed. And I would have kicked the guy real hard. What would he want me for anyway?"

Mia wiped away tears. "He would have been too strong for you."

Daniel had to stop them. "Mia, hold on now. Mr. Crohn knew what to do. We have an understanding. Now I repeat the safety lecture. Look around you, don't daydream, don't trust people you don't know. For now, that's the way it has to be. We will solve this mystery. End of lesson."

Mia looked at him. "You may be the next one, Papa."

"I'm amongst a lot of people most of the time. It would be too risky." No use telling them about the car incident and making them even more worried. "Any questions?"

"Yes." Mia had regained some color. She stood up and leaned her hands on the table. "Can we start with supper? I wouldn't like us starving."

Daniel just stared at her. "You are turning more and more into your Mama." *Kids are unbelievable. Thank God for their resilience. And my ever-alert Guardian Angel.*

Chapter 11

Later that night Daniel ran the events of the afternoon through his mind again. To endanger his children aside from himself someone must cover or hide a crime of some importance. Drugs, lots of money, smuggling, probably all of it. It had to be widespread to involve different cities like Seattle. What about Portland? *Do I need a bodyguard again?* And he would have Julian with him. But he certainly would not be any safer here. Inspector Lankin better put some pressure on the to-be-kidnapper. Thinking about what could have happened to Julian made Daniel's stomach turn into a knot. Maybe the boy with the bomb would be a better candidate for giving up the person who texted him. He was scared and not as hardened as the other men. And there was his cell phone. Nowadays techies could retrieve all sorts of messages. How long would all of this take? Daniel's patience was getting shorter by the day.

In a previous situation, he had been able to talk to the suspect. If Daniel could convince the boy of the seriousness and the danger he had put the children in, maybe he would realize how close to a murder he had come. Does this kid have anyone looking after him? Daniel sighed. That was always the question. But he would try to get the inspector's permission to talk to the boy. With that thought, Daniel finally crept under the blankets. *Let me be unconscious for a while.*

☙❧

On Wednesday morning Daniel heard Mia running up and down the stair earlier than usual. Was she nervous about the *Carmina* rehearsal? He yawned and threw off the blankets. His sleep had been amazingly deep with only wisps of places and faces he didn't recognize. *Time to get real again.*

Mia had already boiled eggs when Daniel came into the kitchen. The coffee pot made its usual popping noises. "You're going full out this morning. Why the hurry?" Daniel asked. Compared to yesterday Mia seemed to have regained her good spirits.

"I'm so excited, I couldn't sleep any longer. Besides, I'll miss school today, so I did some writing ahead of time."

"Mia, you're too perfect, relax." Daniel grabbed his mug and filled it with coffee. "It's only the first rehearsal."

"Yes, and my first time on stage with you conducting." She put plates on the table.

Julian, sleepy-eyed, slumped down the stairs. "You have all the fun, Mia. I'll have a history with all the boring dates."

Daniel grabbed bread out of the toaster. "Eat your breakfast. You'll feel better."

Julian slid onto the chair. "I'm not going to practice to-day."

"Why not?"

"Mia has three hours of fun, so I'll have one hour of TV instead." Julian bit purposefully into his toast.

Mia giggled. "The piano will be so sad."

"Oh, bull—" Julian stopped himself just in time after looking at Daniel's stern face.

"Ahem, delete that word forever. Okay, have your show. One hour, no more. Mrs. Gantrey will tell me." Daniel had a hard time not laughing.

∞

After Julian had left for school Daniel collected his score and notes for the rehearsal, as well as the taped voicemail for the inspector. He needed results more than ever.

Mia, with the *Carmina* book under her arm, stood ready to drive along with him. "It will be different from drama class," she said. "Busier for sure."

Daniel had to agree when they stepped into the Symphony Hall. "Forty-five more people," he muttered. "It's going to be noisy." It took a while for the musicians to settle and the stage manager to reorganize the tiers for the singers. Between chatter and laughter, they finally found their places. Daniel knew it would take more time than usual to achieve the quiet he needed to start.

When it finally happened he called out, "Good morning, everybody. This will be a good performance—" he stopped, smiled, and continued "—eventually." Which created laughter from all around. "This being the first rehearsal it might involve some repeats. Orchestra and choir need to stay together." He motioned to the choirmaster. "Your tempo might not be my tempo, so tell the singers to watch me closely." The choirmaster nodded and trotted up the stage to instruct his group.

All right, here we go. Daniel looked at the orchestra, then at the choir, and raised his arms for the downbeat. To his surprise, they all came in together with a strong "Oh, Fortuna!"

After a while, he noticed one soprano voice a bit too loud for his taste. It stuck out instead of blending in. Maybe she wasn't aware of it. But he did not need a soloist just yet. He stopped after the first chorus and called the choirmaster. "Who is the lady with the loud voice?" he asked.

The choirmaster smiled. "Your daughter, Maestro."

Daniel's mouth fell open. "No kidding. Tell her to hold back."

Still smiling the man went back to the stage.

Big surprise, Daniel thought. Since Elvira's death, he had not heard Mia sing at home. Was she practicing when he was at work? Or had he just not paid attention? Her voice must have developed in the meantime. Maybe it would be solo material. For now, she had to be aware of her strength. He hoped it did not rattle her to be criticized by her father. *I'll talk to her later.*

He kept working through the music until lunch break. The soloists, a soprano, tenor, and baritone, would arrive after it.

The restaurant was filling up quickly. Singers crowded in talking and looking for spaces to sit. When Daniel came through the door all eyes turned to him. He smiled and waved. A waitress ushered him to a table with two seats. *Rescued.* Where was Mia? He needed to assure her that softening her voice was not meant as a critique. Finally he saw her coming in. He waved her over. She did not look happy.

"Sit down, Mia. Have some lunch. Why do you look so sad?"

She fiddled with the dessert menu. "I didn't sing very well."

"Not true. I'm glad your voice has developed. All you need to do is hold back a bit in a choir."

Mia looked at him. "Okay, but I've worked hard since

Mama died so she would be proud of me. I want to be a strong mezzo-soprano."

Daniel patted her hand. "And you will be. You might turn into a solo singer for recitals, opera, or solos for a chorus like this one. For that, you will need a voice to fill the house."

"So I'm okay?" Mia still looked doubtful.

"Yes, you are. Just realize that you'll have to face stiff competition. Learn as much as you can. You know I'll support you."

Mia nodded, then smiled. "I'll only have dessert. That's my soul food for today. Can I go over to my friends?"

Daniel chuckled. "Get going, diva-to-be."

✎✎✎

The three soloists were waiting when Daniel arrived back at Symphony Hall. He shook their hands. "I'm glad to see you. We'll start with you, way-ward monk, then the swan, ready to be eaten and the temptress."

"Happy to meet you again, Maestro," the baritone said. "This will be fun."

"Except for me." The tenor sighed. "I'm on the dinner table."

The soprano patted him on the shoulder. "Only temporarily."

Daniel enjoyed their bantering. "Okay, let's start. I think the masses are ready."

As rehearsals progressed, Daniel had to call out instructions for the stage settings. "I need the singers for the swan scene to sit around the table with forks in their hands. Do we have a pretend swan?" He knew this would create laughter in the audience. But Orff's work showed all about medieval times and customs.

Daniel took the soloists through their parts three times,

then dismissed musicians and singers. "Tomorrow the whole thing. Prepare yourselves," he told them. On his way out he heard a girl talking to Mia.

"Your dad is picky. He repeats a lot."

"He has to," Mia answered. "He wants it to sound the best it can be for the composer and the audience."

Daniel chuckled. "Well said, my clever daughter."

Since Mia decided to drive home with one of her soprano friends, Daniel went on his way to deliver the voice tape to the inspector. *Maybe I can convince him to let me visit the arson boy in jail,* he thought.

Inspector Lankin was not impressed with the idea. "Only next of kin and his solicitor are allowed to see him," he reminded Daniel.

Daniel did not give up. "Did any of his parents see him? Does he even have parents?"

The inspector shrugged. "He told us he doesn't know where they are. Maybe he doesn't want them to know. We couldn't find any address."

"I'm sure anyone caring for him would have reported him missing by now," Daniel said.

Inspector Lankin turned his head and looked out of the window beside him. "We're searching now for a guardian or a foster home."

Daniel pushed again. "Even more reason for me to see him. He might tell me more than a policeman."

The inspector gave one of his deep sighs. "Okay, Daniel, just for you but I want you to record the session. We record all our interviews anyway, so, it's no different."

Daniel got up. "Thank you, Inspector. When can I go?"

"Right now. Let's get it over with." To Daniel Inspector Lankin sounded like he might regret his decision. He called an officer to accompany Daniel. "Stay with him," he ordered.

I won this one, Daniel thought. On his way to the cell,

he tried to organize his thoughts. Again he remembered Jason from years ago and how this helped to unravel the mystery. Daniel would be calm and understanding. *Maybe I should be a psychologist.*

❧

The boy he saw in his cell looked pale, sat hunched over, and kept his eyes on his tightly clasped hands in his lap. Daniel sat down opposite him.

"My name is Daniel. What's yours?" he asked.

The boy did not look up. "Why is my name important?"

"Because someone named you to make you important."

The boy only shrugged.

"A couple of years ago I helped a person like you," Daniel continued. "I'm not the police, just someone who cares about young people who get themselves into trouble. So, what's your name?"

The boy looked up, his blue eyes still defiant. "Alex."

Baby steps. "Okay, Alex, I bet someone is very worried about you. All of a sudden you disappeared. Who could that be?"

Alex shrugged again. "Maybe my foster mother."

"Does she live nearby?"

"On Polk Street."

Daniel knew he had to be careful of how many questions he would ask. But he tried again. "Is she good to you? Like, feed you right?"

Alex looked down again. "I guess."

"So, what about this bomb, did you get paid for it?" Daniel held his breath.

"No, never." The boy's voice turned angry. "I got cheated."

I'm making progress. "Why would anybody want you to do things like that?"

"I didn't ask and I needed money. Now you know." Alex crossed his arms over his chest.

Daniel sat back. "I know how that feels. When my father died I had a really tough time. What did you need money for?"

"I never get an allowance, even for a candy bar." Now Alex sounded like a grumpy child. Then he looked up. "My father died too, and my mother couldn't cope."

I'll have to go easy now. "Did you even realize what a bomb like that could do? You could have killed the girls."

Alex twisted his hands together again. "I thought it was like fireworks to scare them."

Daniel got up. "Yeah, I'll bet that's what the man told you, right? Did you ever hear his name or his voice?"

Alex shook his head. "Nope."

"Okay, I'll go now. Can I come back again, Alex? Just to talk?"

The boy nodded and looked up. "Can I have my blue bag with my homework?"

Daniel was surprised. "I'll see what I can do. Stay calm, okay?" *I think he can be saved.*

He handed the tape of the conversation over to the officer. "You seem to have a knack with kids," he commented. "I'll take this over to the inspector."

On the street again he had to stop for a minute. Alex was not a criminal, he was hurt and troubled. He had been barely aware of the possible outcome of the fire. His foster mother needed to be found. In the meantime, Alex would stand trial as a juvenile

They parted ways and Daniel drove home. Thoughts tumbled through his mind. Was it only upbringing which turned kids into what they became? He had heard from loving, caring parents whose son or daughter went astray. Rebellion? Genes? Bad influence despite a stable family? This made him wonder whether he was even able to raise his own children to be responsible, good adults. So far both of them had listened to his advice whenever needed. *I will have to try hard that it will continue. Oh, Elvira, where are you when I need you?*

Chapter 12

On his way to *Carmina's* rehearsal the next morning Daniel still recalled Alex's pale face and listless eyes. Mia had been quiet when Daniel described his visit with the boy.

"He had a lonely life," she said. "But that's no way to make money."

"True," Daniel agreed. "He has to go to jail. But I got more information out of him than the police. I'm going to see him again. He needs a friend. Who knows, maybe it will lead to an end of our problems."

Mia stayed silent for the rest of the drive. At the theater, she brightened up. "I'll hold back my voice," she said with an impish smile. Daniel chuckled at that.

Two hours later he stopped the rehearsal. "I'm happy so far," he told the musicians. "I only want to hear the soloists once more after lunch. For now, have something to eat."

On the way to the restaurant, he called Inspector Lankin. "Did you have time to listen to the tape, Inspector? Any news on the boy?"

"Yeah, we found his foster mother. She didn't report him missing because she has other kids to take care of, so she said. But your voice tape didn't match any of the men we have in custody."

Daniel's good mood crumbled. "Disappointing. Thanks

for checking. I want to see Alex again soon."

"Only if you get more info out of him," the inspector said and hung up.

Let me think. Coffee! No voice comparison, nothing on the maker of the bomb, nothing on Alex's cell phone. And none of the prisoners were talking. They must be deadly afraid of someone. *Do I have to wait for another hit? I would probably be next in line again. Darn it all!* Daniel stirred sugar into his coffee cup. The menu didn't look tempting. A second cup would be it for now.

Mia walked in and sat down opposite Daniel. "How did I sound today, Papa?" she asked.

He sipped his coffee. "You fitted in nicely. Now don't hold back in your lessons or solos."

Mia nodded. "Okay, but you look down. I thought you were happy with us."

Daniel sighed. "I am. Only the inspector hasn't found anything to help us. Not even on the latest incident with Julian. I'll change the day for his piano lessons." He related the conversation he had with Inspector Lankin. "I'll see Alex again, although I doubt that he knows much more than before."

"What about the guy who tried to kidnap Julian?"

"He should be in the system, I'm sure. He's being held and will be tried." Daniel stopped for a moment. "Come to think of it, the boss behind all this has lost four of his soldiers. He must be angry by now. If someone doesn't talk soon, we'll be hit again."

"Might he give up?" Mia looked hopefully at Daniel.

He shook his head. "The criminal mind doesn't give up. He seems to have them working mostly in construction, that's all we have so far. They certainly have all the vehicles to transport stuff, whatever that is. Maybe the police are checking them out."

Mia got up. "I'm going home to make sure Julian is okay."

"Right, see you later." Daniel rose too. *The soloists are waiting.*

⌘

The next morning Daniel kept busy going over *Aida* scenes again and sorting out the music he had chosen for London. His agent, Gwen Curtis, had not told him yet whether they agreed with Daniel's choices. He didn't foresee any problems and he liked working ahead of time.

Daniel had promised Julian that he could attend the *Carmina* performance that night. "I can hardly wait." Julian jumped from one foot to the other. "Can I sing along with it? Really quiet?"

"Only if you sing in your head," Daniel cautioned him. "I don't want to hear you behind me."

"What about tomorrow evening?"

"Same thing, Mr. Eager Beaver. You can sing at home." Daniel couldn't help feeling proud of his son's interest in the music.

⌘

To his surprise, the audience filled the theater quickly that night. *Carmina Burana* had not been on the program for some time, people seemed to be looking forward to it. With Julian dancing around him, Daniel changed in his dressing room.

"Can I see Mia from where I'm sitting?" Julian asked for the second time.

"You can see the whole choir," Daniel assured him. "Now calm down. I'll show you where you go." He steered his son through a side door and pointed to a seat with a sign *Reserved.* "Sit there and don't move until the inter-mission. The lady beside you will watch over you, okay?"

"Yes, Papa. I promised I won't sing."

Daniel waited until Julian sat down and waved to him. He had recruited one of the ushers to sit with Julian for safety reasons. One failed kidnapping attempt was more than enough. The oboe's A sounded, time to concentrate on the performance.

When Daniel bowed to the audience he heard Julian whisper, "I can see Mia." Daniel glanced at him and put his finger across his lips. Julian nodded.

The audience enjoyed the performance and even ap-plauded after each solo number. Daniel had to appear a few times before they started to leave. The usher brought Julian to his dressing room. He could hardly contain him-self.

"This was super great, Papa. The different instruments and the swan with his high voice and—and—"

"Stop, Julian, slow down. You can see it all again to-morrow. Let's wait for Mia, then go home." Daniel changed into his street clothes. Julian was still squirming around.

"How do you know which instrument has to play next?"

"I have the score and I memorize. Here comes Mia. My stomach growls, let's go." Daniel knew both kids would chatter all the way home.

☙❧

After breakfast the next morning Daniel got a phone call from Inspector Lankin.

"We had an incident last night. They found our would-be-kidnapper dead in his jail cell."

Daniel sat down. "How? How was that possible with all the security?"

The inspector grunted. "Unless someone bribed the warden, I don't know. Maybe someone was afraid he would talk. He got shot with a small arrow, possibly poisoned."

Daniel got up again and paced around. "A quick order of a fast and quiet death. No wonder none of the others are talking. If this guy has his spies everywhere, he will know that I have talked to Alex. You have to make sure that he's safe. I'm seeing him again today. Maybe he remembers some details. He has no knowledge of my problems or a connection to the kidnapper. So that person's death doesn't mean anything to him." A thought occurred to him. "Do you think you might have a mole in your ranks? People do a lot for money."

The inspector snorted. "Impossible! My men are honest cops. I trust them, never had reasons not to."

Daniel softened his voice. "Okay, I see your side. But, as you said before, what about the wardens? Can they be bought? Or could someone have stolen a police uniform and marched right in?"

Inspector Lankin was quiet for a moment. Then he said, "You have quite an imagination. I still say none of my officers are involved. But..." Daniel heard him sigh. The inspector continued, "I guess in this world anything can happen. We better keep an eye on the other prisoners. I don't need any more corpses in jail cells."

Daniel rubbed his forehead. "I'd better look out too if I see Alex."

"Right. Now back to work." The inspector hung up.

Daniel looked at Mia and Julian. "What are you doing today?"

Julian shrugged. "Not much, just waiting for tonight."

"And I'm studying and practicing a new song," Mia said.

"Good. I'm visiting Alex once more, so stay safe and get ready for tonight." *I'm not telling them about the prisoner's death, at least not yet.*

∽⌒∾

"One less who could have talked," Daniel muttered on his ride to the jail. "Maybe they won't let me see Alex, after all the jail is a crime scene."

By the time Daniel arrived, things were calm again. Since Alex was kept in another cellblock he was allowed to see him.

The boy sat hunched over like the last time, but he looked up when Daniel came in.

Daniel pushed the chair closer to the table. "How are you holding out, Alex?"

The boy shrugged, also like before.

"Do they treat you right?"

"I guess."

He seems to use the same words and gestures. "Did you remember anything about the text you got about the bomb? What exactly did it say?" *Come on, tell me something.*

Alex studied his hands. "It said 'go to the post office, ask for Clark to give you a parcel, tell him, the big one.' He did, I took it and threw it into the gym. That's it."

Aha, another step forward. "Which post office was it? Can you describe this Clark or pick him out of pictures?"

Alex looked up. "I guess."

"The more information we get the faster the police can locate the man who used you. We have to find him before he does any more damage." *Particularly to me and my family.* Daniel pushed the chair back. "When do you have to go to court?"

"Tomorrow, I think." Alex looked worried.

"If I can make it, I'll be there, okay?"

The boy nodded. Daniel heard a soft, "Thank you." He waved to Alex and left. He doesn't even know what kind of a rat's nest he has gotten himself into, Daniel thought. Now I can tell the inspector a bit more. But today was Sunday, so no use in trying. Maybe they found it all out on Alex's cellphone already. For now, Daniel had to think of this evening's performance of *Carmina* with all the excitement of Julian and Mia again.

Chapter 13

At the second performance that night Daniel again had a sympathetic audience. Not a full house but close to it. Julian was quieter this time.

"I'm listening to every instrument," he stated. "That way I can hear where they're going."

"Be my guest," Daniel said. "But don't forget the whole effect. That's what I have to aim for." Secretly he was proud of Julian's ideas and effort.

∽∾

On their way home later that night Mia looked sad. "Twice is not enough for all the work. Why not do it once more?"

"Scheduling, Mia. We're not the only ones in the theater. It's not all for me to decide. Tomorrow rehearsals start again for the international concert, twice here and once over at the concert hall in Oakland over the bridge." Daniel felt for Mia. Her singing on stage had been a huge experience for her.

Mia fiddled with her purse. "Could I audition for the opera chorus, Papa?"

Daniel looked at her. "You can try. But what about school? The rehearsals are mostly in the morning."

Mia frowned. "I might not be good enough anyway."

"Hey," Julian chimed in. "You should audition because you're good."

Daniel knew Mia would give it a lot of thought.

ᑔᑊᑔ

"Oh, you again." Inspector Lankin didn't look happy when Daniel entered his office the next morning.

Daniel's calm mood faded. "Yes, I thought you might be interested that Alex told me all about the text on his cell phone, also the post office where he picked up the parcel, and the name of the person who gave it to him. Your department doesn't seem to get any closer to solving my problems."

The inspector stared at him. "How do you know? I understand your frustration but you're not the only case we're working on." He sat down. "We got the text from Alex's cell phone and the area from where it was sent. Knowing criminals, that's probably not our bad guy's place of command."

Daniel took a long breath. *I better check my temper.* "I'm glad the techies found it. But you have to admit I was somewhat helpful."

"Hm." The inspector shuffled papers again. "They must have met before. How else could anyone know Alex's phone number to send him the message? Alex didn't tell you that, did he?"

Daniel raked his fingers through his hair. "Then someone has approached him before, maybe at school or on the street. But why him?"

"We're asking his foster mother that as we speak."

Daniel stared open-mouthed at the inspector. "You mean that this unsavory individual has his nose in foster care for recruiting vulnerable kids?"

"Where else? Even though he's not supposed to get any

info about them, there is always a way in."

Daniel shook his head. "And all this is going on to get back at me for reporting a bad driver? And maybe—just maybe—discovering a gang of criminals? Hard to believe. Anything on the prisoner's death?"

Inspector Lankin got up. "We're working on it. Daniel, I'll let you know what we find out from the foster mother. Go to your music. Your kids are in school, so relax."

Daniel checked his watch. *Music, my way out of any problem.* "Thank you, Inspector. This has to come to an end sometime." He gave him a quick wave and went out. *Yes, sometime. How much patience do I have to show? If it just involved me I could deal with it, but with the kids? But me getting all huffy doesn't help.* On his way to rehearsal, he promised himself to have faith in the police system. The next hours were going to be full of the best sounds instruments could make. He would wallow in it.

At the theater, Daniel heard the familiar sounds of musicians warming up on their parts and already felt better. *Our problems will end but music will not.* His phone rang: Gwen Curtis, his agent.

"Just wanted to let you know that London likes most of your choices except for Brahms' *Second Symphony*. They want something bigger, flashier, like Saint-Saens' *Organ Symphony*."

"Good Lord, really? It's one of my favorites, but it leaves not much time for anything else."

Gwen was in a hurry. "Let me know soon, okay?" She hung up.

Daniel scratched his head. Good thing he had selected two smaller pieces for variety. *All right, whatever they want. Now back to my work here.*

In Brahms' *Fourth Symphony* Daniel found a dual personality. The music started softly, almost like a lullaby, but soon it turned into dark clouds that threaten to cover the sun. Since Brahms' sickness barely let him attend the premiere, he must have known that his end was near. Even though the dreamy theme came back often, the struggle in the music dominated. The second movement again seemed to be full of unanswered questions. Only the third movement turned boisterous like a good time at the Bierstube. Finally, the music came back to a pensive mood and doubts until the strong character of Brahms made its peace with life as well as death.

Daniel was reminded of his own struggles to keep his life and the lives of his children stress-free, joyful, and safe. But, as he so often found out, that was utopia. He needed strength to keep both his kids and himself on even ground and his mind in reality. Only in the theater was he allowed to dream.

Later, during lunch, Daniel thought it better to leave Inspector Lankin alone for a while. He had his hands full with case after case, and Daniel had almost accused him of not helping him. But he was curious about the foster mother's interview. Would she sell Alex out for money? Maybe she met the main culprit who was behind all the trouble. Maybe she could even identify him. Daniel's head started to throb. He needed to stop assuming things. The only true reality was his music, note by note, score by score. He swallowed the rest of his coffee and switched his mind back to Brahms. He remembered a few small bars he meant to correct in the second violin section. How easy was his job against the one to figure out criminal minds?

✎∽✎∽

During rehearsal, the librarian came up to Daniel. "I got a call from Karl at the stage door. A man wants to speak to you urgently. He claims it's about your daughter."

Cold shivers ran down Daniel's spine. "Did he mention

her name?"

"No, he didn't."

"Tell Karl to keep him there. I'll call my daughter first." Daniel shook with anger. Was this again a ruse? Mia answered at the third ring. "Are you all right, Mia?" He had a hard time controlling his voice.

"Yeah, what's up, Papa?" Mia sounded concerned. "I couldn't answer right away."

Daniel took a breath. *Thank the Lord.* "That's all I need to know. Take special care. I'll tell you later." He dialed the inspector's number. "If you're quick you can pick up another of my enemies at the theater's stage door."

"Right!" The inspector hung up. Daniel could only hope that Karl was able to hold the man there. There was nothing else for Daniel to do. He closed his eyes and willed his heart to stop racing. In case the man had disappeared Karl would have had a good look at him to identify him.

Daniel had to get his breathing back to normal before he returned to the musicians. "Sorry for the interruption. A personal inconvenience. Let's start the last movement." *I'm not allowing criminals to break my work into pieces. I* won't *give them that pleasure.*

At the end of the rehearsal, Daniel didn't quite know where to go first: home to see Mia or to the police station to find out what happened with the man at the stage door. Even if the officers had been able to nab him, he would be like the others, not talking. Daniel had to get home. Before that he needed to talk to Karl.

He sat in his booth munching on a sandwich when Daniel came around the corner. Karl looked up. "Maestro, that strange man walked off. He was weird, hedging. No way was I going to let him see you."

"So the police didn't come fast enough?"

Karl wiped his hands. "They came and I gave them a description of him. Maybe they found him."

Daniel nodded. "Let's hope so. Thank you for being careful." *Well, we tried.*

ॐ

He heard Mia's voice when he opened the back door. She was singing, that is, practicing. Her voice sounded strong with a certain warmth which he had seldom heard in a young girl. He had missed it for a long time. He tiptoed into the kitchen. *Tea, coffee? Why not tea for a change?* He heard Julian come into the house and braced himself for the usual slam of the back door. To his surprise, it closed softly.

Julian beamed at him. "I was quiet, wasn't I?"

Daniel ruffled his hair. "I can't believe you were."

"Mia said, if I slam the door when she's practicing, she'd bop me."

Daniel sat down and chuckled. "Bop you? How nicely said." *I only have to come home to laugh again. How good is that?*

Mia appeared at the kitchen door. "I'm planning spaghetti and meatballs for supper. Agreed?"

Daniel finished his tea. "Okay. Kids, I have work to do. If you need help with supper, let me know." He looked at Mia. "This morning someone wanted me to believe that he had a message about you. The police might have caught him, I don't know."

Mia shook her head. "Good thing I was in school. I'm extra careful now. Only my main teacher and the principal know about our threats. So they look out for me too."

"I'm happy with that. See you in an hour."

In his study he sat down. He needed to think through the events of the day. Why did the man at the stage door want to see Daniel face to face? *Harming or even killing me in front of Karl would have been stupid. Killing Karl first and then me? Unthinkable. If either of us had survived we would have identified him. Another incompetent soldier?* Daniel shook his head. Karl could now be in danger too because he gave the police his description. How far would all of this lead? The inspector had not called him, so, the guy probably took off before the police arrived.

He got up and put on a CD of *Aida's* last scene. He found his hands automatically moving to the music. The Portland engagement was coming up quickly and he needed to know every phrase, every note. Taking over someone's conducting work was always tricky. But Daniel knew he would enjoy it.

After the death scene of Aida and Radames, Daniel had to wipe a tear off his cheek. Elvira's death still seemed to be so close. He needed to steel himself against his feelings, especially in front of the musicians.

Daniel's phone rang. Inspector Lankin's voice boomed at him. "You want some news? I have a bit for you. See you tomorrow morning."

"Hold on, Inspector, not so fast. At least give me a hint." *Don't hang up on me.*

"The news is connected to the foster mother, the post office, and the guy at your stage door. We also have some fingerprints. Figure it out. All right, I'm ready to go for supper. Good night."

Daniel sat stunned for a few minutes. But he had detected almost a chuckle in the inspector's voice. Was he baiting Daniel? But he left Daniel again to his own assumptions which he didn't want to make. Did the police get the man at the theater? Did the foster mother give up names? What about the clerk at the post office? Who's fingerprints? *All right, stop. I'm not taking this to supper and bed. I'll wait until tomorrow.*

cᴓcᴓ

After a restless night, Daniel wasn't sure if this day was worth getting up for. On the one hand, he could hardly contain his curiosity to hear the inspector's news. On the other hand, he had butterflies in his stomach. Would his hopes for some real answers be dashed again? Alex's trial day was also on his mind. *I might not be able to go there, depending on the time.*

At breakfast he told the kids, "Well, here goes nothing—or everything. Send some good thought to the universe to speed up catching the real troublemaker."

"Is the universe up in the sky?" Julian asked.

"Yes, and all around us. Often it decides our fate. Hard to understand, I know." Daniel swallowed the last of his coffee and got up.

Mia and Julian gave him a hug. "Good luck, Papa."

He swore to himself to listen calmly to Inspector Lankin.

On his way to the police station, Daniel recited the inspector's words—foster mother, post office, the man at the stage door, fingerprints. How were they connected? Was the post office guy the same man at the theater? Was the foster mother in debt to someone and had to give Alex's cell phone number away? Whose fingerprints? Daniel had to remind himself to cool down and let the inspector do the talking.

In the waiting room of the police station, he was met by the same woman he had seen on his first visit.

"Hello, Maestro. How nice to see you. You must be an early riser, not like other artists." She gave him a wide smile.

Daniel had a strange feeling about her demeanor. Something looked false. *She smiles with her white teeth but not with her eyes.* "My artistic endeavors require rehearsals in the morning," he told her. "No sleeping in."

Her smile didn't falter. "Of course, how silly of me not to know. The inspector is waiting for you." She pointed down the hall.

Daniel shook his head. Could she have been the woman waiting for Mia that night and giving him that strong push? But why? A dedicated policewoman? He had to laugh at himself. Of course she wouldn't wear those pink sneakers to work. Proper shoes were needed here. *Whatever gave me the idea that she could be involved?*

Inspector Lankin was deep into a telephone conversation. He waved Daniel in. With the words "Call me back in an hour," he ended the call. He sat back and looked at Daniel. "I hope you realize that you get special treatment here. Me calling you, telling you what's going on. However, your status and being a single father caring for your children shifted my rules a bit."

Daniel took a minute to get over his surprise. He had expected the inspector to be as short and to the point as possible. "Thank you, Sir. I'm grateful that you understand what I'm up against." He sat down across from the inspector. "I think that the hints you gave me yesterday are all connected. But how?"

Inspector Lankin got up. "Let's see now. Three people are in custody: the race driver who ran down the lady, the one who broke into your house, and now Alex. The other threats didn't show enough evidence to hold anyone, including the Seattle event. Neither did we get any voice match from your tape."

"I agree," Daniel said. "But what about Alex's foster mother?"

"A woman from Social Services convinced her to hand over Alex's cell phone number explaining that they needed to keep in touch with foster children. The mother described her with long blond hair and sunglasses."

Daniel shook his head. "Didn't she ask for

identification?"

The inspector sat down again. "Apparently she showed her something, possibly fake. I'm sure so are her looks."

Daniel slid his hand along the polished desk. "Clever. That way nobody can identify her later. Wigs are available. We deal with them in the theater all the time."

"About the guy at the theater," the inspector continued. "He is the same man as the one in the post office."

Daniel got excited. "So you caught him after all. Now we know someone connected to the bomb in the parcel."

"Yes, thanks to Karl's description and Alex remembering the post office clerk. He told us that he was handed the parcel with the order to give it to Alex. He didn't know what was in it."

"Then why did he come to the theater? Just to make me anxious about Mia? Only more exposure of him, not very bright." *Are they actually that stupid?*

Inspector Lankin nodded. "They all claim they only obey orders by texting, no personal contacts."

"Except maybe at their construction sites?"

The inspector shrugged. "That's where we are going now. There must be quite a few of them. The only lead we have now is a full palm print at the side of the cell door. The shooter of the kidnapper must have leaned again it. Careless, because the arrow had no fingerprints on it. That means he only wore one glove. We have to find the person to match it with."

Daniel let out a long breath. "You have been busy, thank you for telling me. It gives me some hope. If the woman from foster care was a fake you have to find her too. Never ending, isn't it?"

Inspector Lankin got up. "We will eventually find them all. Stay alert, you and your kids."

"We will. I'd better go and do my work. Thanks again." Daniel pushed the chair back, nodded goodbye and closed the door. *That gives me a lot to think about. Somehow things seem to be going forward. But I better expect more tricks coming my way.*

∽∾∽

All the way to Symphony Hall Daniel tried to fit together the information he had heard from Inspector Lankin. One thought popped up again and again: how could anyone have known about him reporting the race driver except the inspector? The first person he had seen had been the policewoman at the front desk. But she didn't know any details unless she had picked them up from the chatter around her. Or she had somehow listened in on a telephone connection. Why was Daniel so suspicious of her? Because she acted like a fake? That didn't make her a spy. Then why? *I have to stop, this is too far out. Concentrate on your music.* Daniel needed to go through the whole program from Bizet to Rimsky to Brahms. That should chase any other thoughts away.

And it did. At lunchtime, he felt like taking a nap. Instead, he headed for the coffee urn. To keep his promise to Mia he also opted for a Greek salad. Lately, she reminded him of keeping a balance in his eating habits. Daniel smiled to himself. *She's so much like her mother.* While spreading the salad dressing he remembered Alex's court day. Damn, there had been no time for him to go. Daniel could guess the outcome: juvenile detention. *I'll see him soon. He needs someone to tell him there is a way to better his life.*

Deep in thought, he picked at his salad. Someone came to his table. He looked up. "Oh, John. Everything all right?"

The concertmaster smiled. "Yes. You mind?" He pointed to the chair.

"No, of course not, sit."

John sat down. "I hope you don't mind me asking. I heard about threats made against you and your family. Is it serious? It must be scary."

Daniel pushed his salad bowl away. "It's been a problem but the police are working to get a handle on it." *I'm not going to go into details. The less the musicians know, the better. Why is John so interested?*

"I just heard about the man at the stage door from Karl," John continued. "What did he want?"

Daniel sipped his coffee. "No idea. The police caught him. I have tried not to let this get into my work."

John chuckled. "Yeah, we don't feel any difference. Da capo as usual."

Daniel laughed too. "Good. Let's get back to the rest of the concert. Just don't spread any of my problems around. I'll try and stay alive." *All I need is the orchestra hovering around me speculating.* It occurred to Daniel that Karl knew nothing about the other threats, only of the man at the door. How did John find out about them? *I'm paranoid again. Faithful John wouldn't try to get more info out of me, would he? And why? John is a musician not a spy for someone. Discard that thought.*

The rest of the rehearsal went well and Daniel felt good about it. "One more of this tomorrow," he told the musicians. "Then three performances, two here, and the Sunday matinee in Oakland. For that one, we leave here in the morning. It will be an all-day job. Just a reminder. I hope all of you can make it." Sometimes a Sunday performance clashed with orchestra members—family obligations, teaching, even though the performances were arranged long ago.

On his way home, Daniel remembered trips with the orchestra into different cities. It always took a lot of planning and work, especially when it involved plane rides.

After a tour like that he always felt the need for a holiday. This time they only needed two buses.

When he got home Daniel heard Julian practicing. Mia sat at the kitchen table. She looked up at him with tears in her eyes.

"What's the matter, Mia? What happened?"

"My singing teacher is moving to Santa Monica in the summer. What am I going to do then?" She wiped her eyes. "I hate getting a new teacher I don't know."

Daniel sat down beside her. "Honey, you have come a long way already. You just continue. A new teacher doesn't mean to start all over again."

"What if they want or have a different technique that could ruin my voice?"

Daniel thought for a moment. "Could your teacher recommend someone that teaches as she does? If you're aiming for a singing career you'll need different teachers along the way. Some can only go a certain way and then you need a better one. It's the same with all soloists. We'll find a good one." Daniel hated to see Mia upset. He also knew that she had to get used to change. He put his arm around her shoulder. "Cheer up, kiddo, I also went through that. It's a bit scary but it's a natural process."

Mia wiped her eyes again. "Okay, maybe you can help find a good one? You know so many people."

"Ask your teacher first if she knows someone, then we'll see. Agreed?"

Mia nodded. "Sorry, Papa, you have enough to think about, but I'm anxious about it."

Daniel patted her hand. "Understandably. But keep on with your work."

"Can we go out for supper? I didn't prepare anything." She still looked forlorn.

Daniel couldn't help smiling. "If that'll soothe your pain, we certainly can do that. Better?"

Mia gave him a lopsided smile. "Okay, thanks." She got up. "I have work to do."

Julian came into the kitchen. "What's wrong with Mia? Is she crying?"

Daniel explained why Mia was sad. "Oh, bummer." Julian headed for the cookie jar. "I hope I'll keep my teacher for a while, although he's pretty strict." He looked thoughtfully at his cookie. "Is she going to find a new one?"

I might as well prepare him too. "Yes, she will. After a few years, you might need a new teacher too. The first one might not be able to teach you more than you need. But you have time yet." He looked at him. "No more cookies, we're going out for supper. Get your homework done."

As usual, Julian's reaction was, "Yayyy!" with a hop and skip up to his room.

Chapter 14

At the restaurant over her favorite meal of stir-fry chicken Daniel noticed Mia's face brighten up. After an additional treat of cheesecake, she turned to him. "Papa, I saw conductors on TV. They didn't use a baton, just their hands. Can you do that?"

Daniel stared at her in mock horror. "What? You want to take away my only defense against eighty-plus people staring at me?"

Mia laughed. "Papa, they don't attack you."

"That's because I have my stick waving at them. Who knows what any of them might do if they don't agree with me?" Daniel enjoyed pretending fear about the age-old joke of the conductor's weapon.

Mia shook her head. "I guess it's your good-luck charm."

Daniel chuckled. "Yes, it is. When I started I had the fear that I would lose the baton and it would fly away ending up on some musician's head. Luckily that never happened."

Both kids laughed out loud at the vision of a flying baton piercing a musician's head.

Shortly before leaving the restaurant, Daniel's phone rang. He heard the inspector's voice.

"I want you to give a statement about the harassment of the stage door guy. Make it big like claiming emotional stress worrying about Mia on top of your other threats. We need all we can get. Come in tomorrow."

Daniel promised he would be there. He stood quietly for a minute. Yes, he would give them a statement all right with all the correct words of what he was going through.

"What was the call about?" Mia asked.

"Just the inspector. I'll see him tomorrow again. Let's pay and go home." It had been a busy day of music and parenting with a good ending. Daniel yawned, he was ready for bed.

☙☙

The next morning, on his way to the police station, Daniel tried to formulate in his mind the words for his statement. Oh, yes, he would let them know how he had felt on hearing Mia's name from the man at the stage door.

The woman at the front desk tried to smile at Daniel but something wasn't right. Why is she so nervous, he wondered. She pushed papers around as if searching for things, dropped pencils, and frowned.

"I'm here to make the statement the inspector wanted," Daniel said. "Is there a place where I can do that?"

The woman looked up. "Ah—yes—of course. The officer will take you."

Maybe a bad day at the office? In the interview room, he sat at a desk and put down his thoughts onto a page as clearly as possible. *Okay, done. But will it help resolve any of my problems? I'd better get back to work.*

☙☙

The last rehearsal went well, although Daniel made sure of all details. He reminded the musicians to write notes on their scores. As if they don't already know, he thought. In Daniel's mind, a lot of the beauty of music lay in its details: small intonations, quick ideas, musical sparks that would lighten up a few bars. He didn't want to miss them. "See you all tomorrow night," he called and wrapped up his score.

His next step was to see Alex. Daniel felt bad because he had not been able to be at his trial. Junior detention might not be as grim as prison but still meant a loss of freedom. Someone needed to tell Alex not to give up and think instead of his future. After a short interview with the guard who thought Daniel should have made an appointment, he was led into the visitor's room. He couldn't hide his surprise at seeing Alex.

"Lord, have you grown? You're so tall." Daniel shook Alex's hand. *I have never seen him upright before, that's why.* "How are things going, Alex? You all right?"

"Okay, I guess." Alex sat down. "Very organized into hours, outside and inside."

Aha, more words. "Are you keeping up with your studies?"

Alex shrugged. "What for?"

Daniel looked at him. "For the rest of your life outside this place. You want to live, work, and be a person like everyone else, even better."

Alex gave another shrug. "Everybody knows what I did. They don't want me to be around."

"Not true, Alex. If I were you, I would go back to school and finish grade twelve with good marks. By then you'll know what you want to do. But it's up to you."

Alex looked at his hands. "Why do you care? You're famous and have everything."

Daniel had to laugh. "Famous? Not quite. I also have my share of troubles, partly with your help. But I care about young people who were stupid just once. They shouldn't suffer the rest of their lives." He didn't know if he had convinced the boy but then Alex looked up and said, "Maybe. Thanks." After a pause he continued, "I remembered something from the post office. There was another man in a dark suit."

Daniel's ears pricked up. "What? Why didn't you tell me before? What did he do there?"

"He was looking through the mail. I didn't think he was important."

"He might well be. Remember, any little detail can make a difference." Daniel got up. "Think it through what I said. I'll see you again."

Outside he thought, it would be a success if he changes his attitude to learn again. Another man in a dark suit, the lawyer? The one that killed the would-be kidnapper? Interesting.

ೲ

The house was quiet when Daniel arrived. Both kids were still at lessons. *Wonderful, peaceful, good for a leisurely cup of tea.* With a steaming mug of tea in one hand, he opened the newspaper on the table. He seldom got a chance to read it except on weekends.

As he leaved through the pages he stopped at a picture with the caption "Why be unemployed? Build houses." The image showed a burly-looking, smiling man holding various tools and other workers carrying wooden planks. Daniel jumped up to get a magnifying glass. This was after all a construction company hiring people. As the inspector would say, "One of many." Who was the man in the background all dressed up, again in a dark suit? He popped up for the second time today.

Daniel stopped. He needed to get the name of the company and the boss in the front of the picture. They only gave an e-mail. He could find out that way or better yet, he would call the newspaper and the reporter who took the ad. Daniel grabbed the phone. After a few different connections, he got the reporter.

"I don't know any names," he said, "Only the one for the company 'Built Right.' The boss wasn't very happy. He yelled at the guy in the background, 'Get out of the picture, you idiot'." The reporter still chuckled about it.

Daniel thanked him and hung up. Well, maybe I've hit on something, he thought. He called the police station and told the officer to alert the inspector to the ad. Hopefully, he would notice what Daniel saw.

The door slammed. Julian was home. "Julian!" Daniel was not pleased with the noise.

"But, Papa, Mia isn't singing."

"Bad excuse, Buddy." Daniel didn't feel like arguing with his son's logic. His mind was occupied with people in dark suits. Why was this one told to get out of the picture? Clearly, because he wasn't supposed to be seen. Because he was a killer? Even if this was a coincidence, it was worth looking into.

∽∾∽

Mia opened the kitchen door with a big smile. "Guess what, Papa."

"What? Tell me. I'm still wondering about supper. Any ideas?"

Mia rolled her eyes. "Half the menu is already done. But listen. My singing teacher is planning a recital with me and four other students."

"Wow! When?" *Another chance for her.*

"Not sure. But soon." Mia's eyes sparkled. "We have to practice hard and she has to get a place to perform." She opened the fridge door. "See? Hamburgers ready to be fried and salad."

Elvira, how did you raise this girl so well?

Since Daniel had no performance that night he decided after supper to catch up on his exercising, namely walking. After he crossed the first intersection in his neighborhood he heard the sirens of an ambulance. *What now*? He jogged towards the sound and saw people milling around. He sidled up to a woman and asked, "An accident?"

She shook her head. "No, a man fainted on the street. My neighbor couldn't get him up, so he called the ambulance."

Daniel looked closer at the man on the stretcher: long curly, dark hair, with his baseball cap resting on his chest. *Where have I seen him before? What's the race driver doing in my neighborhood? Shouldn't he be in jail? Did he plan to visit me—again?* With more questions on his mind as before Daniel decided to keep on walking for a while. Should he inform Inspector Lankin about this? *Never mind, let me clear my mind, I'm walking.*

Back at home Daniel called the inspector. He should know about one of his jail bird's doings. Inspector Lankin was not happy. "Daniel, really. Do you think I'll have the time to read newspapers? I've barely time to..."

"No, no, Inspector," Daniel interrupted. "Listen, this is new. Our speed demon fainted on the street in my neighborhood, ended up in hospital. Why isn't he in jail?"

After a moment of silence the inspector said, "He was bailed out by his girlfriend."

"I didn't know that. But what is he doing in my neighborhood? Looking for me?"

"Look, Daniel, it's late. Go to bed. I'll check out the hospital. St. Francis?"

"Yes, most likely. Let me know, please." Daniel heard the usual inspectorial sigh.

"Yeah, yeah." The inspector hung up.

No matter how annoyed he gets, *I'm the victim here*

and my kids, Daniel thought. I gave him two items connected to my case. It better count for something. He headed for the brandy bottle and poured himself his favorite treat. *I might as well reward myself.* He tried to relax in his chair and listened to Mia and Julian discussing the weekend. I should take them along for the Sunday concert, he thought. It would do them good to listen to a whole evening of music. He sighed. Crimes, threats, performances, *Aida* coming up, almost too much to digest—except the music itself of course.

⌘

Friday morning was again free for Daniel except for working on scores of upcoming concerts. He also wanted to get in touch with the ailing conductor in Portland before the start of *Aida*. The more he knew ahead of time about the progress of the opera the better.

The conductor was happy to hear from Daniel. They talked about the details concerning the singers, the staging, and the orchestra in general. Then Daniel asked, "Charles, I have a question. My son will be with me during that time. Can you find a babysitter for him when I'm working?"

"Oh, no problem," Charles answered. "We have a nanny for our two kids. She doesn't mind having one more. Besides they will enjoy a different playmate."

Daniel was relieved. "Thank you so much. I'll need all the brain cells I have without a thousand questions from Julian."

Charles laughed. "See you soon. I appreciate you coming."

I'm surprised at the man's happy mood, Daniel thought. Being in the middle of cancer treatment must drag him down but he certainly doesn't sound like it. The phone jangled. *One of the kids?* No, the inspector's voice boomed at him.

"Just so you hear some news. Our jailbird conked out from an overdose even though he claims he doesn't use drugs."

Daniel rubbed his forehead. "He got help I'm sure, just like the kidnapper-to-be."

"Yeah, but this one will live. He's back in the jail infirmary because he had a gun with him."

Daniel's throat felt tight. "Was he on his way to me—again? Thanks for letting me know." So, this race driver had a gun with him, in my neighborhood, he thought. But if he was on a mission, why poison him? If there was a plan, it escapes me. I should think about the performance tonight. At least there is a reliable plan.

Right now, he needed lunch. Soup? Eggs? Sandwich? Okay, scrambled eggs on toast. Sounded like breakfast but in a pinch, he would choose eggs anytime. Elvira used to tease him about it saying that he might have been brought up in a chicken coop. He chuckled about it even now. He could use some reassurance from her right now. *If there is any way from where you are, please keep the kids and me safe.* Because the children were still in school Daniel would take a nap. It wasn't often that he had that opportunity.

೧೪೦೪

On his way to the theater that night the traffic was heavier than usual. With the music humming through Daniel's head, he tried to pay attention to the cars around him. Halfway to his destination, he noticed a silver Mercedes following him. *Could it be one of my musicians? Able to afford a Mercedes? Probably not. I'm not deviating from my normal route.*

Shortly before the entrance to the theater's underground garage, the Mercedes seemed to fall back, then drive by. Good, Daniel thought, just to be on the safe side, I'll notify the police about it. He parked and got out of his car. He had just finished his phone call when he heard screeching brakes and a revving motor. The Mercedes came roaring around the bend.

Daniel barely had time to dive in between two other vehicles when the silver car crashed into the driver's side of his own car pushing it into another parking space. The Mercedes squealed into reverse and screamed out of the garage.

Daniel came slowly out of his crouching position gasping for breath. Two security men ran towards him. "My God, what happened? Are you okay, Maestro?"

Daniel held onto the car beside him. "They wanted me dead," he mumbled.

"Why, in God's name? We'll call this in right now. Did you see who it was?"

Daniel tried to breathe normally. "Only that it was a silver Mercedes." He walked over to his car. He was able to open the passenger's door and retrieve his bag and scores. *If I hadn't stood outside to make the phone call I would be—what? Dead? Half dead?* He closed his eyes.

One of the security men handed him a plastic cup with water. "You better get something stronger than this, Sir. You have to conduct."

Daniel straightened up. "Yes. Thank you." He gulped the water down. "Let them tow my car to the police garage for evidence. At least I'm in one piece." Then he heard police sirens. *Oh, great. More wasted time.*

Two officers rushed in. "Sir, what happened here?"

"Someone tried to kill me again. But I have to conduct a concert with whatever energy I still have." Daniel just wanted to get upstairs.

"We need a statement from you. Can you do that?"

Daniel needed to stall. "Can we do that during the intermission? These two security guards can tell you some of it already."

The officers looked at each other, then nodded. "Okay, go ahead. But we do need your statement today."

"Yes, you will. Excuse me now." On his way up in the elevator Daniel felt numb. His mind seemed to be empty. *Let me sit down in my dressing room*, was all he could think of. Before he arrived the manager ran towards him.

"Thank God, you're all right, Maestro. Please, rest for a bit, it's still early. Can I help in any way?" His face looked flushed.

I don't want to talk to him. "If someone can get me a brandy that would calm me down."

"Of course." The manager disappeared.

Daniel sank into his chair and stretched out his legs. At last, they stopped shaking. He took a long, deep breath. *They have failed again.* There was a knock at the door. "Your brandy, Sir," he heard a voice. "Come in." The worried face of a stagehand appeared around the door. "Great. Thank you. And—I'm okay."

The strong drink opened his throat and warmed his insides. *How many more times is this going to happen? I'm so tired of it. Maybe the rest of my car will give us another clue. There has to be a way.* He checked his watch. *Time to remember the concert.* He grabbed his scores. *If these people think they can keep me away from giving the audience the music they came for, they're badly mistaken.*

The concertmaster met him on the way. "You can wait a bit if you need to."

"No. I'm ready. Let's start." A moment after the oboe's A he strode up to the podium. The audience and musicians applauded. *How word gets around. So much support, amazing.* Daniel bowed and gave the musicians two thumbs up. *Criminals won't survive, music will last for-ever. Let's hear the Russian Easter.*

Rimsky Korsakov got Daniel a standing ovation. The following Bizet's Children's Scenes went the same way. Daniel's mind felt steady and grounded again. This was all worthwhile: the rehearsals, research, poring over manu-scripts and scores. During intermission, he went to get some water. The police officers were waiting. *Let's get this over with.*

Daniel gave them his history and the details from to-night. "This is serious," one of the officers commented. "Any idea who's behind it?"

"If I knew I would solve it," Daniel said. "Or at least the inspector would. Maybe we get closer now." He looked at his watch. "Am I good to go?"

"Yes, thank you, Sir. Good luck from now on." The of-ficers left.

Daniel knew the audience would be getting antsy, but he called the police station. To his surprise, Inspector Lankin came through.

"I'm surprised you're working," he said. "We found the Mercedes, only it's burnt out."

Daniel's mood sank. "So, no evidence left?"

"I wouldn't say that," the inspector continued. "They had an iron bar put in front of the car that didn't burn. They just made sure it would do the most damage to you and your car."

Daniel paced around. "Honestly, we have to find this nest of vipers. I've had enough."

"Right. For now make music. Come by tomorrow. We're on it." The inspector hung up.

Daniel stood quietly for a few minutes. The police had been busy, they had found the car. Was there hope to find anything on it to help to identify the driver?

The concertmaster looked around the corner. "Are you okay to go on, Sir?"

"I'm fine. Just talked to the inspector. Let's go on. Brahms is waiting."

During the performance, Daniel felt closer to Brahms than ever. He was facing death with no second chance. Daniel had come through many close calls but he would live.

After the applause had settled down the manager came to the front of the audience. "Our Maestro was attacked in the parking garage and barely escaped with his life. However, it did not stop him from giving us a most memorable performance of three amazing composers. I would like you to give him an extra hand."

Of course, the clapping started all over again. Daniel felt a bit embarrassed. Give me a raise in salary, he thought. But he had to laugh. *That's not going to happen.* He shook the manager's hand and finally made his way outside to a waiting taxi. *Home*, he thought, *I want to go home and go to bed.*

Chapter 15

Daniel arrived to a dark and quiet house. He crept through the back door as silently as possible. No way was he going to wake up the children. He would explain everything tomorrow. Right now he needed to sit down and replay in his mind what had happened.

Since he had crouched between two cars he had not seen the person in the Mercedes. Daniel could still hear the crashing and ripping of the metal. Only when the car reversed he had noticed a head, round, big, no hat or cap. That was all, nothing of any help. License plates? Everything had happened so fast and he had been too stunned to look for it. *Again something or someone has saved my life. I feel like a cat with a few more lives to spare.* He could hardly keep his eyes open. All he could hope was that his dreams didn't show it all over again.

∾∾∾

A knock on his bedroom door woke Daniel up. He kept his eyes closed until he heard Julian's voice. "Papa, Mia wants to know if you're making pancakes today."

Daniel groaned. His Saturday morning job in the kitchen. "Okay, I'll be down." He had to take his time to wake up properly. His night had been full of blurred images and noises he had tried to get away from. *Right, breakfast.*

Mia had already organized the ingredients on the countertop. "Hey, you could have made them already," Daniel teased her.

"Ha, your job for today." Mia gave him an impish smile.

I should be happy to do this, Daniel thought. *It could have been different.*

"You make good pancakes, Papa." Julian topped two of them with strawberries.

Daniel knew he had to tell them. "Both of you, I want you to listen." Their eyes were on him, big and questioning. "I came home by taxi last night because my car is a wreck." He lifted both hands. "No accident, at least not by me." He gave his kids a short version of the evening's event.

Mia broke into sobs. "Why can't the police do something? They'll kill you."

Daniel needed to calm her down. "So far they have failed. The police will find more evidence on my car and on the iron bar. They will be caught."

Mia wiped her eyes. "I'm getting nightmares about it."

Julian had been quiet all this time. His eyes were big and dark. "What now, Papa? They'll try again, right?"

Daniel swallowed the rest of his coffee. "They have to figure out another plan first. In the meantime, the police might catch the driver. Let's just keep our safety rules in place as always. Maybe you should stay close to home today."

"I'll go over to my friend Evelyn's house if that's okay. That was the plan." Mia gathered the dishes. "What about Julian?"

"Jason and I want to play in their yard. Can we?" Julian looked up hopefully.

They need some fun. "All right, as long as you don't tell anyone about this. I need a quick walk through the park. Wait until I'm back, okay?" Daniel felt like moving his body, walking, jogging, to get his lungs working.

At the entrance to the park, he slowed down. He was going to enjoy nature, looking at the flowers, listening to the birds. *All the indoor work I'm doing needs a balance,* he thought. *I'm sure, nobody expects me to walk around here on a Saturday morning.* He sat down on a bench. The sounds of the nearby fountain on the lake turned into music. It reminded Daniel of various compositions created about waterfalls and fountains like this.

When he noticed three people standing nearby in deep conversation, he took a closer look. He recognized one of them, the woman at the front desk at the police station, the one that was so nervous the last time he had seen her. But neither of the two men was familiar. At that point the woman spotted Daniel, quickly looked away, and all three headed down the walk. *Hey,* Daniel thought, *not even a wave from her or one of her big toothy smiles? Maybe she was in shock to see me here. Why? Were the two other men police officers off duty or her friends? I'm getting more and more suspicious of her.*

Daniel got up. *Should I follow them? Wouldn't do any good. Waste of energy.* Then he remembered the inspector saying to come by today. Daniel trotted home, told Mia and Julian to go to their friends, and called for a taxi. *I need a car to go whenever I want to,* he thought. *Let's see what the inspector has to say.*

ⅭⅯⅭ

The police stations looked deserted, no reception lady. An officer looked around the corner.

"Oh, hello, Mr. Abogado. I'm so glad you're in one

piece. The inspector just got in." He pointed down the hall-way. "Go ahead."

Inspector Lankin stood by the window looking out. Without turning around he said, "What took you so long? I thought you would be waiting here biting your finger-nails."

"I needed to take a walk in nature as did your lady from the front desk." Daniel needed to let him know.

"Well, it's Saturday, her day off. Does that bother you?" A bit of a smile crossed the inspector's face.

"Lord no. But she pretended not to see me. A bit odd. Never mind. Do you have any news for me at all?"

The inspector sat down. He sorted through some pho-tos. "The damage to your car fitted the iron bar perfectly. We rescued most of the license plate numbers and traced the owner of the Mercedes. We're interviewing him later."

Daniel was surprised. "You have been busy. Might he be the same man from the construction firm in the paper?" *Wouldn't that be perfect?*

The inspector shrugged. "He could be. But since he seems to have money to spare on wrecking cars, he prob-ably used one of his underlings for the job yesterday. He could be a link but not the boss."

Daniel nodded. "I have the feeling that the company and maybe another one are a front for their business. From whatever they are selling—drugs, money laundering, and I messed with it."

The inspector squinted. "Aren't you a smart one? But mostly correct. Extortion is also a good business nowa-days. We'll know more after the interview."

Daniel got up. "I would like to be a mouse in the corner listening. I have work to do. Thank you, Sir. Will you let me know what you find out?"

"Will do. Do you need armor?" He again gave a tiny smile.

"No, but a car. I'll get a loaner and—send you the bill."
With a laugh, Daniel closed the door behind him.

Outside again he called his previous car dealer. At least
he would be mobile again.

eↄeↄ

The Mazda sedan felt just right. Nobody knows what
car I'm riding in, Daniel thought. I feel a little safer.

Back at home he told his children, "I want you to come
with me on Sunday for the matinee concert in Oakland. Be
ready at ten o'clock. We all go in two buses. It will be interesting for you."

"Can Evelyn come along?" Mia asked. "She loves that
music."

"I guess we can squeeze her in. But ask her parents."
Hopefully, it should be safe enough.

eↄeↄ

That night the second performance went well again, the
audience loved it. Daniel had to endure more questions
from the musicians. He tried to avoid details. *None of their
business. I know very little about the real problem myself.*
He was sorely tempted to ask the inspector how the questioning of the owner of the construction company went.
But he held back. Maybe I'm bugging him too much, he
thought. The lawyer could be the clue. He killed the prisoner and disappeared until he showed up in the newspaper.
I wonder what the police are doing about that.

eↄeↄ

The next morning turned out to be more stressful than
Daniel expected. Being at the theater on a Sunday at ten

didn't agree with his body clock. Luckily Mia and Julian were ready and excited. They talked about the trip with the musicians and that it would give them a chance to ask questions about how they chose their instruments and how they studied.

"Since I am going to lose my singing teacher they might give me some tips," Mia said. "Or they might know somebody really good."

Daniel looked at her. "I can do that. I already tried."

"Yeah, but you're my father," came her answer.

Teenagers and their logic.

It took some time to stow the instruments and settle the musicians into the two buses. The children wanted to sit up front but Daniel didn't let them.

"In any accident, the people in the front seats get hurt the most. Sit in the middle." *If anyone wants to shoot us he's going to aim into the front window at the driver.* Daniel couldn't help but be overly cautious. He moved into the back of the bus on the long seat. That way he could have a quick look at the *Aida* score again. He had to be in Portland in two days. Would he know more about his attacker from the inspector before then? Daniel would certainly question him on Monday.

Mia and Julian had already found musicians to answer their questions. I'm happy with that, Daniel thought, as long as they know when to stop. He hoped he didn't have to explain anything more about the Friday night's event. Right now he just wanted to enjoy the ride. The chatter of the people faded into the background and *Aida*'s overture took over. It didn't take long and Daniel's hands moved to the music. Until he heard a voice saying, "He's doing it again."

Daniel looked up. "Doing what?"

The trumpeter laughed. "Conducting, Sir."

Daniel put down the score. "That's what I'm supposed

to do. This gives me the chance to go over my next assignment."

"But without an orchestra?"

Daniel leaned back and smiled. "How little you know about the secrets of conductors." After the chuckles had died down the driver announced, "We have arrived, Ladies and Gentlemen."

While everyone piled out of the buses and retrieved—what they called—their tools, Daniel went ahead to inspect the theater. Of course, the Paramount Theater was not as big as Symphony Hall, he thought, but it has a good roomy stage. The manager and librarian appeared and shook his hand.

"We'll start setting up right now," the manager said, "then you have time to inspect everything before settling down."

"That's all right. We'll all have some lunch somewhere first." Daniel's stomach reminded him.

The manager's eyes lit up. "I already arranged a lunch for all of you at a restaurant around the corner." He pointed outside. "It's large enough for your orchestra."

Daniel was surprised. "Wonderful. Does that come with a glass of wine?"

The manager smiled. "Just say the word."

"Okay let me talk to my trusted band." *And look for my kids.*

Mia and Julian with Evelyn behind ran towards Daniel, excited and laughing. "We heard quite a few anecdotes," Mia said, "and got a few good tips too."

"And finger exercises for pianists," Julian added.

Every bit helps, Daniel thought.

The musicians trooped over to the restaurant. They were met with a beaming owner and a score of waiters and waitresses. Daniel hoped that everyone knew better than to let their consumption of beer or wine result in a bad performance. But he also knew that music came first to all of them.

When Daniel came out of the restroom a while later he saw one of the waiters scurrying by. He hadn't seen this one in the line-up before. Why was that man running? Because of all his experiences, Daniel's guard came up. *Are the children all right?* Mia, her friend, and Julian were still finishing some ice cream. Some of the waitresses started collecting dishes and money. Daniel looked around but couldn't find the strange waiter. *Probably nothing. I might not have paid enough attention to all the servers.* He checked his watch. *Time to get organized.*

The concertmaster stood up already and called, "Ready to go. We should start."

Nice to have someone to take over, Daniel thought. He turned to Mia and Julian. "You're listening to the concert, right? I want you to stay close. You can select the seats you want." He heard Mia's friend whispering, "Is he always so bossy?"

"He has his reasons, Evelyn," Mia said. "Besides, I love seeing him conduct."

Daniel smiled. *Good girl.* He still couldn't get the odd waiter out of his mind. He hadn't seen him serving anyone. But now his thoughts needed to be on the performance. No matter where he conducted or how small an audience he might have, he had to do his best.

To his surprise, the theater filled up faster than he had hoped. When he bowed to the applauding audience he stared right into the eyes of the strange waiter. He was sitting in the middle a few rows up. He did not applaud. How stupid, Daniel thought. Now he has alerted me. Okay, Mister, whatever your plan, you can't rattle me.

The first part of the performance was rewarded with clapping and whistles. During the intermission, Daniel tried to

keep his eyes on his kids. Just in case, he thought. But the
waiter had disappeared and didn't come back.

Chapter 16

The second part of the concert was again well appreciated with applause and whistles from the younger music lovers. Daniel was happy. Mia came up to him.

"You sure have to work hard to keep them all together, Papa."

"Luckily they all know their part. I just remind them of the tempo and volume," Daniel said.

Julian piped in. "Yeah, but how do you remember all the different instruments in the *Russian Easter*?"

Daniel shook his head. "I really can't explain that, Julian. I expect them to come in. That's why we rehearse and memorize. You need that too in your playing."

Julian sighed. "I guess so."

"Me too," Mia added. "Words and music."

Mia's friend Evelyn said, "I so loved that music. It was powerful. But I think I'll stick with math."

Mia groaned. Julian gave another sigh. "How can you?"

Daniel looked at his watch. He glanced over to his concertmaster. "Are we ready to go?"

John nodded. "Almost." He turned around. "The bus drivers caught someone lurking around the buses, but he disappeared."

Daniel held his breath. "Dark hair, looking like a waiter? They better check the tires. He caught my attention before."

John looked puzzled. "When? How? Are you psychic?"

"No, it's just a lot of experience. Let's go." *I wish I was.*

The bus drivers didn't find anything wrong with the tires, but they found a note on one of the windshields. "You're not off our list. Be aware."

"What does that mean, Maestro?" one of the drivers ask.

"Someone likes to annoy me," Daniel said. His heart started pumping fast again. "For now we should be safe, I think. Just drive us home. And give me the note." He knew that the so-called waiter was one of the underlings of the *boss*. It was too obvious. Despite this new development, Daniel dozed off.

Something woke him up. The bus had stopped. Daniel heard various voices, then the bus driver's, "My gas tank is empty. I filled up before we left."

Daniel got up and went over to him. "Someone either siphoned it off or cut your gas line." *The waiter, the note.* "The guy you saw sneaking around."

The second bus had stopped behind them, the driver came over. "I have a full can in the back that should be enough. Unless the line is cut. Let's look at it."

Daniel grumbled, "My very thoughts."

After checking under the hood, the driver swore. "Damn it all, it's cut."

"I know who did it," Daniel said. "I can identify him." Daniel shook with anger. *What a nerve to follow me around and involve other people.* The drivers stared at him. He knew he had to give them an explanation. "The guy in the waiter's outfit wasn't there for serving. He was the one you saw lurking around. When you spotted him, he didn't have time to get to the second bus."

The second driver scratched his head. "I can transport some of you in my bus but not all. I'll get into trouble with the safety board. Let's call for another bus."

Daniel felt responsible. *They're after me and everybody suffers.* "I have another idea. Let's call a few taxis. I pay, it's faster and you can share." He walked back to get Mia, Julian, and their friend who had waited wide-eyed and worried.

It took some time for taxis to arrive and to transfer musicians and their instruments. Daniel stood by and watched. It *was supposed to be a great Sunday. The concert had been but now I have another note to identify.* "Let's take the bus. At least that one seems to be safe." The first bus driver decided to stay and wait for a tow truck.

Daniel tried to calm himself. Even though there seemed to be no end to the harassment he needed to keep a cool head. He wanted to get home and prepare for tomorrow. He had two jobs to attend to…talking to the inspector and giving him the note and meeting with his assistant conductor. Since Daniel had to be in Portland for five days he hoped that the assistant conductor would get a start at rehearsing for the end-of-the-season concert. He had three composers in mind: Schubert, Korngold, and Grieg. Enough variety to interest most of the audience, he thought. Daniel had already engaged a violinist for the Korngold concerto. In the music department, everything seemed to be organized and enjoyable. Why can't my personal life be that way? Daniel thought. Because I can't abide lawless people, the one big fault in my life.

☙❧

The next morning Daniel was surprised to find Mia and Julian acting quite normally. Shouldn't they still be worried? But they just looked at him and smiled.

"Did you sleep all right last night?" Daniel asked.

"It took me a bit longer to get to sleep," Mia answered. "But then I dropped off." She looked at Daniel. "We weren't too scared yesterday because you were not."

Julian nodded. "Yeah, Papa, you just took over."

Daniel sat down with his coffee. "Thank you for your confidence. Yes, I was angry because this time they involved other people. I'll talk to Inspector Lankin today. I hope for some news that makes sense. In the meantime—" he dropped two sugar cubes into his coffee, "keep your eyes open as always." He got up and gave both kids a hug. "You two make me proud."

After they had left for school Daniel sat quietly for a few minutes. His children were so steady, so grounded. But they were so young. *Amazing. What a blessing.* He got up. *Time to face the inspector. Will he finally have news to shed some light on the whos and whys?*

On the way to the police station Daniel's stomach filled with the usual butterflies. *Do I expect too much? I don't want to be disappointed.* The woman at the front desk smiled at him as before. Good actress, Daniel thought. "Is the inspector in?" he asked.

"Yes, go right in, Sir."

White teeth again. Inspector Lankin's door was open. Daniel knocked and stuck his head around the corner.

"Well, well, the man I was thinking about." The inspector smiled. "Anything new?"

Daniel took a breath. "That's my question too. But I have a story for you." He handed him the note. "Unfortunately, my fingerprints are on it." He told him about last evening's event. "I can identify the man. He was quite brazen, sitting in the audience."

The inspector read the note and called an officer. "Take this to the lab, urgent." He sat back. "Good thing it didn't happen in the middle of the Golden Gates Bridge. Now something else. The construction boss admitted to knowing the lawyer because he uses him in case of legal problems. But he claimed he has disappeared, of course. He choked up a bit when I told him about his fingerprints at the jail cell. 'I didn't tell him to kill anyone he told me. I think he's part of a criminal gang but not the head of it. Like the others he's scared.'"

"So, we have to catch him red-handed before we can charge him." *Another downer.* "What about the one who got drugged? Has he recovered?" Daniel was itching to hear more.

"Yes, and is charged with weapon possessions, some more jail time, no bail."

Tell me more. "What about the burnt-out car? Did they find anything of importance?" *Butterflies again.*

The inspector smiled again. "It's amazing what the forensics can locate. The trunk wasn't as burnt as the rest. They found parts of tools in it, a hammer, screwdriver, tire wrench. But—" he raised two fingers, "we found two diamonds imbedded in melted plastic."

Daniel's jaw dropped. "Di-a-monds?"

The inspector's smile got bigger. "They are most likely in the diamond smuggling business, got a bit sloppy or one of the soldiers got greedy and saved some."

Daniel still couldn't believe it. "Drugs, yes, but diamonds? How would they get them? This could be big."

"Just like drugs," the inspector said. "You make deals with the proper people in the trade, wherever they are, and sell them again."

Daniel just shook his head. "As far as I know, diamond centers are mainly in Antwerp and New York. So this has to be international."

The inspector nodded. "Mind you, before it gets here, the business has gone through a few cities and places. But even raw or rough-cut diamonds can be quite lucrative. We're hauling the construction boss back in. I want to see his reaction to the two diamonds we found."

"I wonder where the lawyer is right now," Daniel said. "Probably gone for good."

"We have alerted airlines, buses, and rail lines since we have a fair picture of him, thanks to your newspaper."

Daniel was stunned to hear the word "thanks" from the inspector. "According to Alex he was also seen in the post office, so the clerk must know him."

"Okay, let's get him back here, too." Inspector Lankin seemed to enjoy this like going on a hunt.

Daniel felt better, too. At least a few things had been discovered and could be followed up on. He pushed his chair back. "Time to tend to my business. I'll be out of town from tomorrow until the weekend. But I'll take my son with me."

"What? Another target?" The inspector frowned.

"He was a target here already, remember? At least he will be safe with a family I know."

The inspector grabbed the phone. "Hm. Good luck."

On his way back to his car Daniel mulled over the news he had just heard. Diamonds. For that kind of business to succeed it really wouldn't need a lot of people plus transportation like construction trucks. Unless they figured that nobody would connect dirty dump trucks with diamonds. They could also be stashed easily in small places: car seats, handbags with double bottoms, even empty canes. How would anyone know? Maybe the crazy driver was a delivery boy being late. Who was the mastermind whom nobody knew, only by texting? Probably using disposable phones like disposable cars. *That's what I want to know, as soon as possible.*

∽∾∽

At the theater, the assistant conductor was already waiting with a stack of scores under his arm.

"You look ready to jump right in," Daniel said.

"Yes, I'm excited to give this music a whirl. A great program I've been waiting to finally direct, at least for a while."

Daniel smiled. *Sounds like me twenty-five years ago.* "Let's take a look at the masterpieces. Haydn first, Symphony Number 84."

They worked on the score, movement by movement.

The time went by so fast that Daniel forgot how his assistant might feel. "Let's only work on Haydn and Grieg," Daniel suggested. "Leave Korngold to me and the violinist. Lunchtime." Grieg would have to wait until after coffee and BLTs.

Daniel was pleased that his assistant knew the scores quite well. It only took another two hours to make sure of the details embedded in Grieg's *Holberg Suite.*

After a few more questions Daniel's assistant folded up the scores. "Good luck with *Aida*, Daniel. It's going to be a handful."

"Yes, but also a challenge. Have fun with your rehearsals." Daniel needed to get home and organize for the flight tomorrow. Julian had to be ready to go, too.

Both children were home when he arrived. "Papa, when are you coming home again?" Mia asked.

"As far as I know Sunday evening late. We have a matinee that afternoon. Why?"

Mia frowned. "Our recital is Sunday evening. But you're not back then."

Ouch! Daniel felt bad. "Tell you what," he said. "How about you being the last one to sing? By that time we might be here. You start at eight o'clock, right?"

Mia's face lit up. "That might work. You're great, Papa." She hugged him. "I want to know if I have improved."

Daniel had to smile. "But your teacher would tell you."

Mia shook her head. "That's different. She hears me all the time. You don't."

"You will tape the recital, I hope." Daniel wanted to make sure.

Mia nodded. Julian piped up, "Of course. That is for later as a keepsake when you are famous."

That created a chuckle from Mia and Daniel. Julian pouted. "I know, you'll be famous."

Daniel turned back to Mia. "You're going to be at Mrs. Gantrey's, okay? Make sure not to be at our house in the evening. Keep the alarm on. Any questions?"

"Don't think so. It will be fine, Papa. Concentrate on *Aida*."

That sounds like Elvira. "You can call me if you need to. Julian, are you ready with packing?"

Mia laughed. "He was all packed up already yesterday."

"Because you told me to," Julian protested. "You're pushy."

"Okay, kids, I'll do my packing now. Keep the peace." What a mother hen, he thought. She'll be a great mother herself someday. Daniel climbed the steps to his studio. He chuckled. *At least my kids are normal siblings.* Since he would be away almost six days he needed to have enough clothes to look decent. He wondered what Julian thought to be important to take along. Mia probably had a hand in it.

The phone rang. The inspector. "Can you come down? We have a waiter you might be able to identify."

"Really? You bet. I'll be there in twenty minutes." *The gas-line cutting waiter from yesterday? How did they find him?*

The woman at the front desk of the police station put on her usual white smile which never reached her eyes. "You know your way, Sir," she said.

An officer took Daniel downstairs into the same room where he had identified the bad driver before. Inspector Lankin waved Daniel over. "Here we go again. Choose your friend."

Daniel was again amazed at how many look-alikes they had found. *I'll never forget the face of the guy staring at me in the audience yesterday.* "Number three."

"Thank you." The inspector waved him aside. "Wait." Upstairs he ushered him into his office. "Before you go on your trip some news. We have charged the construction boss with aiding and abetting in your attempted murder. It was his car that had been built for destruction. The guy you just identified is one of his workers. That's all I can tell you for now. I think he'll be safer in jail than outside, to go by the last victims."

"Even that isn't secure anymore. Did you mention the diamonds?" Daniel had to know.

The inspector grinned. "He got pale. I'll tell you more sometime later. Now go on your trip."

"That was fast work. How did you find the waiter?" *I need to know before I go.*

"We found him at work. His spit was on the note you gave me. He must have fastened it on the windshield that way." The inspector couldn't suppress a smile.

Daniel laughed too. "Being a criminal doesn't have to be smart. Now I can concentrate on Portland. Thank you." He almost skipped down the steps. Two more people snagged. Someone had to talk sometime, either to get a deal or save his own skin.

Chapter 17

The flight from San Francisco to Portland was short and uneventful. Julian couldn't stop talking about the size of the airplane, inside and out.

"I've never flown before. This is exciting." He wiggled around on his seat to look out the window.

"Yes, you did," said Daniel. "You were one week old."

"Wow, I sure don't remember. From where?"

"From Munich in Germany. You were born there while I was conducting." Daniel still remembered the feeling of panic that night.

"Wow. That must have been confusing. Mom must have been brave. Do we get snacks?"

"As soon as you settle down, maybe." Daniel was glad to have Julian looked after at the conductor's family. He would have more questions than Daniel could ever have time to answer.

At the airport in Portland, they were met by a tall lady waving at them. She introduced herself as Lydia, the librarian of the opera house. Daniel had not expected to be greeted. Usually, he found his way by taxi to his hotel. But he was pleased to meet a pretty woman instead with dark blue eyes and shoulder-length dark, curly hair.

"I will drive you to the hotel and make sure the room is right for you," she said as she wound her way out of the airport parking lot. "We can't have you sleeping on a hard mattress and conduct with a sore back."

"I'm totally surprised." Daniel looked at her sideways.

Lydia smiled. "Orders of our conductor."

"We'll unpack quickly and I'll deliver my sidekick here to his destination then make my way to the theater," Daniel said.

Lydia shook her head. "I'll drive you, Maestro. I'll wait downstairs in the lobby."

"Really?" Daniel couldn't believe it. "Don't you have other work to do? I can manage."

Lydia smiled. "This is my work now. Take your time. No hurry."

What a reception, Daniel thought.

At the hotel Lydia disappeared after inspecting the room. Daniel still shook his head in wonder. "She is nice," Julian commented. "Looks nice too."

Daniel glanced at him. "Well, well, my son, the connoisseur." But he agreed. Lydia was a pretty woman and had an easy way about her. "Let's get a move on, Julian. I'm curious about the theater, the staging, and the people in it. Also we can't have your host waiting too long."

"Why can't I stay with you, Papa?"

Daniel knew that was coming. "I have to work and need all my concentration, Julian. I expect you to understand that. You'll see a performance later."

Julian sighed. "Oookay."

Lydia got up from a chair when Daniel and Julian came down again. "Second stop the Maestro's house," she announced.

ℂℂℂ

Conductor Charles Emmet's house looked impressive with columns in the front and a wide set of stairs to the front door. This would be too imperial for me, Daniel thought. The door opened before they had a chance to ring the bell.

"Come in, please," Charles beamed and looked at Julian. "Welcome to your new playmates and our nanny." He shook Daniel's hand. Daniel had not seen him for a few years but he could not miss the hollow look around his eyes. His clothes were hanging loosely around him. "How are you holding up, Charles?" Daniel asked. "You've shed a few pounds."

Charles shrugged. "It comes with the treatments. Today is fine but tomorrow I get another infusion which will flatten me the next day. I can go with you to the theater today." His wife, Carol, came from the kitchen and, after greeting Daniel, ushered them into the dining room. The next hour was filled with lunch, talk about past years, and, of course, *Aida*. Daniel could hear children's voices and their laughter. *Julian must be all right.*

Even though he didn't want to push it, Daniel was more than ready to get to the theater. Charles must have noticed it. He got up. "Let's go and have a look at my so-far-creation."

When they reached the Hampton Opera Center Daniel's eyes widened in surprise. "Good Lord. The outside looks like a ship with all its riggings."

Charles chuckled. "Yes, like it's waiting to sail off. They wanted something unusual. I think, you'll like the interior. It has good acoustics."

Daniel had to admit, the inside was pleasing. The railing in front of the upper seats wound around in a half circle ending close to the stage. Between rows of seats they had left additional space for a more comfortable audience experience. He wouldn't know about the acoustics until he heard the music.

"I like it," he said. "Right now I'm interested in the

stage settings." He walked around and up onto the stage. The usual temple for the first act was in place as he expected. Even a chariot stood as if waiting for action. Very nicely done, he thought. The stage would be filled with Radames' soldiers ready to go into battle.

Daniel turned to Charles. "Is Amneris' room big enough for the dancers later on?"

"Oh, yes. The ballet is very good. Does this look okay to you?"

"Excellent," Daniel said.

The stage manager came around the corner. "Hello, just checking." He looked at Daniel. "Welcome to our big event. Glad to have you." They shook hands. "Is there anything you want me to change?"

Daniel shook his head. "Not so far." *Although it would add to the atmosphere to have a statue of Radames. I better not grumble already.* "It looks good. Make sure everybody is ready tomorrow at ten a.m. or earlier."

"We'll be, Maestro." The manager disappeared again.

"Talented people to work with," Charles said. "The orchestra knows that you're starting at ten. I'll be at the hospital, unfortunately."

Daniel put his hand on his shoulder. "That's why I'm here, Charles, rest easy. I'm glad you're doing as well as this. Might as well go back to the hotel and work some more."

Charles laughed. "Workaholic!"

☙❧

Daniel picked his son up again. "The kids are okay," Julian said. "Maybe a bit young for me. The girl is smart."

Daniel chuckled. "Too young? Are you the old, wise man already? Let's get you to the playground for a while."

The boy beamed. "Right on."

Two hours later the restaurant at the hotel came in handy for a good supper. Julian looked ready for bed.

Against his normal habits Daniel got up early the next morning. He had to admit, he was excited and ready to start rehearsing. He was looking forward to meeting the soloists and hearing the orchestra. With sleepy-eyed Julian in tow he went for breakfast.

"This is work, Julian," he explained. "Sometimes early in the morning. I'll show you the Opera House and then take you to the Emmet family."

Julian's eyes lit up. "Can I stay longer with you?"

Daniel gave him a stern look. "You know why not, right?"

"Ookay." Julian buttered his toast. "What is the music like, Papa?"

"Verdi's music is melodious, emotional, and powerful with lots of arias and choruses. You can listen to one of my CDs."

"But I have to play with those kids." Julian still wasn't impressed.

Daniel got up. "Let's look at the theater now." He braced himself for his son's questions.

Of course, they came pouring out of Julian's mouth. "Why did they make it look like a ship? What about the funny ceiling inside with pieces of wood? They can't see you down there in the pit, Papa."

Daniel had to explain the outside of the building, the ceiling for the acoustics, and the pit for operas. By that time the stage crew arrived. Daniel had to get his son to the conductor's family and brave more inquiries in the car.

When he finally got back to the Opera House musicians drifted in through the stage door, chatting and laughing. Good, Daniel thought, they're on time. He heard a beautiful soprano voice warming up with scales and snatches of arias. A dark-haired, tall man rushed in and stopped in front of Daniel.

"Maestro, I'm so glad to see you again." He grabbed Daniel's hand.

Daniel shook it. "Robert Donath, it's been a few years." He knew that he had a good tenor.

From then on the other soloists joined them. Daniel remembered the soprano and got introduced to the alto, baritone, and bass. Great, he thought, and it's not even ten o'clock.

As soon as the orchestra had settled down and the soloists waited on stage, Daniel got up on the podium and looked at them all. *It must feel strange for them with a different conductor standing here.* "Good morning, everybody. Today I would like you all to work as you do at every rehearsal. Unless I stop, keep going. We go right from the beginning. Any questions?"

"Full voice?" the soprano asked.

"Unless you have a problem, yes. Tomorrow is dress rehearsal or costume party, as I call it." Chuckles lightened the air. With all musicians' eyes on Daniel, he raised his arms and the prelude to *Aida* began.

Once through it, Daniel stopped. He took a breath. "This piece of music tells the whole story of Aida, as we all know, starting with her feelings of being a slave. Which was well done, by the way. Now we meet Radames, the hero, with his love for Aida. Bad choice, because Amneris loves him too. Then Aida's father appears as a prisoner and things get tragic. We have to go into more tempo and passion here. Later the emotions soften again, almost to a whisper."

Daniel knew he had to hold back with changes. This time he didn't create, he was filling in for a good conductor. But if something didn't sound equal to the score or the action on stage he needed to look at it. The second try went better and he continued. The tenor impressed Daniel, good voice, good acting.

After the first act he gave everyone a fifteen-minute break. So far, he was pleased with the rehearsal. However, the really emotional parts were still coming during the rest of the opera.

He took a few minutes to call Mia. "Everything all right, Mia?"

She giggled. "Yes, worrywart, we're all fine, no suspicious actions to report."

Daniel laughed too. *How typical of her to say that.* "Don't forget, call me if you need to." They chatted for a while then Daniel knew he had to get back to his work. Now he had to combine the dancers with Amneris' actions. Daniel loved the ballet music. It fitted so seamlessly into the Egyptian scenes. And all went well, no collisions between staging or dancers. The only thing that made his eyes pop was the live tiger cub Amneris had on a lead. *I guess she needed a royal pet, at least it's not fully grown.* During a pause after the ballet, Daniel heard a commotion backstage. *What now?* "Everything okay?" Daniel called. A stagehand came forward.

"Some guy had snuck into the dancers' dressing room. They chased him out."

Daniel paused. "Are you sure he's really gone?"

"Yes, I escorted him outside," the stagehand answered.

Enamored with the pretty girls? Or looking for someone else? Am I really safe?

Chapter 18

When lunchtime came around Daniel walked up to the stage. He wondered about the space for the soldiers and extras for Radames' upcoming victory celebration. As long as they were not moving too much it would be all right. The librarian Lydia came up to him.

"Maestro, you made me cry during the prelude."

"I'm sorry, Lydia." He couldn't disguise his surprise to see her.

"You put something into it that almost broke my heart," she continued. "It was different from the other times I heard it."

How nice to tell me. "Thank you, that helps me. I did something right." Daniel couldn't help admiring her dark-blue eyes, again. "I hope, the rest will go well."

Lydia nodded. "I know, it will. I love our Maestro, but I think you have more energy," she looked away, "not surprising with his sickness. I'd better get back." She turned and disappeared backstage.

Daniel smiled. *Nice to see her again. I hope she doesn't just flatter me. But she looked sincere. Well, back to work.*

The rest of the rehearsal went ahead with some small corrections. By three o'clock Daniel knew that it would be a good performance. The concertmaster shook his hand.

"Good work, Maestro. Different from the assistant conductor."

"He's still learning, but it was good for him. I need to sit down somewhere quiet with a glass of wine. Come with me."

They went to a nearby pub and found a cozy corner. Daniel studied his glass of wine. "I know, it's a bit early for it but I needed some libation. Besides, we did a lot of good work. We deserve it."

With the concertmaster enjoying his beer it generated an hour-long conversation about *Aida*, music, and conductorship in general. Daniel felt that having a good relationship with the first violinist helped everyone. Yes, Daniel was the Maestro but without the full cooperation of the musicians through their concertmaster, Daniel's work would be hard. He had known jealousies and intrigues before. It never did the music any good.

Finally Daniel looked at his watch. "I better pick up my son. He's being entertained at Maestro Emmet's house."

The violinist pushed back his beer glass. "I look forward to tomorrow. Sometimes dress rehearsals go sideways. That's supposed to bring good luck for the performance. See you tomorrow night."

಄಄

When Daniel arrived at the Emmet's house Julian was busy teaching the girl piano. Daniel didn't want to laugh to make his son feel bad. But it was amusing to hear him explaining proper fingering.

On the way to the hotel Julian commented, "She's a natural."

Now Daniel had to chuckle. "You're turning into a wise know-it-all. She's only five years old."

"Papa, if she gets lessons now she'll be great in no time."

Daniel opened the door to the restaurant. "Right now we need supper." *How did he turn into such a confident little person? Only ten years old.*

At the hotel, Daniel was debating whether he should call the inspector for some news. But he didn't realize how tired he was. He had weathered the first rehearsal with just a few changes. The performances would come close to his own ideas. Yes, the dress rehearsal. He had memories about some of them: voices gone, sickness, lights not working, staging moving at the wrong time, all due to nerves. *We'll see. Right now I need my beauty sleep.*

❦

The next morning Daniel took the opportunity to call Mrs. Gantrey. He didn't want to disturb Mia in school. Mrs. Gantrey sounded as cheerful as always.

"Mia is a nice girl, good company," she said. "Everything is fine. I'll tell her you phoned."

Now a call to Inspector Lankin. Daniel needed news, preferably good.

The inspector let out a sigh, as usual. "In short, all the men we have in custody will be charged. The one who cut the gas line probably with mischief since he didn't cause injury, just delay."

"He should pay for the taxis," Daniel suggested. "Just to teach him." *Let him do something.*

The inspector grunted. "None of them have talked so far, claiming not to know anything except through texting."

Frustration crept up into Daniel. "So, they'll gladly go to prison for their boss. Any closer in the diamond trade?"

"We are on it." The inspector seemed to run out of time.

"But we have a lead on the lawyer. No criminal is perfect, we'll find a hole."

"Okay, I'll try and stay out of trouble." Daniel knew that this was all the inspector, would tell him. *Can I be hopeful?*

Since the dress rehearsal didn't start until eight o'clock that evening, Julian was antsy. "Can we go somewhere, Papa?" he asked.

"What do you have in mind?" Daniel needed to save some of his energy for the night.

"There is a shopping center near the Emmet's house. They have a fair with rides for a few days. Can we go there?"

"All right, for a few hours." *I guess, he can't just sit around.*

⁊

At the crowded parking lot full of various booths and rides with their musical noises Daniel again felt the need to stay safe for Julian and himself. He scanned the people around the rides: mostly mothers with children, fathers being at work.

"Can I choose a ride, Papa?" Julian tugged at his sleeve. "That one where I can fly."

Daniel had to smile. As a child, he used to pick that one too with the seats high up on chains. The attraction was the music, Strauss waltzes. Julian beamed. Soon he was waving every time he flew by.

Daniel kept an eye on the people standing nearby. He spotted a few men, one older really scruffy-looking one who swayed with the music. Daniel walked closer. The ride was almost over. The man put his hand into his jacket pocket and pulled something out. He stared at it and looked up to the slowing Star-Flyer. Standing beside him

Daniel saw a toy dinosaur in the man's hand. *What is he up to? Who is he waiting for?* Everything inside him already knew. The ride stopped. Julian scooted down the ramp. The man ran up to him and pushed the toy into his hand. Daniel jumped in and grabbed him by the arm.

"Why did you give my son this toy?" He yelled over the noise around them.

"Because—because I like him," the man stammered and tried to free his arm.

Daniel turned and pulled the dinosaur out of Julian's hand. He pushed it against the man's chest. "Here, take it back. He has toys enough."

"No, no, he needs to keep it," the man protested. People had gathered around and stared. A security guard ran up.

"Anything wrong, Sir?"

Daniel pointed to the man. "He waited for my son to come down from the ride and forced this toy into his hand, which I don't appreciate. My son has been a target before."

At that moment the old man pulled his arm loose and started running.

"Hold on there!" the guard shouted and sprinted after him. Daniel was ready to chase him too but the guard caught the man and pulled him towards the office. Daniel heard him shouting, "Let's see, what you and the dinosaur are all about."

Daniel grabbed Julian's hand. "We should go into the office and sit down for a few minutes." He needed to slow down his heartbeat and think. *Was it just a toy from an old man? Maybe something he had found and wanted to give away? But why to Julian and not some other boy?* Daniel had learned to trust the red flags in his mind

Daniel and Julian walked back to the office. A worker pushed a loaded cart through the door. Daniel stopped him.

"Is the security guard in the back? I would like to talk to him."

The worker pointed to a door. "Yeah, he's in there. He brought an old man with him."

Daniel knocked on the door, the guard came out. "Oh Sir, everything okay?"

"I would like to know what's going to happen. Have the police been notified?"

The guard shrugged. "Is that necessary? He didn't hurt anyone. He seems to be a bit befuddled. He says someone gave the toy to him."

Daniel's temper rose. "Aha, so there is something else. I wonder if there is anything special with that dinosaur. I would like it to be checked. My son almost got kidnapped before, so I'm a bit suspicious."

The guard still seemed unsure, then he nodded. "Okay Sir, but shouldn't you stay here to talk to the police?"

Daniel shook his head. "I'm not able to. I have a dress rehearsal to conduct. I'll give you my card, let them contact me. You can tell them what I told you. I have to go."

The guard looked at him open-mouthed. "Are you the new conductor for the opera?"

Now Daniel had to take a breath. *An opera lover?* "Yes, I am. Let me know how this turns out, please."

Julian had been standing quietly beside his father observing. He turned to Daniel. "Do you think the man was a bad one? How does he know me? We are in Portland."

"I wish I could explain that Julian." He tried to smile. "Maybe the dinosaur was full of diamonds?" *No use making him afraid of every move we make. I'm surprised he's not screaming.*

Julian shook his head. "He wouldn't have given that away."

"Just joking. Let's get home."

All the way to the hotel Daniel ran the last episode through his mind. Why a toy? Because Julian was a child. Why did he insist that Julian keep the dinosaur? If the man wanted to harm him, why not do it? Something had to be in or on the toy. Drugs? Poison? He was reminded of the attempt on Mia, years ago. Julian's hands looked fine, no rash or burns. Hopefully, the guard informs the police. What about this thing of someone giving it to the old man? Who? "Let's get some supper and get you to the Emmets. It's going to be a long night."

"I would have liked to keep the dinosaur," Julian said quietly. "Could I get it when they have looked at it?"

"If it's evidence to a crime, no. We'll have to wait." *He still likes toys. After all, he's still a child. And I have to clear my mind: dress rehearsal.*

Chapter 19

Once Daniel was on his way to the Opera House he made up his mind to forget the afternoon's event, at least for now. Julian was safe and the rehearsal better be good.

The theater hummed with people, instruments, last minute checks on the staging and—nerves. As usual, Daniel thought. Just the right atmosphere. The mezzo-soprano, Amneris, came up to him.

"Do you mind if I sing a bit quieter tonight? My voice is a bit shaky." She looked worried.

"Do what you can, Terry. And don't be nervous." *Also as usual.* Daniel wondered if everyone would be ready by eight o'clock. A sudden quiet filled the theater when Daniel stood on the podium. He noticed many people spread throughout the seats. Probably the opera critic among them, he thought. He called out, "Is everyone ready?"

"Yes," from the pit, and "Yes," from the curtained stage. *And definitely "Yes" from me.*

If there remained any residue of anxiety left in Daniel, it melted with the music. Except for a short coughing spell coming from Amneris, some refitting of two costumes, and a wobbly column in the first scene, all went well. Maybe Terry was right, Daniel thought. Her voice might have a problem. Do we have an understudy handy?

At the intermission, he found Amneris in the Green Room sucking on cough drops. "Why don't you sing half voice for the rest of the night?" Daniel suggested. "How about the understudy?"

"I hope it's not necessary," she answered. "I'll gargle all night. I don't want to miss this opera."

What can I say? "Let's keep going then."

By the end of the evening, everyone breathed a sigh of relief and agreed that it had been a good dress rehearsal. That doesn't ensure good performances, Daniel thought on the way home. But he was happy and felt proud of his work as—what he still called—a fill-in. *It could have been close to perfect if the old man and the dinosaur hadn't thrown another rock into the way. How can I find out the real reason?*

♋♋

The next morning, after breakfast, Daniel's phone rang. A stern voice asked for his name.

"We would like you to come to the police station. You had a complaint yesterday about an old man with a toy dinosaur. We want to hear your side of the story."

"Of course I'll come. I'll bring my son too, he was the target. Give me your address." *Yes, the guard did keep his word and called the police.* A feeling of relief ran through him. "Let's go Julian. We might find out the truth about the dinosaur."

At the station, a policewoman ushered Julian away. "It's okay," Daniel told his son.

The officer asked about the appearance of the man, his behavior, and the toy. He seemed to be satisfied with Daniel's answers. "Good thing your son didn't keep the toy. It was filled with powdered drugs which would have seeped through pinholes and eventually poisoned him.

Apparently, someone wanted this to be a slow process and make him sick."

Daniel had to take a deep breath. "What kind of drug?"

"Cocaine."

"My Lord. That's plain evil. I knew something wasn't normal. Just another attempt to wear us down, through my son. What about the person who gave the man the toy?"

The officer leaned back. "All he would say was that it was a tall man with a black beard who gave him two hundred dollars."

"Any fingerprints on them?"

"Only the old man's."

"How would he have known where we were at that time?" *My Lord, they followed us. What about the intruder in the dancers' dressing room?*

The officer nodded. "They must have tailed you for a while. The fair was a good spot. But why?"

Daniel told him about some of the attacks during the last months and the reason for them. "I can't believe they followed us all the way here."

The officer got up. "The old man is being charged with distributing drugs but to find the real criminal is doubtful. I'm sure the beard was a disguise." He gave Daniel some paper and a pen. "Write all of this down, please."

Daniel took his time remembering the details. Who knows, maybe after all these incidents the *boss* can't help but show his real face, with or without the beard, he thought. He handed the report back and got Julian. He told him about the reason for the dinosaur.

Julian looked worried. "I'm getting scared, Papa. Will they find the real guy? I mean the one who put the drugs into the dinosaur."

Daniel put his arm around the boy's shoulder. "I hope so with all my heart. In the meantime, I'm going to keep you safe." *If I can.* He needed to inform Inspector Lankin about this. *Maybe he might have some good news as well?*

☙❧☙

The inspector didn't say anything for a while when Daniel told him about the afternoon's attack on Julian. "But you're in Portland," he finally said. "How did they, whoever they are, know that?"

Daniel didn't know how to say this but he needed to. "Inspector, someone in your station listens when I'm there and relays what he or she hears. I know you don't believe this and I wished I didn't either. But that's one explanation I can't get out of my head."

Again, Inspector Lankin was silent. Then with his usual sigh, he said," Do you have anyone in mind?"

"I have no proof so I don't want to say. Even if I told you, you wouldn't believe me. Now tell me, do you have anything new?" *Anything to brighten the day.*

"Yes, some, but let us keep working. I'll tell you more when you're back. Take care of your work—and mainly of yourself."

As Daniel ended the call two words reverberated in his head: Yes, some. Did the inspector really find something important? Was there real hope? Would the kids ever be safe? *I'll have to try and get my head back to the performance.* Daniel hoped that Maestro Emmet could be able to attend. It would mean a lot to Daniel to get his approval. *Might Charles ever be conducting again as much as he used to?*

☙❧☙

On his way to the theater that night Daniel tried to be cool and confident on the outside but his heart was pounding more than he wanted it to. Even though the dress rehearsal had been quite smooth, there was no guarantee of the same for the performance. *Hey, you're the master here, chill out. It will be the greatest Aida ever.*

The Opera House filled up quickly. Good sign, Daniel thought. Maybe someone listened at the rehearsal and advertised. As he walked to the dressing room Charles Emmet came around the corner. Daniel stopped. "What a wonderful surprise to see you. How do you feel?"

Charles chuckled. "You didn't think I would miss this, did you?"

"I hope you'll hear it as you had it in your mind," Daniel said.

Charles shook his head. "No, Daniel. I know you well enough. There will be changes and I can't wait to hear them." He clapped Daniel on the shoulder. "Break a leg or a baton." He waved and walked away.

Daniel felt good. He changed into his *fancy clothes* and smoothed back his hair. He was ready and all the rest better be too.

He was expecting the sound of the oboe when Lydia scooted towards him. "I just wanted to wish you luck, Maestro. I know everything will be wonderful."

"Thank you, Lydia. I think so too." *How nice of her to think of me. Maybe I should ask her out for a drink afterward.* He waved at her and made his way to the orchestra pit. Then the manager cornered him.

"Amneris can't sing tonight, the understudy is ready to go."

Daniel nodded. "I've had a hunch since yesterday. Here we go. Hopefully, the other one is good."

"Yes, she is," the manager assured Daniel. "She attended every rehearsal and sang in the back room along with it."

That's comforting.

The audience applauded when he appeared, and he didn't lose any time. The prelude started.

Everything up to the intermission went well. The new singer for Amneris impressed Daniel. He went up to her. "You're doing great, Julia. This is a good opportunity for you."

Julia beamed. "But I'm sorry for Terry. She's backstage crying."

"Maybe she's able to sing tomorrow or Sunday," Daniel said. "Enjoy your chance." Singers and their throats are in a constant battle, he thought. That will happen to Mia too. Julia needs more roles like this. And now to the finale.

Strong applause greeted Daniel when he appeared again in the pit. He hadn't seen Charles and hoped that he was okay for the rest of the performance.

As the drama unfolded with Aida torn between her love for Radames, her father, and her homeland, Daniel was totally taken into the music and actions. Even though he knew the emotions on stage were after all make-believe, the love shown between the soprano and tenor gripped him more than he thought it would. At least they could die together, not one left behind. *Good thing I'm too busy to dwell on it. Dredging up feelings about Elvira's death isn't healthy. I have children to raise.*

After Amneris' chant on top of the lovers' tomb and the curtain slowly coming down a few seconds of silence stayed with the audience. Then it erupted in bravos and cheers. Daniel stood quietly. He realized that perspiration was dripping down his face. Or were those tears? Smarten up, he scolded himself. As the tradition required, he would be called on stage after the singers had taken their bows. Daniel wanted Charles to be with him too. And there he was. Someone had brought him around to get on stage. Everyone connected with the performance applauded them. Ladies carried bouquets of flowers to the singers.

Overwhelming, Daniel thought. He pointed down into the pit. *Don't forget the ones who supplied the music.*

When the curtain finally came down for the last time tears flowed from most female singers. The success had everyone over the top. Daniel led Charles into the lobby. His ears were still humming. He wondered what Charles was thinking.

Charles turned to him. "I couldn't have done it that well, Daniel," he said. "You have a different energy. It showed."

Daniel looked at him. "You started it, built the house, I just furnished it."

Charles shook his head. "All I can hope for now is that I can get back to my health and continue in the fall. If not…" he stopped and smiled, "we need another conductor."

"Not me, Charles. I'm already all over the place."

"I know, just ribbing you. But thank you." He grabbed Daniel's hand. "I think my bed is calling. I'll see you tomorrow."

Mrs. Emmet appeared at the door. After a short chat she touched her husband's arm. "He needs his rest now." They waved and went outside.

Daniel stood and closed his eyes. His insides still vibrated. What a performance. He knew it would take a while for him to calm down. He heard a voice. "Maestro, are you all right?" He opened his eyes and looked right into Lydia's blue ones.

Daniel just stared. "Heavens, Lydia. Yes, I'm fine." *What happened?*

"Your eyes were closed. I…I thought you weren't well." She looked apologetic. "Sorry."

"No, no. I sometimes do that to relax. I need to get a drink somewhere. Are you free to come along? We'll probably see the rest of the orchestra doing the same."

Lydia took a breath. "Are you sure? Yes, I've finished for the day. Thank you."

Daniel walked towards his dressing room. "I need to change. Give me a minute." His shirt was damp, he wanted his normal clothes. Daniel also felt hungry. A late supper would be great. *There must be a restaurant around here.*

Lydia was waiting at the front door. "I know a pub around the corner open until late," she said. "Would that be okay?"

"Lead on," Daniel said. It's been a while since I had a drink with a lady, he thought, even if it happened to be in a crowd. Then he remembered Sonja in Seattle. But what a difference between the two. He didn't quite know what it was, but he liked it.

At the pub, Daniel found many of the musicians already celebrating. They started cheering when he came into the door. He knew he had to join them. He waved to the group and said, "Thanks for your excellent work tonight. I need a breather. You have a place for your book lady?"

Lydia held a seat for Daniel. He ordered an omelet. Lydia smiled. "Eggs at night?"

"Why not? Meat is too heavy right now." With a glass of wine Daniel's adrenaline faded. He was glad he had asked Lydia. Between drinks, food, chatter all around, and her questions about his career and how he knew Charles Emmet he enjoyed his success. Finally, he couldn't help yawning. "I should go. How are you getting home?"

"I'll get my car and drive home. Three of the violinists are going in the same direction." Lydia got up. "I really enjoyed talking to you, Maestro. Usually conductors don't bother with lowly librarians."

"Hey, don't forget, your job is essential. See you tomorrow." Daniel waved to her and the remaining musicians. *What a night.*

Chapter 20

Since Julian stayed over at the Emmet house for the night the hotel room felt desolate to Daniel. *No one breathing but myself.* He stood quietly and looked out the window. Snatches of music still tumbled around in his head. Yes, it had been a success. Can it be repeated tomorrow and Sunday? In the parking lot outside cars still came and went. Daniel saw two people under the lamp post. Were they arguing? One pushed and punched the other. Then a spark and a *pop* followed. Did he just shoot someone? Daniel grabbed the phone.

"A man just got shot in the parking lot," he yelled at the desk clerk. "Check it out."

That's as far as I will go, just reporting. I'll get into another mess otherwise. What if they want me to make a statement right now? I want to go to bed.

The phone rang. "Can you come down, Sir, the police are already here and want to talk to you." *There I go again. Why am I always involved? Do I have a target on my back so I can't be missed?*

The police waited downstairs, talking to the people at the desk and the parking attendant. Daniel told them what he had seen and heard. Then questions like "Can you describe the men? How tall, what clothes did they wear?"

Daniel had to smile. "It was midnight and dark, all clothes looked black. I just happened to look out of the window, practically ready for bed."

"Can you make a statement to that effect? Let's say, tomorrow morning?"

Daniel sighed. "All right. I'll do that."

One of the officers looked at him. "You are the conductor from tonight. I was there. Fantastic. Quite a success."

Small world. "Thank you. It went very well. And now you're working this late?" Daniel didn't know what else to say. The officer shrugged. "Filling in for someone." They departed and Daniel heaved a sigh of relief. Finally. he could go to bed although sleep would be a question mark. Police seem not far away from me, he thought, never mind where I go. Was this incident a coincidence or not? I'll probably never find out. I still have to try my best to get some sleep.

ↄ৩ↄ৩

Morning arrived too quickly for Daniel. He wasn't sure how he had slept. Between fuzzy dreams of people, cars, and himself standing on a podium conducting he had been wrestling around. It also occurred to him that he had never checked his cell phone last night. *I'm getting old.* He found three messages: one from Mia wishing him well for the opera, one from Inspector Lankin ,and one wrong number. The inspector? Even before breakfast, Daniel dialed his number.

"You disturbed my Saturday morning, Daniel," was the first thing he heard from the inspector.

As usual, Daniel thought. "You called me to call you, Sir. What's up?"

"In your case of the dinosaur and Julian, the man with the black beard has apparently appeared before."

"When? Where?" *Tell me more. It sounds like the inspector is drinking something, coffee?*

"One of our jailbirds remembered seeing someone like that, of course, from far away, at his construction site. Hard to keep invisible with a prominent black beard." The inspector chuckled.

"Could anyone else regain their memory, like Alex? It still will be extremely hard to find that man with all the other beards around. Anything else you found?" *Do I expect too much?*

"We are looking at a sighting of the lawyer who disappeared. Other than that we are digging. Have a good second performance." The inspector hung up.

Yes, that was important now, also picking up Julian. Daniel wasn't quite sure what to do with him. Maybe go to the zoo? Oh yes, the police station. *Breakfast first and coffee.*

ఌఁ

It didn't take long for Daniel to write his report at the police station. The officer remembered the incident with the toy dinosaur and the old man. Daniel tried to joke about it.

"Luckily I'm leaving on Sunday. You don't want to see me too often. I seem to attract the police. I hope you get the shooter at the hotel."

The officer smiled. "Yes, another job to do. Have a good flight back home."

Now to pick up Julian.

He was again full of questions about the opera, the audience, the singers. "Mr. Emmet said it was faaabulous. When can I see it, Papa?"

Daniel promised, "I'll take you to the Sunday Matinee. But afterwards, we have to leave and fly back home. Remember Mia's recital?"

"Oh yeah. Then I have to say goodbye to Emma and Manny before that. I sort of got used to them." Julian looked sad.

"You can keep in touch with them by email," Daniel said.

Julian shrugged. "Guess so."

"Should we see some animals at the zoo?" *I've got to do something with him.*

"Like elephants and lions and tigers?" Julian's eyes lit up.

"That's it. Let's go." Daniel hoped for a visit without threats from a man with a black beard. Although he knew that he would keep his mind and eyes on alert.

After getting a map at the entrance of the zoo, Daniel found the way to the lions, Julian's first choice. *Unless they are born in captivity or rescued, they shouldn't be here,* Daniel thought. *They're magnificent.* Out of habit, he kept looking around. Amongst so many people anyone sneaky enough could come too close. He decided everybody just seemed to have fun visiting the animals. He hadn't seen any man with a black beard. However, every time an unsavory person came close his adrenalin shot up. *What a way to live.*

The tigers were next, then the elephants. Julian, as usual, had questions about everything he saw. Finally he asked, "Is it lunch yet?"

Daniel looked at his watch. "Yes, and then we go home. Don't forget, I have another *Aida* tonight."

"So, no monkeys?"

Daniel shook his head. "But you have your choice of lunch." He turned around to see two men standing together and staring at him. *Wait a minute.* He glared back at them.

The men left. *Spies or opera lovers? Probably the first kind.* Since they had gone Daniel tried to dismiss the thought. *My head has to go back to the performance. And I need a little breather until then.*

He dropped Julian off at the Emmet's house and went back to the hotel. He wanted some quiet and to shut his eyes. Amazing how tiring walking around a zoo could be. Almost like meditation, he went through all the actions and music as he lay stretched out on the bed. *May it be as good as yesterday.*

The chime of the telephone woke Daniel. He rubbed his eyes. *Another call to scare me?* The desk clerk asked, "Can you come down, sir? A lady is asking for you."

"Does she have a name?"

"She says it's *Sonja* and you know her."

Oh Lord. Not that *Sonja. I'm not ready for this.* "Tell her I'll see her at the theater at seven o'clock. I'm busy right now." She has quite a nerve to track me down here, Daniel thought. She'd better have a good reason. Since Seattle, she should know how much I hate interruptions. Daniel decided to get a bit of supper. At least he could gather his thoughts over it.

The restaurant was filling up quickly. The waiter ushered Daniel to a table in a corner by the window. No sooner did Daniel sip his coffee when someone in an evening dress approached his table. "Good evening, Maestro."

Daniel leaned back. "I told you to meet me at the theater, Sonja." *I don't like surprises like this.*

Sonja tried to smile. "I'm sorry, I couldn't wait. I need to tell you something."

Daniel drank his coffee. "Not here. I need some peace before an important performance. You should know that. All else can wait unless someone is going to try to kill me—again. "He couldn't disguise his anger.

"It has something to do with that. But—okay. I'll see you at seven. I'll be in the audience too." She turned and walked away

Daniel crumpled his napkin. *I don't believe this. She waited until now to tell me whatever is so important?* He looked at his salad with chicken and shrimp. *I'm not missing my supper even if it might be my last one.*

Chapter 21

On his way to the Opera House Daniel tried to keep his mind on the performance. Even if Sonja—for whatever reason—had dire warnings, it could not impede his concentration. Knowing Sonja's mind she might just want to make sure she wasn't forgotten. How could he? He would see her at the Seattle year-end concert.

To Daniel's dismay, Sonja waited already at the elevator on his way up to his dressing room. *Right, let's get this over with. I need to be civil.*

"You are determined, Sonja. This has to be good. It would be better to tell me your secrets after the performance."

Sonja nodded. "I know and I apologize. But your life is important to me and I came across the truth about your almost accident in Seattle."

Daniel's ears couldn't help but perk up. "If this is a long story we better meet afterward. My mind needs to be clear of disasters right now." *Just go!*

"All right Maestro. Where?"

"Around the corner at the pub. Enjoy *Aida*." Daniel looked at her and saw tears in her eyes. She turned away.

"Until later then."

Daniel sighed and raked his fingers through his hair. The accident in Seattle is history, he thought. Why now? He took a bit longer to get changed. With each piece of clothing he took off he made a piece of *Aida* move into his mind. He breathed deeply and felt his calm slowly coming back. This needed to be another successful performance.

The manager met him halfway to the stage. "Amneris can't sing yet. Her doctor advised her to wait until tomorrow. She is backstage though."

"She's better off to save her voice. We have a good extra. What else?" *Anything to worry about?*

"No, all is clear. Almost a full house." The manager beamed.

Daniel clapped him on the shoulder. "That's what we need." *All right, I'm fine now and ready to go.* The audience cheered as he marched up to the podium. He looked at the musicians and motioned a thumbs-up. The prelude started.

As usual, the music transported Daniel into the life of Egypt and away from his own questions. The soloists were in good voice and their arias were rewarded with applause.

By intermission Daniel knew that all was well, at least opera-wise. He stayed out of sight of the musicians just to keep the feelings created by the performance—elation and a kind of wonder. Somehow this *Aida* was different from others. Was it because of what he himself had gone through during the last years? Elvira's death, Charles Emmet's sickness, Daniel's own problems? Whatever the reason he would forever take this as a model for all the ones he would ever conduct.

Just about at the end of the intermission, Lydia peeked into the door.

"Maestro, again really wonderful."

Nice to see her. "Yes, I'm glad it is. Did you cry again?" *I need to tease her.*

She smiled. "I try not to, but it's hard because of the music." She turned. "I'll let you get on. See you tomorrow."

She could have stayed. But yes, it is time for the rest of Aida.

When the curtain closed the applause again overwhelmed Daniel. After many bows and handshakes all around he finally made it up to his dressing room. It would be hard to get back to reality and—Sonja.

When Daniel arrived at the pub he saw Sonja already waiting at a table. *This better not take too long.* He sat down. A waiter set a brandy in front of him.

"I ordered it for you, Maestro. I know you like brandy." Sonja tried to smile.

"Thank you, but let's not waste time. Tell me in the shortest way possible what I'm supposed to know." Daniel tried not to be angry but he really didn`t feel like socializing with Sonja.

"Okay." She folded her hands in front of her. "You might remember me being beaten up by my now ex-husband. He was the one trying to run you over. He had asked me when the concert would be over, in other words when you would walk home." She stopped and took a sip of wine. "I know this because he told me after 'I'm still going to get him, if not me then someone else.'"

"So he's one of the gang trying to make my life interesting." *I should have known, never mind drunken driver.* "Then why did he beat you up?"

Sonja took another sip of wine. "He thought that I had warned you. Maestro, there are others after you, too."

Daniel almost laughed. "Don't I know it? Everywhere I go plus after my kids."

"I didn't know that. Oh, and he yelled that he now had lost his standing in the group."

Daniel finished his brandy. "I believe that. A few others have been killed for failing to do me in. I'm the pebble in their boots." He turned around. "If you don't mind, I would like to join my musicians. But thank you for clearing things up."

Sonja got up. She had tears in her eyes again. "By the way, *Aida* was amazing. Congratulations. I'm glad I came."

Daniel held out his hand. "I'm happy your ex-husband is off the street. I'll see you soon in Seattle."

She grabbed his hand and shook it. "I'm looking forward to it."

Daniel waited until the door had closed behind her. *I didn't really hear anything new. It just confirmed what I had already thought. Maybe Inspector Lankin should get in touch with the police in Seattle. Since Sonja's ex is already in jail, they might find out more about his association with the diamond smugglers. Every little bit of info could help.*

He walked over to the musicians who cheered him with glasses raised. Daniel breathed easier.

✂✂✂

On the way back to his hotel Daniel thought again about Sonja's tale. What a mixed-up situation. And how convenient for her husband since Sonja knew Daniel's habits well. Her ex should be safe behind bars for now, although punishment for wife beatings was never too severe. Apparently not important enough. Would he reveal anything about the boss of the gang to the police? After all, he would be angry that he was demoted. Daniel didn't believe it. Just like the others: too scared.

By the time Daniel went up to his room, he had decided to put Sonja's interlude into the back of his mind. *I have one more Aida to do and then prepare to leave afterward.* He would pick up Julian in the morning to make sure his luggage was packed for the flight home. Of course Julian wanted to see the matinee performance. *Could I ask Lydia to sit with him? He needs someone to keep him in his seat. I'll try that tomorrow.* Daniel checked his cell phone. Mia had called saying that everything was all right. *Good, I'd better get some sleep.*

Chapter 22

At Daniel's arrival at Charles Emmet's house the next morning Mrs. Emmet greeted him with a sad face. "We took Charles to the hospital last night. The pain got worse and the side effects of the medication…He was in bad shape."

Daniel's heart sank. He grabbed her hand. "I'm so sorry. I thought he was doing quite well."

She nodded. "You already know what can happen. You went through it. I'm going to the hospital now. Julian is ready to go."

"I am so grateful to you for taking care of him. I'll see Charles before I leave." Daniel had a hard time finding the right words. He could see hope in Mrs. Emmet's eyes. Yes, there was always hope if only for a short time. They shook hands. Daniel took Julian and both waved to the two children and their nanny.

Julian was quiet and looked sad. "Is Mr. Emmet going to die like Mama?"

Daniel sighed. "I hope not, Julian. They'll take care of his pain and adjust the medication." *What can I say?* "Let's get our luggage together and take it to the theater because we are leaving from there." To lighten Julian's mood he gave him his phone. "Call Mia. Tell her we'll try and make it to her recital." Julian beamed. *How quickly one can change a child's mood.*

After lunch, Daniel decided to visit Charles in the hospital. He took Julian along. If there was a problem with that he would have to deal with it then and there. Daniel tried to push back any memories of Elvira's hospital visits. This was a friend who needed support.

The nurse advised him to only stay a few minutes. "He is quite weak and needs rest. Is this your son, Sir?"

"Yes, and a friend of Mr. Emmet. He'll be quiet."

The nurse nodded. "Go in then."

As Daniel expected Charles was connected to many tubes. His eyes were closed. He seemed to sense Daniel's presence and smiled. "What are you doing here?"

"To wish you the best recovery, Charles. Let this be only a small setback." Daniel touched Charles' hand. The hand that used to swing a baton and directed eighty plus musicians, he thought.

Charles looked at Julian. "I'm glad to have met you, Julian. Keep practicing."

The boy nodded. "Thank you for looking after me. I like your kids."

Charles smiled then his eyes closed again. Daniel motioned Julian. *Let's go.* He touched his friend's hand once more. *Lord, let him live a little longer.*

Outside again Daniel tried to get his thoughts back to the tasks at hand: luggage and theater. With any luck he would see Lydia to ask her to sit with Julian.

He met her at the restaurant filling her coffee cup. "You're early, Maestro."

"I had to run other errands. Julian wants to see the matinee. Would you possibly be able to sit with him? He tends to roam."

Lydia smiled at Julian. "I should be able to. Everything is quite organized."

"Thank you. I'll pay for your lunch." *It's all I can do.* After Daniel ordered the food for himself and Julian they talked about the outcome of Mr. Emmet's hospital stay. Daniel also thought about not being able to see Lydia anymore after today. It had a funny feeling to it.

As if reading his mind Lydia asked, "Where are you off to now after *Aida*?"

Daniel lined up all his assignments. "Seattle isn't too far away. Come and see the concerts."

Lydia looked surprised. "What an invitation."

Daniel laughed. "I'll invite anyone who cries at my *Aida* prelude."

She laughed too and raised her coffee cup. "I'll try my best. Thank you. I better tend to my business. Let me know when Julian is ready."

"She is nice, isn't she?" Julian commented.

"Yes, and you behave sitting with her." *I need to slow down my thinking. She just has a pleasing way about her.* "Finish your lunch, I have work to do."

☙❧☙

Until people started filling the theater Daniel kept checking all details on stage and off. Julian pulled at his sleeve. "I thought everything was organized, why do you have to check it all over?"

"Because this is the last performance of the opera. It has to be as good as the other ones."

Julian looked around. "There is Lydia. Can I go with her?"

He already has a crush on her. "Okay, see you after, be good." Daniel went to his dressing room to change. *All right, say goodbye to Aida in the best way possible to honor Maestro Emmet.*

❦

Daniel wasn't sure how to leave at the end of the performance. As a custom he would stay and have a drink with the soloists and musicians. But he needed to get to the airport to be home in time for Mia's recital. "Fatherly duties," he mumbled. He decided to make it as short as possible.

After the applause had stopped Daniel shook hands with all soloists and explained why he was in a hurry. "All I can say is thank you for your great work."

The tenor said, "Why don't you take over here?"

Goodness, Charles isn't dead yet. "You would have to clone me, Robert. My dance card is full until August. Who knows what might happen?"

Lydia and Julian were waiting at Daniel's dressing room. "Papa, that was so sad. How could they put them in a tomb?"

"I tried to explain," Lydia said.

"Thank you for taking care of him. But we have to leave soon." Daniel shook her hand. "Maybe we'll see you sometime?"

"I hope so, Sir. But never mind a taxi. I'll drive you to the airport."

Daniel's mouth fell open. "Are you sure? There is no need for it."

"I picked you up, I'll bring you back." She smiled. "Mr. Emmet's orders."

During the drive Julian kept the conversation going with more questions. Daniel wouldn't have known what to talk about. Something bothered him but he didn't know exactly what. At the turnstile, they shook hands again and waved goodbye. *I might not see her again.*

As soon as Daniel sat in his seat he couldn't keep his eyes open any longer. Julian also yawned and pulled the blanket around him. Even before the plane left the ground Daniel drifted off. His last thoughts were "Get us home safely."

∽∾∽

After landing in San Francisco Daniel and Julian took a taxi to the church where Mia's recital was taking place.

"We almost made it," Julian said.

"Yes, only half an hour late. Let's creep in quietly." Daniel opened the front door carefully. He could hear a girl's high voice. *Not Mia, good.* A small group of people, maybe thirty, sat in the front pews. All the proud parents, Daniel thought. He saw Mrs. Gantrey as well. The voices were good. A young man sang a Schubert Lied. That will be a good baritone soon, Daniel thought.

Julian nudged him. "Mia is next." Daniel sat on pins and needles. *With her dark hair loose, she looks like Elvira.* The piano started and Mia came into the song. She had chosen Norina's aria from *Don Pasquale* by Donizetti.

I'm like the other parents, Daniel thought, surprised. Her voice is quite mature and able to express emotions. He was annoyed that his eyes watered. *Good Lord, tears?* "She's good, isn't she?" Julian whispered. Daniel nodded.

Mia beamed as everyone applauded with even a few whistles. The teacher announced that Mia would sing one more song, a Spanish love song. All Daniel could think was Wow! Spanish? Listening to it he remembered his father singing it many years ago. *Moist eyes again.*

After the singers had taken their bows, he went up to the teacher. "I have to congratulate you. Your students are very good."

Mrs. Frank blushed a little. "Thank you. They have worked hard. Mia is really progressing and so is Nathan. I'm really sorry I'm leaving."

They chatted for a while until the singers came out again. "I'm taking them out for a treat," Mrs. Frank said. "You're invited."

Daniel shook his head. "Sorry, no. We're just home from Portland. Let me talk to Mia."

Mia glowed and Daniel hugged her. "Great show. You surprised me. You're getting good. Where did the Spanish song come from?"

"My teacher found it for me since you and Mama are Spanish. Am I really getting good, Papa?"

"Definitely, you're on your way, kiddo. Now, enjoy your outing, see you in the morning."

Mia hugged Daniel again. "I'm glad you're home again, Papa."

Daniel was glad too for two reasons: Mia's success and going home to get a good night's sleep. Tomorrow would be a busy day again, checking in with the assistant conductor's rehearsals and—hopefully—new information from Inspector Lankin.

⁓⁓⁓

When Daniel came into the kitchen for breakfast the next morning Mia and Julian were already sitting at the table chatting up a storm. "It sounds like we were away for months."

"It felt like it." Mia filled Daniel's cup with coffee.

Between toasts popping and Cheerios spilling both children kept on talking. When Julian started to explain the incident at the carnival's parking lot Daniel interrupted. "We'll talk about it later today. Right now you need to go to school. But, Mia, I'm proud of your singing. Off you go." Telling the tale of the old man with the dinosaur needs more than Julian's version, Daniel thought. Even outside he could hear his son chatting away. He had to smile. *What a pair.*

Daniel savored his second cup of coffee and the quiet around him. He decided to call Inspector Lankin to make sure he would have time to talk to Daniel. But the inspector wasn't in yet. *All right, to the theater first.* Daniel needed to start with Korngold's violin concerto. He had not met the violinist yet. Some really good ones had an ego to match, so he was eager to talk to Carlos Florenso.

The assistant conductor met Daniel in the hallway. "Welcome back, Maestro. I read some great reviews about you and *Aida*."

"Thank you. How have you been coping? Did Mr. Florenso show up?"

"He's waiting already. Quite a character." The assistant smiled.

That's all I need, a character.

The violinist got up from his chair when Daniel entered the Green Room. "Maestro, finally I meet the Great One."

Daniel chuckled. "Don't flatter me, Carlos. It won't get you a better review." They shook hands. The violinist laughed. "I don't expect anything special—except a drink before I start. I'll have to calm my nerves."

"It's only a rehearsal, Carlos. We can have breaks." *Butterflies are common, he's never met me before.* "I'll start with Haydn. You can listen first to get to know me." Daniel turned to the assistant conductor. "Any questions before we begin?"

"No, Daniel. I think I got a good start."

Daniel knew he would sit with the score on his lap taking notes. *Like I did years ago.*

Most of the rehearsal went quite well. Daniel knew that Haydn usually sounded pleasant and easy to listen to. However, there were nuances for a conductor to discover and hear—small sparks of wit that shouldn't be ignored.

Those details his assistant could only find out by listening and studying the scores.

During lunch, Daniel joked with Carlos about not drinking coffee. "It doesn't help your nerves."

"Okay, decaf it is. But I feel better already. I think I know what I'm doing. Particularly with those shrimps in my salad."

At least he isn't eating burgers, Daniel thought. I wonder how many times he has played this concert.

But Carlos took command of his violin once the music started.

Daniel stopped after each movement. The first two had an easy, song-like pace. Whenever he felt Carlos' eyes like a question mark concerning tempo, Daniel tried to explain why he had slowed down or used *rubato* in certain places. Once or twice Carlos didn't agree right away.

"Each conductor feels differently about this," Daniel said. "But let's do it my way this time."

Carlos nodded. He did a great job on the last fast, joyful movement.

As rehearsal time ran out Daniel told the musicians, "Grieg will have to wait. We'll do all of it tomorrow." *My next stop: the inspector.*

Chapter 23

The police station was busier than usual with officers walking around all talking at the same time.

Daniel asked the woman at the desk, "What's going on? A crisis?"

"Close to it." She looked downcast. "A murderer
slipped through our fingers."

"Ouch! Is there any time at all to talk to the inspector?"

The woman shrugged. "I can try and ask him." Her
hand shook while she pushed a button. After a short while
she nodded to Daniel. "Okay, go in, but tread carefully."

Daniel knocked at the inspector's half-open door.

"You might as well add to my misery, Daniel." Inspector Lankin sat bent over a stack of papers.

"I didn't intend to," Daniel said. "Just reporting back
from Portland."

The inspector sat up. "Yeah, yeah, I know. We had a
serious setback. But in your case, I might have something.
Sit down."

Daniel's hope rose. *Wouldn't that be wonderful?*

"As I said before," the inspector started. "We smoked
the lawyer out of his hiding place and good thing we did.
He needed treatment, someone shot him."

Daniel could hardly sit still. "Again because of his fail-
ure to stay out of sight? Why didn't he?"

The inspector shrugged. "Who knows? He still won't tell us who the head of the gang is. 'Nobody knows' he said. Hard to believe." He stopped and flicked the pen between his fingers. "Since you had the dispute in Portland concerning the black-bearded man, we got in touch with the police there. The old man might still be a lead, however small."

"I wish them luck. Will the lawyer now be charged with murder?"

The inspector nodded. "We have to make sure he doesn't get killed in the meantime." He stopped again. "We're showing pictures of the construction crew at various diamond centers. Maybe someone will recognize one of them." He got up.

Daniel knew he had to leave. They needed to chase the missing murderer. "Thank you, Inspector. We'll get them." What else could he say? *Now back home to my fatherly duties.*

✧✧✧

On his way to the theater the next morning Daniel remembered to check the music for London. He had forgotten because of all the other activities. Of course first on his list was Seattle again: the Chamber Orchestra and the Symphony. *I better make sure I know what I'm supposed to present. But first another rehearsal.*

Daniel heard Carlos already practicing when he walked into the foyer. He wondered if Carlos had thought about the corrections. Daniel's cell buzzed. Mia.

"Julian is sick, the nurse is looking after him. He threw up once. Maybe it's stomach flu."

Daniel's chest tightened. *No, not now.* "What if they send him home?"

"Then I'll go home too, just do your job, Papa." Mia sounded calm enough.

"Okay, if it gets worse call me and the ambulance. No use taking chances."

"I will, Papa. See you later." Mia hung up.

Daniel scratched his head. Julian had been fine this morning. Could it just be a one-day stomach thing or—was it connected to Julian holding the poisoned Dinosaur? But that was four days ago.

The concertmaster looked around the door. "We're ready, Maestro."

"Coming, John. Had a phone call. Let's go." Grieg's *Holberg Suite* was first in line. That was if he didn't get interrupted with Julian's sickness. Daniel had often wondered who Holberg was to have music written about him. He'd found out that Holberg was regarded in Denmark and Norway as the father of poetry and literature. He was also a professor and later a baron. Reason enough for Grieg to honor him with his music.

Except for a few changes in expression details rehearsal went well. Daniel took Haydn next to have more time with the violin concerto after lunch. At noon he called Mia. When she didn't answer his stomach cramped. Was she still in class, on her way home? Picking up Julian? Daniel tried again.

Mia picked up on the second ring. "I'm just home now with Julian. He's okay I think, just didn't want to stay with the nurse. I made him lay down on the couch."

Daniel breathed again. "I'm glad you took him home. I won't be late. Thanks, Mia." *Maybe I can concentrate on Korngold now.*

Carlos waited already, ready to go. "I'll concede to your wishes, Maestro. I made notes on the score." He smiled but Daniel noticed some nervousness.

"You wouldn't have much of a choice, Carlos. You'll do well." And he did, he even impressed Daniel. He shook his hand. "Good job, Carlos. The audience will like you. Prepare an encore."

Carlos beamed. "Thank you. I got used to your corrections."

Daniel chuckled. "People usually do. Another conductor might think differently about it." He turned to the musicians. "One more run-through tomorrow, then performances on Friday and Saturday. We have another concert as a year-ender: two long pieces, Tchaikovsky's Fifth and Liszt's Hungarian Rhapsody. Prepare already, please."

On his way home he realized that he should talk to the president of the London Symphony to make sure they hadn't made any changes. Then Seattle, the first stop-off. Mia and Julian were coming along so they all could fly from Seattle to London. Inspector Lankin should also know that Daniel and family would be away for three weeks. Someone besides Mrs. Gantrey had to keep an eye on the house. *No end to it.*

Daniel found Julian in the living room watching TV. "Hi, Papa"

"How are you feeling now? Any more stomach troubles?" *Julian still looks a bit pale.*

Julian turned the TV off. "Not much, just a little funny. Maybe I'm hungry?"

Daniel called Mia. "Do we have chicken soup in the house?"

"Why, Papa?"

"Because that's the all-time remedy according to my mother and your Mama." *Nothing better than old-time cures.*

Mia came back. "Only canned soup will have to do."

"Better than nothing." *Maybe then I can take a breather?*

രൃൃൃ

The next morning Julian felt better and went to school under the careful scrutiny of Mia. Daniel called the inspector. He thought it was important to tell him about Sonja's story.

"Okay, what now?" came the inspector's growly voice.

Daniel explained Sonja's visit and her husband's membership in the group out to harass Daniel in Seattle. "Since he is in jail for beating up his wife, he might be the person to question further about this group."

"Hm. Willows might get to it. Thank you." The inspector hung up.

He probably didn't have his coffee yet. At least he knows. Daniel remembered Andy Willows, the detective hovering over him in Seattle. He was sure he was going to meet him again during the concerts. Now to the last rehearsal. So far nothing had gone wrong.

To Daniel's surprise he spotted two fire trucks in front of the theater. A shiver ran down his back. *Fire in the Symphony Hall? Who would do that?* The firemen stood around talking. Daniel approached them. "What happened? Where is the fire?"

"No fire, Sir," one of them answered. "It must have been a false alarm. We checked everything, nothing wrong."

"But something set the alarm off."

The fireman nodded. "It can happen, maybe bad wiring. We're looking into it."

"Can I go on with the program? Nobody lurking around?" Daniel still wasn't sure.

The man motioned to the stage door. "Yes, go ahead. We checked the building. We're leaving pretty soon."

Daniel felt a lump in his stomach: *coincidence or organized to aggravate him? Just a fluke? In my life nothing is a fluke*. The musicians drifted in with puzzled looks. The concertmaster joked, "I'm all for a hot performance but not in this way."

Daniel knew he had to get to his music to keep his mind steady. "Nothing we can do; all seems to be in order now. Let's get started."

Except for some settling-down time and a few repeats the rehearsal went well. Daniel was grateful that the musicians concentrated and let the music take over. He reminded them, "You have tomorrow off from me. Friday and Saturday are the performances, then rehearsals for the year-end concert." He still had this urge to look over his shoulder now and then.

All right, another call to the inspector? What could he do? Unless fingerprints had been left somewhere he couldn't help anyway. Was this done to interrupt Daniel's conducting? What about his own house? He called Mrs. Gantrey.

"Could you keep an eye on my house, Mrs. Gantrey, just until I get home? Something might go on, I'm not sure."

"I'll go over and check," she offered. "All seems to be quiet."

I'm getting paranoid again, Daniel thought. Most likely it was an electrical glitch. He tried hard not to assume that this incident was meant for him personally. He needed to work on the music for the last concert here as well as the pieces for Seattle and London. Especially London's evening and outdoor programs, quite different from each other. Daniel had to make sure to be undisturbed in his study for a few hours.

At home he went through every room to make sure that no surprises would spring on him.

The door slammed and Julian appeared. He smacked his bag on a chair. "You have no idea how much homework I have. I missed some stuff and have to do it now. I need some cookies or ice cream to keep up my strength."

Daniel laughed. "You had fun in Portland. Now it's back to work. Get on with it."

"But so much." Julian already munched on a chocolate chip cookie.

Daniel grabbed a mug with tea. "I have to get about ten long pieces of music ready. I think you can manage."

"But I'm only ten, Papa."

Mia stood in the kitchen door. "I heard that. Let's do our homework together. I have a lot too."

Bless you, Mia. "I'll slave away in my study—without interruption until supper. Agreed?"

"Okay, Papa," came from both kids.

Daniel closed the door behind him. *Where to start? The one for the next concert—Tchaikovsky's Fifth Symphony.*

Chapter 24

After an hour of poring over and humming along with the first two movements Daniel got up and stretched. *I'm going to turn into a hunchback if I'm not careful.* He needed some tea to loosen up his throat. With all the emotions in the music it tended to dry out. No one was more connected to and believed in fate than Tchaikovsky. Most Russians were, but through his music, he spelled out his feelings of doubt and inadequacy. What else was left? Fate.

Daniel sighed. *Is it my fate to be harassed and threatened all the time? No, it's not! This will end. Back to the last two movements.*

When he finally listened to his CD of the symphony led by one of his favorite conductors, Valerie Gergiev, he heard a knock on his door. "Supper, Papa." *How time flies.*

Hours later, in the middle of Liszt's Hungarian Rhapsody, the phone rang. Inspector Lankin's voice sounded raspy. "Go to Alex tomorrow, Daniel. You know him better than we do. He remembered a bearded man in his school. See what you can get out of him. I'm losing my voice. Good night."

Daniel leaned back in his chair. Alex must have found out somehow about this Mr. Blackbeard. Being in his school? Looking for recruits? Maybe it's one step closer to solving the mystery of diamonds and greed.

಄಄಄

Since the next morning was free of rehearsals Daniel had time to visit Alex at the Youth Detention facility. The warden allowed him to come in after lunch. Daniel was looking forward to meeting Alex again and finding out if he had continued with his studies.

Alex's eyes lit up when he saw Daniel. "So, you did come back."

"Yes, and I'm sure you have grown again. Are you getting on all right? How about your studies?" Daniel got the customary shrug. He got right into the reason for coming. "I heard you remembered a fellow in your school with a black beard. Was he there often or just snooping around?"

"I saw him talking to the principal only once," Alex answered. "But he talked to some of the teachers too."

"How did you even find out that we're looking for him?"

Alex sat down. "My foster mother came and told me. I don't know how she knew." He shrugged again. "Maybe she knows some guys like that."

Wouldn't surprise me. "Did you hear the teachers call him by name?"

Alex shook his head. "I don't know what they were talking about. I didn't really listen, just saw them. Maybe the principal still remembers him or one of the teachers does."

Daniel put his hand on Alex's shoulder. "You might have helped us in this. The man could be the one making my life miserable and who enticed you with the bomb. I'll get back to you. Thank you, Alex, for remembering and— keep up with your studies."

Alex laughed and they shook hands.

Daniel felt like speeding right down to Alex's school and asking the teachers about the bearded man. But he remembered that this was Mia's school as well. This might put her in danger again. Back to the inspector.

This time the desk in the police office was occupied by an officer. *Her day off again?* "I need to tell the inspector some new information," Daniel said.

The officer grinned. "He won't yell at you today. His voice isn't back yet."

Daniel smiled. "He doesn't have to talk, I'll do it this time."

Inspector Lankin sat at his desk bent over photos and papers. He motioned Daniel to sit down. "Tell me," he rasped.

Daniel related the story Alex told him. "I'll leave it in your capable hands to question the teachers. It wouldn't bode well for my daughter if I do it."

The inspector nodded. "Tell Officer Duncan what you told me. He needs to know what to ask." The inspector coughed. "Arrr, darn. How about going with him?"

"If you think it helps, okay. Don't you need two offic-ers?"

"Yeah, you're just back-up." He swallowed a cough drop.

Daniel waved. "Get better soon." *It must be a burden for him not being able to raise his voice. Just like me not be able to raise my arms to conduct. Now to find Officer Duncan.*

On the way to the school officer Duncan asked Daniel about the man they were looking for. "I've heard some of the stories from the inspector. But what exactly happened in Portland?"

Daniel related the details. Duncan shook his head. "Who would do that to a child? They must be really afraid that you know too much about their business and went af-ter your son."

"Since Alex remembered the incident at school," Daniel continued, "I want a better description of the man, not just that he has a black beard. What did he talk to the teachers about? I can only guess."

"We'll find out." Duncan stopped the car in the school's driveway.

Children were outside for recess. Daniel felt uneasy. "I'll stay outside. They might know me, it's my daughter's school as well."

The students looked with interest at the police officers walking into the school. Daniel heard comments like "Are they arresting someone?" Big laughter when some boys mentioned names. Probably unpopular teachers, Daniel thought. He walked around. All he could hope was that the principal and teachers had a good memory. What were they talking about with Mr. Blackbeard? Did he leave a phone number or an address? Most likely not.

Daniel kept his eyes on the entrance door in case the officers wanted him for something. He could hardly contain his impatience. He paced around the grassy area. *Good thing I have a day off, no time lost.*

Finally the officers appeared again. "We'll tell you on the way back."

"Did you get anything at all?" *Can I hope?*

On the road the second officer said, "All they remembered was his first name, Rupert. He offered work for any graduating student. But no phone number or address. He had said he would come back at the end of the school year."

Daniel let out a breath. "Could they describe him more? Like how tall, how old, clothes?"

"Yeah, they told us a few things. But the best way is to wait until he appears again, one month away. We'll have to be there."

"That could be a tricky wait. But better than we had before." Daniel leaned back in his seat. "Rupert is probably not his real name. The teachers should have figured that he wasn't real. His behavior looked fake. Why didn't they call the police?" *Was there really enough security in schools?*

❡❡❡

Inspector Lankin listened to the officers' report and twirled his pen between his fingers. "We have to get the techies on it and dig up all data on a Rupert with a possible criminal record." His voice still sounded hoarse. "Okay, Daniel, don't expect a miracle. But we might have a timeline."

Daniel needed to say something. "Thank you, Inspector, for your officers and their time. We're grasping at the proverbial straws but it's a bright spot in the gloom."

The inspector nodded. "Now get back to your music."

"Yes, Sir." Daniel had to smile. In other words, "Get out and leave me alone."

❡❡❡

Back home Daniel stood for a moment thinking. Could this small mistake of Blackbeard topple him? Remembered by a student he recruited in the school he had visited? That would be ironic. But Daniel knew he could not pin his hopes too strongly on this good outcome. This man was still full of revenge continuing to hurt Daniel and the children. So, what else could he do to keep safe?

Daniel sat down at the kitchen table. With his limited knowledge and time, he needed to leave it to the police. Officer Duncan had mentioned something about more of a description of the bearded man. Daniel had to keep his trust in the police techies to tune into cyberspace.

His stomach growled. Soup, sandwich, coffee? Best to do it all. Then he had to work on Seattle's concerts. He also needed to contact London about a change of the first piece on the program. Instead of Tchaikovsky's Polonaise, which he had done too often, he decided on Borodin's *Prince Igor Overture. They want drama, they'll get it.*

❦❦❦

The next morning Daniel tried hard to concentrate on the rehearsal of Korngold, Haydn, and Grieg. The idea of having a lead on the bearded man interfered with his normal thought process. To make himself work hard he started with Korngold. Eventually, the music took over and enfolded him as usual. Carlos was in good form. He turned out to be a commendable violinist.

During a break in Haydn, his cell phone rang. Mia. Daniel stopped. "Take five, I'll have to answer this."

"What's up, Mia?" His heart constricted.

"I have some news about a blond woman who called on me today in school."

Daniel's hand shook as he held the phone. "At school? What did she want?"

"She told the principal that I needed to come along, that you were in trouble. But he came and told me and I called you, and you're okay." Mia's voice wobbled a bit.

Daniel sat down on the steps to the podium. "Good Lord. Where is the woman now?"

"She left when the principal told her that you were fine. She apparently said, 'Oh, then he must have recovered.'"

"Would you have gone with her, Mia?"

"No way, Papa, not without calling you."

Daniel's breathing had slowed down. "What if she had caught you on the way home and kidnapped you?"

"I would have screamed my head off and jammed my keys in her face." Mia's voice sounded angry.

"Did the principal call the police? I mean, this is serious."

"He said he would."

Daniel scrambled up to the podium again. "I'll tell you more about some other blond woman when I come home. Don't walk home by yourself, okay?"

"I won't, Papa. My friend is going with me. See you later." Mia hung up.

Daniel had to take some deep breaths. *What if they had caught Mia on the street? Would there have been people around to help her? They don't stop, are they that desperate?* Mia was safe, he had to push through the rehearsal for tomorrow's performance.

He turned to the musicians. "Sorry, let's continue." *No use getting them involved in my predicaments.* He tried again to focus on Haydn and banish the blond woman into the back of his mind. At lunch Daniel left a message for Inspector Lankin. An attempted abduction was pressing enough to disturb him. Mr. Blackbeard must feel strongly to again send his soldiers out to do his bidding. Daniel refilled his coffee cup and bought a cookie from the tray. He needed something sweet.

The concertmaster came up to him. "I hope the phone call wasn't a bad one. You looked kind of shocked."

Daniel nodded. "Yes, I was. But it's all good now. My daughter knew what to do. Let's leave it at that."

"Okay, Maestro." He put his finger across his mouth.

The rest of the rehearsal went well. The performances would be good. Daniel couldn't wait to get home and talk to Mia, as well as caution Julian again to be very careful at all times.

Chapter 25

Mia was already home when Daniel arrived. She stood in front of the stove dropping vegetables into a pot of broth.

"Well, look at the cook working," Daniel said. *What a wife she will make.*

Mia measured out some noodles. "Just working ahead. I need to go back for singing lessons."

Daniel sat down. "Let's go over your blond woman. Did you see her?"

"No, only heard what the principal told me."

"How did he describe her? Tall, short, thin, fat?"

Mia laughed. "Papa, you sound like the police."

"Yeah, I know. But this is important. I remember hearing of another blond woman connected to Alex, the bomb thrower. That one approached his foster mother to demand Alex's cell phone number under the guise of the laws of foster care. All false, of course. There has to be a connection."

Mia's eyes widened. "He said she had shoulder-length, wavy, blond hair and blue eyes, medium everything else."

Daniel got up and filled his cup with tea. "I'll bet it was the same person trying to get to you."

Mia stopped stirring the soup. "And how can we find out?"

"By sending the police to the foster mother to give us a closer description of the woman." Then something popped into Daniel's mind. "She must have left fingerprints somewhere: on the entrance door, on the principal's door. I guess it's too late now with all the kids touching them."

Mia put on her coat. "Would the police even bother?"

"Don't think so." Daniel looked at Mia. "Do you want me to drive you? It might be safer."

Mia shook her head. "Maybe when I'm done when it's darker."

"Okay, call me."

Julian ambled down the stairs. "Papa, can you help me with some theory? My teacher said I'll need to know that too, not only playing the piano."

I like that teacher. "He's right. Come down here with it. I'll have a look." *Here goes my work on Seattle's music. But I'm a father after all.*

Daniel explained some chords, progression of scales, intervals, and different clefs. "You need to write on the staves as neatly as possible."

Julian sighed. "I understand most all of this but the writing is hard."

Daniel encouraged him to do it slowly. "No need to rush." Then Mia called and he had to pick her up. *This was supposed to be my day off. But there is time after supper.*

✑✒✑

Daniel spent the rest of the evening looking through the scores he had planned for London. He wanted to take a good amount of time on Saint-Saëns' Organ Symphony. London wanted it as the main piece. It was also the longest one with organ and piano. Daniel loved it but he wanted it to be as perfect as possible. For the outdoor performances, he chose waltzes, overtures, and a longer Mozart piece. He had found out that outside weekend audiences enjoyed something lighter, lively, and not too long.

Secretly Daniel had hoped to hear from Inspector Lankin after he had left the message. Maybe tomorrow, he thought. If not, Daniel would try to talk to him. After all, an attempt to kidnap Mia and a possible connection between the two blond women could lead to solving a big part of his problem. Daniel still believed that the woman wore a blond wig and the leader of the gang a false black beard.

What is real in all of this, just to get to me? He also wanted to know if the inspector got any information from the diamond dealers. Did they remember anyone of the smugglers here? Someone had to be the middleman. *I'm thinking like a detective again. But some of that has helped before.* Right now the workload of the day caught up with Daniel. Bed looked quite inviting.

☙❦❧

When Daniel had not heard from the police or Inspector Lankin by noon the next day he drove to the station. He was sure that Alex's foster mother would be of help identifying the blond woman.

The police station buzzed like a beehive. The receptionist ignored Daniel, spending her attention on the phone. He cornered an officer. "Is the inspector available?"

"Barely," the officer answered. "Lots of work." He walked away.

Daniel took a chance and knocked on the inspector's closed door.

"What?" came a bellow.

"Just me, Inspector, Daniel." He heard a growl, then, "All right, come in."

When he opened the door he found Inspector Lankin standing looking out the window. "Of course, you would turn up," he said without turning around.

Might as well come to the point. "Did you get my message about Mia and the blond woman at her school?"

Lankin sat down and looked at him. "Yeah, yeah. The foster mother gave us a similar description of the woman. Now what?"

Daniel knew the inspector was agitated but he needed to voice his suspicions. "I'm sure the blond hair is a wig, probably with dark hair underneath. The black beard will be false too."

"That doesn't bring us any closer to finding them."

Daniel nodded. "True, but it helps to know. Two of the same women involved in illegal actions? Do you want to bet she's Blackbeard's soldier or even his wife?"

The inspector twirled his pen around again. "Well, detective, do you have a plan to find out? Let me know. In the meantime, we have a stabbing and an unknown corpse to investigate." He looked at Daniel. "I'm sorry for your daughter's almost abduction. Right now the lawyer seems to be our best lead. I'll let you know."

Daniel had one more question. "What about the diamond suppliers? Did any of them identify our smugglers?"

"We're working on it." Lankin grabbed for the phone.

Daniel waved and left. At least he would stay in the inspector's mind. The lawyer? Would he be brave enough to talk after almost being killed? Daniel checked his watch. Performance tonight. *I'm a conductor, not a detective. I have a concert tonight. Why am I always being sidetracked?* Despite Daniel's effort to use logic his mind would not stop seeking ways to unravel the case of the two similar looking blond women. What could they have in common? All he could think of was blue eyes. Like the reception lady at the police station. And how many more?

Daniel shook his head. *Time to get back to my job, music.* He left earlier to have more time in his dressing room to check his scores and get his head to tune into Haydn, Grieg, and Korngold.

At this time of the evening, the inside of the theater was quiet. Daniel sat down in his chair and let out a long breath. Mia and Julian were safe at home and here he could think. Yes, it had to be about the performances, not a solution to blond women. He scanned the notes and markings he had made on the violin concerto score and hoped that Carlos would remember.

Daniel went on to Grieg. No problem there. *What if we had fingerprints for her? I have no proof she is the culprit even if I suspect her of—what?* He remembered Sonja. Her husband used her and then beat her up. Could the lady at the front desk be in a similar situation? Maybe a boyfriend or also a husband? *Here I go again.* Daniel stood up. It was time to change, at least into proper performance clothes.

Chapter 26

The performance went well with Carlos getting the most applause. He beamed with a few drops of sweat trickling down his face. "Great job," Daniel said as they shook hands and bowed to the audience. On their way off the stage Carlos turned.

"I have to thank you, Maestro, for your support and the tips you gave me."

Daniel touched his shoulder. "You have the technique and the nerves. Just listen a lot to other players and CDs. Never stop learning. And—stick around."

Carlos nodded. A few of the other violinists also came to talk to Carlos.

Looking at his smile Daniel got an idea. White teeth. He had always wondered how the woman at the police station kept her teeth so brilliantly shiny. In his mind, unnaturally so. What if the two blond ladies had the same white smile? The smile that never reached the eyes. Could that be their give-away? *My Lord, I'm obsessed with this.* Daniel heard the gong for the end of the intermission. First, it was Haydn's turn.

After the virtuosic violin concerto, Haydn's symphony felt easy and relaxing. Daniel enjoyed himself as did the audience to judge by the applause. Carlos came up to Daniel afterward.

"Haydn was fun, Maestro. I could hear some instruments more clearly than before like they were talking to each other."

Daniel smiled. "That was the idea. I have found that music isn't just notes and sounds. There are always conversations going on between the instruments." He was happy that Carlos had heard the difference. Soloists concentrated on their individual instruments, not so much on the orchestra. Daniel remembered that as a boy he had asked, "What did the oboe say?" or "Why did the flute laugh?" His good ear had helped him in later life with understanding the different orchestrations in music.

"Once more tomorrow, Carlos. Play as well as today."

The violinist showed a thumbs-up and left.

While Daniel changed back into his street clothes a calm settled over him as if a load had dropped off his shoulders. Did something happen during the evening? Had a problem been solved pertaining to his eternal worries? That would be unbelievably lucky, he thought.

He still felt upbeat when he arrived home. With a brandy in his hand he relaxed in his chair and closed his eyes. Then he looked across to Elvira's picture. "Did you help somehow, Love? I wouldn't doubt it." *Here I'm talking to a photo again. But she's still close, still surrounds me. How lucky am I.* He checked his cell phone. It showed two messages, one from the inspector and one unknown.

"No, I'm not finding out anything before going to bed," he mumbled. He was going to take his good spirit with him to sleep.

After Daniel did his Saturday morning pancake duty, Mia and Julian decided to go over to their friends. "I might meet with the inspector," Daniel told them. "He left a message. I want you back in the afternoon, okay? I have a performance tonight."

"We know, Papa," two voices came back in unison.

An officer answered Daniel's call. "The inspector is at home today unless something special happens. You can phone him there."

Daniel expected a growl or a bellow from Inspector Lankin. But he had left a message, so Daniel was only responding. To his surprise he got a mellow reaction.

"So, you got curious. As I said before, the lawyer who's recovering in jail must have had a twinge of regret or got mad. He told us that the man named Rupert doesn't have a beard. He only met him once."

Daniel sat down. "It sounds like the beard is only used when he comes out of hiding and takes care of something."

"Yeah, like the school and the old man with the dinosaur."

Daniel felt a surge of excitement. "But the rest of him is the same—his hair, his eyes, his figure. Could we not get a sketch artist to draw his face that the principal and the old man remember?"

Lankin grunted. "If the old fellow can even do that."

"He will if it's a way out for him for his defense," Daniel tried again.

The inspector sighed. "All right, I'll get our sketch lady to tackle the principal and the Portland one to try the old guy. You're full of ideas, Maestro. Maybe you should switch over to be a detective."

Daniel was happy that he had caught the inspector in a good mood. "I wish I could sketch but I'm hopeless at it." Lankin chuckled and hung up.

Drinking another cup of coffee doubts assailed Daniel again. What if there were two Ruperts, with and without a beard? Brothers in crime used whenever the need arose? *Lord, let this be a proper step forward for once.*

ᎧᎧᎧ

The evening's performance went well. Carlos had to give a solo encore. Daniel was happy for him, he was talented and deserved the success. Daniel knew it would help his self-confidence. After Haydn Daniel told him, "You can play for me anytime, Carlos. And don't get rattled by another conductor. Just follow him, at least most of the time. You can put in your own emotions about the piece."

Carlos shook Daniel's hand. "Thank you, Maestro. I'll keep following you. Maybe soon I can work with you again."

"Fine with me. Stay in touch." Daniel knew he wouldn't see Carlos for a long time. He would fly around the world playing concerts and recitals. There was a lot of competition among talented up-and-coming violinists. Carlos would need all his determination and love for music to go to the top.

Now Daniel had to get the year-end concert ready. Then he could think about Seattle and finally London. But in the meantime? He hadn't mentioned to the inspector about the idea concerning the white teeth. He would have laughed him out of his office. And referring to the policewoman at the desk could have been worse. Daniel would have to try this on his own.

On his drive home he tried to relax. *The audience loved both performances, Carlos played as well as anyone could have, and I haven't been so bad myself even in Portland. Isn't that what I should be concerned about? As a conductor?* By the time he drove into his garage he also knew that the lives of his children and his own were most important. After all these months of looking over his shoulder, expecting another attack from somewhere, and worrying about Mia and Julian, a bit of detective work couldn't hurt.

Daniel would contact the principal of Mia's school and get his opinion on the blond lady's super-white teeth. Daniel chuckled. Wouldn't it be ironic? Brushing teeth with the most whitening toothpaste to impress all in the office and her boyfriend and ending up as a suspect? He had to bide his time. Tomorrow was Sunday and Mia had told him that teachers don't give out their phone numbers. He would try and get an appointment with the principal on Monday.

What about Alex's foster mother? Would she even remember the woman who claimed to check up on foster children? Was it even worthwhile to investigate? But Daniel couldn't get rid of his suspicion of the policewoman ever since he had the encounter with the female waiting for Mia. Although he never saw her wearing the neon-pink runners again. *Oh Lord, help me with this one before something serious happens again.*

∾

Sunday morning, after breakfast, Daniel called the kids for a family conference. He needed to know what they were doing: schoolwork, lessons, any concerns he wanted to catch.

Mia and Julian looked at Daniel. "What's this about, Papa? Is something wrong?"

"No, not yet. I only want to find out what your life is like since I can't always be around."

Mia's eyes were big. "You trust us, right? We're all right."

"I know, Mia. But I'm curious about your singing lessons, piano lessons, schoolwork. The school year is almost over. How are you doing? Do you have any concerns?"

Mia smiled. "I'm doing well, I think. I worked hard. I'm just a bit anxious about a new singing teacher. My old one gave me the name of one she really likes. I have to see her next week."

Daniel filled his coffee cup. "You see, that is something I want to know about. I told you I can investigate for another one too. Singers teach and I know quite a lot. How about you, Julian?"

Julian wiggled around on his chair. "I think I'm okay in school. I don't like math but I'm trying. I'm still stuck with some of the theory we worked on." He shrugged. "I can't be good at everything, Papa."

Daniel had to hide a smile. "As a future pianist you have to. Do you still like the piano? I mean, really love it?"

Julian frowned. "Yeah, most of the time. I get mad at myself if I don't get stuff right away."

"What would you do if I took the piano away from you?"

"Oh nooo, Papa, please. I can't—I couldn't do anything else. I would lose my friend."

Now Daniel laughed. "Even if you hate the black keys?"

Julian shook his head. "I don't hate them, they just interfere sometimes."

Daniel finished his coffee. "So, no boyfriend or girlfriend trouble?"

"Nooo," came in unison. "Not yet," Mia added.

"Well, off you go then. Conference is done. Let's go out for supper tonight." He knew that would agree with both of them. *How do I deserve such good children? I thought it would be a lot harder to raise them without their mother. And I know they don't tell me everything.* Daniel sighed. He had to be happy the way it was.

Chapter 27

The next morning Daniel announced, "Mia, Julian, I'll drive you to school today."

"Yaiii," Julian yelled. "What's up?" Mia asked.

Daniel grabbed his case with the scores for today's rehearsal. "I'm going to talk to your principal."

Mia giggled. "Our Papa won't let up."

"No, he won't. I need more description of the woman who asked for you."

Mia nodded. "But I'm not sure what you'll find."

Neither do I. "Right, let's go."

∽∾∽

Daniel didn't get an answer when he knocked on the principal's door. *Maybe teaching?* He paced up and down the hallway and looked at the announcements on the walls. He had to smile. *Takes me back a bit.*

Finally, a well-dressed man walked towards him. "How can I help you? Nothing wrong with Mia, I hope?"

Daniel shook his hand. "No, she's fine. I have a question about the woman who claimed I needed Mia's help and to come with her."

The principal sat down behind his desk. "Please, sit down, Mr. Abogado. I knew something wasn't right. And it wasn't."

"Yes, you did the right thing and talked to Mia first. She knows the safety procedure."

The principal leaned back. "After the firebomb we're careful." He drummed his fingers on the desktop.

Is he nervous because of me? "Did you notice anything special about the woman? Face, eyes, really white teeth? I mean, super white."

The principal smiled. "As a matter of fact, yes. Some of our girls show that too. They do what the TV tells them. And this lady had them when she smiled at me."

Daniel had to be sure. "Is there anything else you can think of? Voice high, low, sweet, scratchy?"

The principal leaned back. "Actually sweet, wheedling I would call it. And really red lipstick. Over the top, I thought."

Daniel got up. "Thank you so much for your time. You've helped me a lot. I'll let you get back to your job. I have rehearsals to go to."

The principal beamed. "So glad to meet you in person, Maestro." He shook Daniel's hand. "Mia is a great student and a talented one."

Outside Daniel smiled. "Just as I thought," he mumbled. "But how to convince the inspector?" "Hearsay!" a judge would say. "Evidence!" the lawyer would ask. *I need her wig. But that's impossible. Sometime this police-woman had to make a mistake.*

Daniel drove to the theater. He had a job to do. Aside from his safety, this was the most important thing.

The theater was already humming with musicians practicing and talking. Daniel would warm up the rehearsal with a Rossini overture to "The Thieving Magpie." After that it would be a few hours of serious music: Liszt and Tchaikovsky. Just before starting Daniel's cellphone rang. He heard an officer's voice.

"The inspector has some news and wants you to come in," he said.

Daniel's heart gave an extra beat. "Very good, but it has to be after three if that's possible."

"I'll tell him," came the answer.

Daniel took a breath. Was it about the lawyer in jail? Rupert the bearded—or not—boss? Someone in the diamond exchange? *Calm down, music first.* He had to make sure he didn't expect too much. Just another baby step would help.

Daniel opened his score. *Let the music steady me.*

Until lunchtime he had covered most of Liszt's Hungarian Rhapsody. Some details could be worked out tomorrow. Tchaikovsky would keep Daniel from thinking too much about what the inspector had found out.

ⰮⰮ

On his way to the police station, Daniel couldn't help being excited. He kept telling himself not to expect a miracle.

The policewoman was back at her desk, smiling and chatting on the phone. Daniel looked at her. *A busy bee and very sure of herself this time.* She noticed him and motioned toward the hallway. Daniel knocked at the inspector's door and heard a "Come in."

Inspector Lankin again stood and looked out of the window.

"Hello, Inspector, taking a breather?" *Let's hear the news.*

Lankin turned around. "Looking out makes me concentrate. Sit, Daniel." He pulled his chair back and slumped into it. "I have two things to discuss. One—the lawyer, two—a suspicion."

Daniel didn't say anything. The inspector looked worried. Daniel thought it better to let him find his words. Lankin fingered a piece of paper then put it down again. "The injured lawyer decided to tell us a bit more. Since they almost killed him, he thought he might as well help us."

"Could he identify Mr. Blackbeard?" Daniel asked.

"Yes and no. He met him once without the beard. Mostly he dealt with the construction boss. We brought that one in again. Yes, he talked to the lawyer but swears that he had nothing to do with beating him up or ordering the inmate's death. This Rupert is probably the one ruling the roost."

Daniel felt a bit let down. "Does the lawyer know where Rupert lives or hangs out?"

The inspector shook his head. "Apparently nobody knows, he makes sure of that. As long as they get their money they don't care. Aside from monitoring the trucks at the construction sites or odd cars, we have to wait for him to make a mistake."

"Any luck at the diamond centers?" *Give me anything.*

"They didn't recognize anyone from the pictures. But..." he held up his hand. "We are after an SUV that travels regularly to the airport and picks something up. It's a rental with a different license plate every time. We are now trying to find the car rental or stopping the driver for some infraction on the road. It all takes time, Daniel."

Daniel sat back. "Well, we have something at least. What about your suspicions?"

The inspector looked towards the window again. "No proof yet, but you might be right that we have a spy in our midst."

Am I going to tell him about the white teeth? Daniel hesitated. He started slowly. "Have you noticed that your desk lady has super white teeth? I mean, really shiny?"

Lankin frowned. "So what?"

"Every time the blond lady comes up, at Alex's mother and at my daughter's school, that's what people remember about her. Also super red lipstick. All we have to do is find the blond wig." Daniel expected an indignant outburst but it didn't come.

Lankin fiddled with his pen. "You never liked her, didn't you? All I noticed is that she takes off at odd times and has an officer take over for her. I'll have to ask her directly." He stopped. Then went on, "She came in one day with a bloody lip and something of a red hand mark on her cheek like from being smacked in the face. She had some ordinary reason for it."

Daniel stared at the inspector. "There you have it. I'm pretty sure now." He got up. "I have taken enough of your time, Inspector. I'm sorry for my suspicions and for you having a mole in your office. I hope you'll find out, one way or another."

The inspector nodded. "We'll keep trying." He grabbed the phone and Daniel closed the door behind him.

On the way back to his car Daniel tried to make sense of what the Inspector had told him. He needed to walk somewhere quiet. A nearby park would do, away from people, cars, and noise. He walked for a while through paths edged with flowers and greenery to clear his mind. The many colors of the flowers reminded him of the colors of the instruments in the orchestra. Deep red: trumpets, white: flute, silver: piccolo, light blue: oboe, darker blue: clarinet, gold: French horn, various browns in the rest of the wind section, yellow: violins, orange: violas, chocolate brown: cellos, really dark: basses. He had to smile. Color, that's what makes the music. He sat down on a bench, thinking again about the inspector's reveal.

Daniel was aware of the fact that white teeth would not be enough to convict anyone. Being absent frequently from work made it more suspicious, although the reasons could be lunch, shopping, looking after someone or meeting someone to get orders. Her being slapped reminded Daniel again of Sonja. Was her husband or boyfriend connected with Rupert? If only one of the other jailbirds would talk. Couldn't they make them by giving them a deal, a lighter sentence? Daniel sighed. *Better get home now and work on the music for Seattle and London.*

On the ride home, Daniel weighed the fact whether he should talk to Mia and Julian about the new development. Why not? They had enough encounters with danger to merit information.

Both were sitting at the kitchen table talking. "Hey, Papa, you're later than usual," Mia said.

"Oh boy, am I now under curfew? I talked to the inspector and took a walk in the park."

Mia put her folder away. "Sorry, but we do get worried. Any news?"

Daniel went to the coffee machine. *I guess I should do the same as I expect from them: call.* "That's what I want to talk to you about." He filled his mug, stirred in some sugar, and sat down. He related the inspector's findings and his own suspicions.

Julian stared at Daniel. "You mean that police lady works with the bad bunch?"

"They cannot prove it yet. But I don't believe in coincidences. It fits too well. All we need are fingerprints or DNA to compare it with." An idea popped into Daniel's head. "What if the lawyer has met her before? He could be a witness."

Julian frowned. "You think he would rat on her?"

Daniel put down his coffee mug. "The lawyer has nothing to lose. He gets convicted anyway. It might even help him."

"If he doesn't get killed like the other one," Mia added.

Daniel got up and rinsed out his coffee mug. "I just wanted to tell you what we have so far. "

"Maybe we can come up with something," Julian said.

Daniel smiled. "Let me hear any brainwaves you might have." He looked at Mia. "Any ideas for supper?"

"Chinese food, if that's okay with you. I came home too late."

Daniel nodded. *Good girl.* "I'll do some work now."

જ⁊જ

In his studio, he took out scores for the Chamber Orchestra in Seattle—Bach, Mozart, and Elgar. These were shorter pieces for a smaller orchestra. However, as usual, Daniel wanted to look through them to remind himself of the details. For the symphony orchestra he needed more work, like Strauss' *Don Juan.*

Daniel scratched his head. It would be nice to talk about all this to someone other than the children. Lydia came back into his mind. She would probably be patient enough to listen to him going on about his music. *I wonder what she's doing. Never mind, back to work.*

જ⁊જ

By the time the Chinese food arrived Daniel had worked through most of the music for the Seattle Chamber Orchestra. He still needed to look at the ones for the two evening performances of the Symphony Orchestra.

Mia asked, "How can you keep them all in your mind and not mix them up, Papa?"

Daniel cracked open his fortune cookie. "I try to select contrasting composers so the pieces are different from each other. My mind just has to switch over."

Julian forked up some sweet and sour chicken. "Awesome. What does your cookie say?"

"It tells me 'open the door to let luck in.' Wouldn't that be wonderful?"

Mia took the dishes away. "Maybe we should believe in it, that might help."

Daniel sighed. "I believe it when the inspector tells me some news that he can take in front of the judge." He got up. "Can you manage?"

Mia gave him a smirky smile. "How about drying dishes?"

"Okay, Miss Mia." Daniel grabbed a towel.

"Yaiii!" Julian shouted and scuttled upstairs.

Mia looked at Daniel. "Did you ever help Mama with the dishes?"

"Yes, I did, many times until you were old enough not to break them."

Mia smiled. "Never mind, Papa, let them air dry. There're only a few. Not enough to put into the dishwasher."

Daniel made a mock bow. "Gracias, Senorita." He still chuckled when he finally settled down with the rest of the music scores.

Chapter 28

Before rehearsal the next morning the manager came up to Daniel. "The first performance is going to be recorded, Maestro. Record companies need new music."

This had to happen sometime. "All right, we better work extra hard." Daniel knew from experience that everyone would be a bit on edge with technicians, wires, and microphones around. But once they started the music would flow.

"You always work hard, Daniel." The manager smiled and walked off.

Just a minor item to think about. Good thing I'm not the sound engineer.

Once the musicians had settled down, Daniel called, "Good morning, Ladies and Gentlemen. We are making a recording of our first performance on Friday. So, keep yourselves and your instruments well-tuned. Maybe we'll become famous." He heard some sighs and groans. The concertmaster winked at Daniel. "I want a gold star."

"I'll put in for extra big ones." This wouldn't be the first time for recordings, but it always put tension into the air. Humor usually helped.

Daniel worked through various portions of Liszt and Tchaikovsky until he was satisfied. After lunch, he would take on the whole Fifth Symphony. That work began with a somber bass clarinet melody. Daniel called it a foreshadowing of the Sixth Symphony, the *Pathetique*. It was up to him to separate the two from each other. Tchaikovsky's heart always lay on the surface, he didn't hold back. Daniel felt like being on a rollercoaster every time he performed it. He needed to convey these emotions to the public, this time to the recording as well.

This created a longer than usual rehearsal. Finally, Daniel noticed the time. "Good work," he called. "Tomorrow all of it from the beginning."

I'll need a nap. Tchaikovsky, you take it out of me.

❧❧❧

At home with the kids safe inside Daniel left orders not to wake him up for phone calls. He stretched out on the couch and drifted off right away.

❧❧❧

When Daniel woke up he found Julian standing at the foot of the couch looking at him. Daniel yawned. "Okay, what's up?"

Julian smirked. "You were snoring, Papa."

Daniel swung his legs off the couch. "No way. I never snore."

"Yes, you do, quietly. The police called, they want you to phone back."

Daniel got up. "That's what I want to hear." His throat tightened. *Something important? Maybe some success?* He sat down again and dialed the station. The officer told him to come by and talk to the inspector.

"I'll be there in twenty minutes." Daniel grabbed his jacket. "Hold the fort, kids. This could be important." *It has to be or he wouldn't have called me.*

Inspector Lankin was talking to the officer at the front desk when Daniel arrived. "You must have broken the speed limit all the way here," Lankin said. "Come in." He slumped down in his chair and stared at Daniel as if searching for something. Then he looked away. "I might hire you someday, Daniel. This is difficult to admit, but you were right. We had a mole and we caught her."

Daniel sat up. "Her? The front desk lady? Oh, my Lord, really? How…"

The inspector raised his hand. "Hold your breath. I'll tell you if you don't interrupt me." He paused. With a quick look towards the window, he continued. "A plain-clothed officer followed her when she left again in the middle of the day. She went to a diner close by, greeted the waiter, and went to the lady's room. The officer waited. She never came out again. Instead, a blond woman appeared and bought some coffee. She also carried a large tote. The officer identified himself and asked her if she could answer some questions concerning a case. She got flustered, the usual 'I know my rights, I don't have to answer any questions,' and so forth. The officer gave her the choice to come to the station. He also noticed a strand of black hair not quite covered by the wig. The rest is history."

Daniel didn't know what to say. This was incredible. His intuitions had been right. It fitted right in with the strange sighting at the park with the two men and her long telephone conversations during her work time. "Don't we have to identify her as the blond woman by the principal?" he finally asked.

The inspector nodded. "We did and he picked her out of three other suspects."

"Did she take off her wig?" Daniel couldn't imagine her doing that willingly.

"She had to here at the station. So far she hasn't said much. We'll let her get over the shock first." Lankin shook his head. "She was a police officer. Where was her pride in protecting the innocent and fighting crime?"

"Money, Inspector, maybe even a boyfriend like Mr. Blackbeard. She isn't going to give him up."

Lankin flipped his pen through his fingers. "There is one way. If she met someone at the diner more than once, the waiter might identify him or her. We're only starting to dig."

Daniel rubbed his forehead. "If they find out that she's in custody they'll try to kill her before she talks or get her out somehow."

"Not going to happen." Lankin looked at some pictures before him. "We took those from her iPhone. Someone is there with her. Just can't see his face." He pushed the photo over to Daniel. He looked at it.

"That's...the fatheaded guy in the car who almost killed me in Portland." *I can't believe this.*

The inspector leaned forward. "Are you sure, Daniel?"

Daniel tipped his finger on the man's head in the picture. "That's all I could see of him when the car sped away."

The inspector got up. "Right. Our lady has to identify him. We'll see to it. Thank you, Daniel."

On his way out the door, Daniel turned around once more and said, "Wow!" That's all he could think of.

✎✎✎

Steering his car through the evening traffic Daniel's mind flipped between elation and doubt. Yes, they connected the policewoman with the blond fraud. But, like the others in jail, she wasn't going to give up the boss or even the ones next to him. That would be a death sentence for her. There should be a way to protect her if she decided to talk. Again, that would be up to the inspector.

Daniel heard Julian practicing the piano when he arrived home. Mia looked at him with big eyes. Daniel raised his hand. "Let Julian finish first, then I'll tell you."

"I can't wait that long," Mia wailed.

"Okay, all I'm going to say is that they caught the blond woman." Daniel heard a wrong chord from upstairs. Julian called, "Is Papa home?"

"Come on down," Mia answered.

Julian scurried down the stairs. "What happened?"

Daniel grabbed a chair. "Sit down and I'll tell you." He related the story between interruptions of "Oh no," and "How could she?"

"Is she the same woman who stalked me at the rehearsals?" Mia asked.

Daniel shrugged. "Probably. Maybe they can find the pink shoes. They're still interrogating her. We'll have to wait for it."

"Waiting again!" came two voices at once.

Daniel felt for them. "Don't forget, this is a major step forward. Be thankful for that."

Julian frowned. "What if she doesn't talk?"

"We have enough evidence to keep her in jail for a long time," Daniel assured him. "She might not want to take all the blame herself and decide to give us information."

For the rest of the evening, Daniel decided to put his mind back into the music for Seattle and maybe even for London.

഑ഽ഑ഽ

When Daniel arrived at the theater the next morning he heard a lot of talking among the musicians. They seem to be upset. The concertmaster came up to him. "Some bad news, Maestro."

"What's going on, John?" *Another disaster?*

"Our first French horn player got attacked yesterday evening and beaten badly. He's in hospital in a coma."

Daniel felt ice cubes attacking his stomach. *Not one of my musicians?* But he dismissed it. "Any idea who and why?"

John shook his head. "They're investigating, of course."

"Was it a mugging? Did they rob him?" *Let it be anything other than a connection with my personal enemies.*

"Yeah, his wallet was gone, but why beat him like that?" John shook his head in disgust.

Daniel put his hand on his shoulder. "We have work to do. Let's calm down."

The musicians finally settled down when Daniel stood at the podium. "Before we start let's give some thought to Donald in the hospital. We're all upset about this, it's a truly horrible situation. Let's hope for a good outcome and with that in mind work on our program. Remember tomorrow's recording session." He felt it sounded a bit cold but until he knew more details, he had to keep the performances in mind.

After a shaky start of the rehearsal, the orchestra concentrated in earnest. The first two pieces didn't need any corrections. Daniel spent more time again on the fifth symphony. With so many shifting details in emotions and rhythms, some could get lost in the excitement of the recording session.

During lunchtime Daniel called the hospital. The musician was alive but still unconscious. Daniel scolded himself. This had to be an unrelated mugging, not a planned attack. Donald couldn't be connected with the diamond mob. It was unthinkable. But why did a plain robbery result in such a severe beating? Were more people involved?

Daniel called the police station. "Do you have any information on the attack on one of my musicians?"

The officer hesitated. "We can't really discuss it, Mr. Abogado. We don't have any witnesses. Hopefully, the victim will regain consciousness and can identify the attacker."

Daniel understood. *I better concentrate on the performances and hope that Donald wakes up. There has to be an explanation.*

∽∾∽

For the rest of the day, Daniel tried to occupy his mind with answering emails and calls to his agent. She was in charge of the flights and accommodations for Seattle and London. But the idea that his first French horn player could be connected to the attacks and harassments of Daniel and his children wouldn't leave him. Donald was a steady first-class musician who never missed rehearsals or performances. Of course, he knew all about Daniel's whereabouts and concerts in other cities. What could be the reason for this betrayal? If it was money what part was Donald playing?

Later that evening Daniel's phone rang. The hospital informed him that the patient had regained consciousness. "May I see him?" Daniel asked.

"Only for a few minutes," came the answer.

Daniel didn't waste time. Within twenty minutes he stood by the musician's bedside. *Again all those tubes to keep a person alive.* Donald's head was bandaged, and his left arm secured in a sling.

"Some ribs are broken too," the nurse mentioned.

Daniel looked at the bruised face of the musician. He opened his eyes and tried a smile. "Maestro, why are you here?"

Daniel bent closer. "When one of my best musicians gets beaten this badly, why shouldn't I be here? I want to know who did this."

Donald closed his eyes. "Don't know. They kept saying 'You didn't do your job'. I don't know what job."

The nurse came back. "He needs rest now."

Daniel nodded. More questions would have to wait. He hoped that Donald would be able to identify his attackers. That wouldn't be easy in the dark with their dark clothes.

On his way back to the car Daniel's cell phone beeped. Inspector Lankin sounded tired. "Come tomorrow, I have news."

"I'll be there. I just visited my musician. He's in bad shape."

"He'll have more surprises coming." The inspector hung up.

"I have enough surprises for one day," Daniel grumbled. "I need a brandy."

Chapter 29

The next morning Daniel told Mia and Julian what had happened the evening before. He put it into the shortest version he could think of. For more details, he wanted to meet the inspector. As Daniel expected, they were shocked.

"I'll bet this was a case of mistaken identity," Mia said.

"Could be." Daniel had wondered about that himself. But so far these men had not made that kind of mistake. He drank the last of his coffee. "I'm off to the inspector. I hope his surprise brings us finally closer to the end of our ordeal. I'll let you know as soon as possible."

On his way to the station, Daniel tried again to temper his hopes. He had experienced too many let-downs.

The police station sounded busy with officers talking to each other. Daniel saw Inspector Lankin listening intently to a plain-clothed man. Daniel waited to not interrupt his concentration.

When the inspector noticed Daniel he waved him over. "You might as well listen to what Officer Hamilton has found out."

Daniel's heart pounded. This sounded like important information.

The officer looked at him. "Your musician who was attacked was the boyfriend of our policewoman. She fell to pieces when she heard that he was in a coma."

Daniel wiped his hand over his face. "Good Lord, I had hoped that he didn't have any connection with that gang."

"He might not have, Daniel. Ms. Clarence told us that she didn't tell him about her secret other life. He only knew her as a police officer." He paused. Then he continued. "It can be that she wants to protect him. But she swore that he didn't know. She was so upset about her boyfriend being punished for something he had no idea about, she is looking for revenge."

"Lucky for us," the inspector grumbled.

Daniel tried to stay calm. He wanted to believe that his musician had been an unlucky bystander. "They probably expected Donald to give his girlfriend information about my whereabouts. I'm sure he talked to her about it. It was part of his daily job."

"But it wasn't enough," Inspector Lankin said. "She failed a few times and now she got arrested. Enough reason to get to her lover to punish her."

The officer smiled. "Yeah, but they didn't figure that she's now so angry that she's going to talk."

Daniel stared at him. "You mean she's giving up names and locations along with the business?"

Lankin shrugged. "We'll have to find out how much she actually knows. She must have met Rupert Blackbeard and some others, also the one she was supposed to meet at the café."

The officer nodded. "That's what we have to find out now." He got up. "Back to the job. Good to have met you, Maestro." He shook Daniel's hand, waved at the inspector, and left.

Daniel took a deep breath. *How did I know that Ms. Clarence was dishonest to the point of almost having me killed?*

The inspector seemed to have the same thought. "I would have never believed that there was a rat in my police station." He looked at Daniel. "I wonder what ticked you off."

"A few small things. But it taught me to listen to my instincts." He got up. "At lot to digest. Thank you, Inspector. Maybe I have some peace and quiet now?"

"Don't relax too soon. Keep your kids safe until we have the leaders under lock and key." He grabbed the phone. Daniel nodded to him and closed the door behind him.

He walked slowly to his car. His head was humming, partly with relief and partly with one question: why was this woman so intent on hurting him and his children for something as simple as reporting a bad driver? This small act must have endangered their lucrative diamond business to the point that plain harassment wasn't enough. Because Daniel hadn't stopped. But now it looked like all of it was coming to an end. He turned on the motor. *Home to some quiet and lunch. And a lot of thought about the performance tonight.*

ॐ

That evening Daniel arrived early at the theater. He needed the hour before concerts to concentrate and make sure the orchestra didn't have problems he might have to deal with. Maybe the sound engineers would have questions. This group was accustomed with the acoustics of the hall from the last time of recording. Daniel liked to watch them work.

After he changed into his performance suit Daniel thought again about his horn player recovering in hospital. He had felt a big rock falling from his shoulders when he heard that Donald had not been involved with the diamond smugglers. He was truly sorry for the injuries. On the other side of it, this had brought about the possibility of catching the whole gang through the policewoman's anger over it. *What kind of a mindset does she have being in law enforcement and being part of a gang of people she would normally arrest?*

As Daniel walked down the hallway, he saw some of the musicians ambling in. Other horn players came up to him and inquired about Donald's state.

"He's recovering and the police are investigating," Daniel told them. Nothing else was important, certainly not Donald's private life. To deal with a betrayal of your girlfriend like that was almost as traumatic as losing someone through sickness, he thought.

By seven o'clock he cornered one of the technicians. "Will you be done soon? The audience usually arrives between seven and close to eight."

"Almost ready, Maestro," the man answered. "We want it to sound good." Fifteen minutes later the crew packed up. They left two sound engineers behind to be on hand if there was a problem. Most of the musicians had already run through passages of the program. This created the noise most of the audience either hated or felt that it was part of the experience. As a boy, Daniel used to pick out snippets of what he would hear later.

When the lights dimmed, coughing and rustling in the audience quietened, and the oboe sounded. *Right, let the music begin.*

Daniel had told the musicians that this concert was important for the recording and for Donald as well. He could feel their tight concentration.

After the lively overture Liszt's Hungarian Rhapsody impressed the audience, the applause seemed to last longer than usual.

During intermission, Daniel called the hospital. A nurse told him that Donald was walking around but would have to stay a few more days. At least he's not losing his career,

Daniel thought. He walked around for a few minutes. Tchaikovsky was vastly different from Liszt. He needed to switch his mind over to the Russian mood.

The audience must have had the same thoughts. A hush fell over them as soon as the lights dimmed again. With the mournful sound of the bass clarinet, the Russian journey began.

As usual, by the last chord, Daniel felt drained. He mopped the perspiration off his face before he bowed to the audience. The applause was strong and lasted a long time. The performance had been excellent. Daniel hoped that the recording would be too. The musicians beamed and some were ready for the pub. Although tired, Daniel wanted to spend an hour with them. His nightly brandy would fit just right. As he listened to the chatter and laughter he again knew this job would be the only one he would ever be happy to do.

Later, on his way home, Daniel realized that this had been one of the best days in a long time. Ms. Clarence was probably talking now, Donald was recovering, and the performance had been a success. No phone calls from the kids, they would be asleep.

At home, he found a note from Mia on the kitchen table. "Julian stubbed his toe, not broken, just swollen. I put ice on it." Daniel sighed. Only a stubbed toe, painful but not fatal. Well, almost a perfect day.

Chapter 30

When Mia knocked on Daniel's door the next morning to wake him, he felt that he had slept through the night for the first time in a long while. He would have loved to continue but he had to keep up the ritual of pancakes. *Fatherly duties.*

Julian still hobbled around with a frown on his face. Daniel looked at the toe. "You'll live, Buddy, keep it wrapped up. Don't walk too much."

"But I want to play over at Jason's," Julian complained.

"Play sitting down," Daniel suggested, "until it doesn't hurt anymore."

Julian still grumbled but dug into his pancake nevertheless.

Daniel smiled. "You know what I mean, right? Sit down and play? At your piano."

"Not fair, Papa, it's Saturday." Julian helped himself to another spoonful of whipping cream.

Mia came up to Daniel. "Papa, I would like to go to a PJ party tonight. Can I?" She looked at him hopefully.

"Where is it? At Evelyn's house?"

Mia nodded.

"What about Julian? I'm at the theater." *I could take him with me.*

"Can Mrs. Gantrey come over?" Another big-eyed plea.

Mia needs her friends. She's been such a trooper. "Okay, call her."

"Thanks, Papa." Mia scooted to the telephone. She beamed after a short conversation. "She's fine with coming over."

Now that's that sorted out I can think about my own business. The trip to Seattle and from there to London was only a few days away. Both kids had to remember to pack for three weeks away from home. Tomorrow would be a good day to remind them of packing. Daniel needed one small suitcase alone for his many scores. He preferred his own with the details marked in, although the libraries would have all of them.

Thinking of libraries Lydia popped back into his mind. Would she come to Seattle? It would be nice to see her again. In the meantime, he had to finish tonight's concert, the last of the season. That would mean afterward mingling with the audience. Another ritual with a glass of wine in one hand and the other one ready to shake the hand of the admiring music lovers. Daniel didn't mind as long as he would have time to wish the musicians a good summer. Many would teach or play with small groups until August.

∽∾∽

Without wires and microphones hanging around the musicians looked more relaxed. Before starting the performance Daniel cornered the concertmaster. "John, in case I shouldn't see you afterward, I want to thank you for your good work. I hope you stay with us for another season." They shook hands.

John smiled. "I have my feelers out, Daniel, but for now I'll be back, and…you're the best."

Daniel clapped him on the shoulder. "Let's get going or the audience will get restless."

☙☜☙

The performance went well, maybe not as tight as the night before. Everybody already felt the holidays coming up. Daniel didn't mind since the audience showed their appreciation again with lengthy applause. *Let me have a breather before I face the masses.*

When his cell phone rang he knew that it was a text. It read "Sorry to send you this but Maestro Emmet passed away this morning. I felt you needed to know. Lydia."

Daniel stood still. His thoughts were a mixture of sadness and gratefulness. He had been with Charles, conducted for him, had seen him happy. Now he was gone, and all Daniel could do was contact Mrs. Emmet and send flowers. He would probably be in Seattle during the funeral. He saw the one bright spot because Lydia had written him. *Never any light without shadow.* Daniel would answer her later. He heard chatter and laughter from the lobby. *Life goes on. Time to go and show myself and smile.*

Applause erupted when Daniel appeared. Someone handed him a glass of red wine. He smiled, shook hands, answered some questions, and felt grateful. *I'm alive, can work, have my family, my music. And I can go home—alive.*

☙☜☙

Mrs. Gantrey sat in front of the TV when Daniel arrived. She smiled. "Did everything go to your satisfaction? You look pleased."

"You should be asleep, Mrs. Gantrey. It's past your bedtime," Daniel said.

She chuckled. "At my age you have the freedom to sleep whenever. I'll go home now. Julian is fast asleep. He told me all about the trip you're taking."

"Yes, it's going to be three weeks. If it's possible, could you keep an eye on the house? I'll tell the police too."

Mrs. Gantrey put on her coat. "Glad to do it, Daniel. Good night now." With a wave she closed the door.

Daniel sat down and looked at the picture of Elvira. "I'm not sure if you're listening, love. But it's just good to talk to you. We had great concerts, important ones are coming up plus a bit of a holiday with the kids. But the death of Charles Emmet really shook me. Maybe I should have expected it, he was really sick." Daniel got up. "You were always a patient listener, love." He gazed at her smiling face. *Now to earthly things.* He grabbed his phone and texted a few lines to Lydia. He needed to be logical and not expect her to come to Seattle. He was hoping to see her again, although he couldn't quite figure out why Lydia was important to him. She was just—nice? Not the correct word but that was all he could think of. *I want to sleep and not think for a while.*

⁊

Daniel took his time waking up the next morning. When he heard Mia and Julian talking, he scrambled out of bed. He would have to tell Julian about Charles' death, then onto packing for the trip. And what about the inspector? Did he get any nearer to the head of the diamond business and closer to the end of Daniel's problems? *I need coffee and eggs.*

Mia stood by the stove when Daniel came downstairs. "How was your party?" he asked. "I'm surprised you're already back."

"Oh, it was fun. We had breakfast early so I came home. What eggs do you want, Papa?"

"Scrambled with bacon would be perfect." Daniel filled a mug with coffee.

Julian scudded down the stairs. "My toe feels better."

I might as well tell him. "I have some bad news for you, Julian. Mr. Emmet died yesterday."

Julian's eyes got big, then he looked down. "So the hospital couldn't help him? Just like Mama." He slid onto the chair. "Then the kids don't have a dad anymore."

Daniel sipped his coffee. "I know this is sad. We'll send them an e-mail and flowers. You got to know Mr. Emmet. That's a good memory, isn't it?"

Julian nodded. "They can talk to their dad like I do to Mama before I go to sleep. Can I have eggs too, Mia?"

Daniel was relieved that his son hadn't lost his appetite. "Now listen," he continued. "We're leaving in two days. Pack your stuff for three weeks. It's summer so no coats, only sweaters."

"And an umbrella," Mia added. "London, you know."

Daniel laughed. He didn't have to worry too much about their baggage, he could put his own suitcases together.

The rest of the Sunday filled up with e-mails and a phone call to Mrs. Emmet. She sounded calm. Daniel knew the real grief would start after the last preparations were done. A call to his agent confirmed that he would not have to expect any changes in London. That left one thing Daniel needed to do tomorrow—talk to the inspector. He wanted to know any bits of news before leaving. Could he feel safe in Seattle or in London or would they try once more to show their power?

∽∾∽

All Daniel could think of the next morning was about any news from Inspector Lankin. He needed to feel secure during his travels. He also needed all of his brain functions in London to make a good first impression. Unfortunately, the children would be on their own most of the time. That would worry him at the best of times. Even with a smart girl like Mia safety was not guaranteed. She had experienced it twice now.

So it was with hope in his heart that Daniel entered the police station. The quietness surprised him. *What? No action, no panic?* A young officer had replaced the woman at the desk. "Can I help you, Sir?"

Daniel smiled. "By now everyone should know me, invading this place much too often. Is the boss available? It's Daniel Abogado."

"Oh, my apologies. I didn't meet you before." The officer looked a bit flustered. "I think the inspector is free right now. Go right in."

Inspector Lankin was talking on the phone when Daniel knocked on the half-open door. He waved him in. After a few "Hm, okay, got you, let me know" he hung up. "So, you're ready to go on another trip," he said and grabbed a folder.

Daniel had a hard time sitting still. "Any news from our ex-police lady?"

"Oh, yes. Hang on, I'll tell you." The inspector took a breath. "Although she's not involved in the actual smuggling business, she was the informer for the boss. Easy, because she would hear what was going on at this station. You were correct on that one. But…" he took another breath. "She gave us a lot of names including Rupert, the Blackbeard. Of course, no address, the big secret about him. She also knew when meetings were going on in New York about diamond negotiations. We alerted the NPD there and they nabbed two men doing business, one of them the boss of the construction company. You don't need to know the details."

Now Daniel let out a breath he had been holding in. "That's a lot. And she told you all this just like that?"

Inspector Lankin leaned back. "Not without a deal, of course. She will claim to have been coerced under duress, threatened, and so on. Of course, she can't deny trying to kidnap your daughter, again done under threat."

"Oh, my Lord, I'm just afraid that Rupert is going berserk, now that he's lost so many workers. Is he going to lash out at me or the kids again?" *He still has his spies.*

Lankin shook his head. "That would expose him. He knows we're onto him. He might take his money and run. We would like to prevent that. Besides, he doesn't have an informer anymore to know where you are."

"So, what's your next step, Inspector?"

"Rounding up as many of his soldiers we can find. I think you can safely travel. Our friend Willows in Seattle is informed too, remember him? He's more than willing to look after you."

Daniel had to smile. "Mr. Willows, the good guy, always guarding me. Looking forward to meeting him again." He got up. "You have made great progress, Inspector. Thank you. Maybe I can concentrate on music now." He reached over and shook Lankin's hand.

"I'll let you know of further developments, Daniel. Have a good trip."

On the way back to his car Daniel felt like skipping. It certainly looked like the whole gang would break up now. All that was missing was Rupert. *He will be found, he wouldn't leave his money behind. There could be a trail.*

The children were home when he arrived. School was done. "We'll celebrate tonight," Daniel announced. "The police caught a lot of the smugglers. The policewoman gave them away."

Julian jumped up and down. "Yaiiii! Let them rot in jail."

Daniel's jaw dropped. "Where did you get that from?"

"His favorite detective show, Papa," Mia answered.

Daniel couldn't help smiling. "Just refine your language a bit, Buddy."

Julian looked down. "But it's so great, Papa. Are we going out eating?"

"Only if you talk politely, no bad words. Did you get your packing done?"

Julian hurried up the stairs. "I'll check again."

Mia looked at Daniel. "Is this for real, Papa? No more worries?"

Daniel poured himself some tea and stirred honey into it. "As long as Rupert is around he'll have his spies still working for him. I don't feel one hundred percent safe but without proper leadership, the group will break up. We should never let our guards down, though."

Mia nodded. "But it will be more fun now."

"I'm a bit concerned about what you two are going to do when I'm working. Running around Seattle or London is not a good idea." It *does worry me.*

Mia smiled. "I already have plans like city tours or the zoo or something else."

"I need to be informed of all that, understand? You're still kids."

Mia smirked. "Maybe Julian, not me. Let's plan dinner, okay?"

Daniel sighed. "Right, Ms. Grownup." *Lord, you blessed me with good children.*

Chapter 31

The first thing Daniel saw at arrival at Seattle airport was Andy Willows waving at them. "Who's that, Papa?" Julian asked.

"A good friend of mine. Let's go and meet him." Daniel knew that he would show up. Forever the bodyguard.

"What a great bunch of kids you've got, Daniel," Willows said and shook their hands.

Daniel winked at him. "Two more for you to look after."

Andy laughed. "Only if they want me to. But, yes, if I'm needed I'll do it."

On the ride to the hotel, Julian chatted away about his piano and the trip to London. Mia quietly looked out of the window. Daniel turned around. "Are you okay, Mia? You're so quiet."

"I'm fine, just thinking," Mia answered.

"Oh, dear," Willows said. "Boyfriends?"

Daniel chuckled. "Wrong question, Andy."

Mia gave him a stern look. "There're more important things than boyfriends."

Andy waved. "My apologies. Maybe later?"

Mia shook her head. "Much later."

Willows dropped them off at the hotel. "I'm looking forward to the concerts, Daniel, both of them. See you then."

Inside the hotel, Daniel looked at Mia again. "Is there something wrong? Andy is a bit of a joker but a great guy."

"I know, Papa. But it would be so great if Mama was here traveling with us."

Daniel stopped. *So that's what's bothering her.* "Yes, honey, I know you miss her right now to talk to. We just have to pretend she's with us, maybe even looking after us." He put his arm around her shoulder and gave it a squeeze. "Let's go up."

Mia's mood brightened when she saw that she had her own bedroom.

"Ladies first," Daniel said. "Why don't we go for breakfast? Then I have to be off for rehearsal. You want to stay here?"

"I think so," Julian said. "I'll hang out here."

Mia nodded. "Yes, I'll sort some clothes."

⌘⌘⌘

After breakfast, Daniel grabbed the scores for the Chamber Orchestra music. It would be a tight run. Since he needed to conduct two performances with the Symphony Orchestra as well he had to squeeze in two more rehearsals with them. In his mind at least two rehearsals were essential for a good performance. That's why he decided to start with the first one already this morning.

During a brisk walk to the theater, Daniel tried to direct his mind towards Bach, Mozart, and Elgar. Some musicians had already arrived and greeted Daniel.

"Great to see you again, Maestro. It's been a while."

Since Daniel worked with them only three times a year he had to admit, it was good to see them too. Then he heard a familiar voice.

"Good morning, Maestro. I'm glad you made it safely." Sonja smiled at him. "How was your flight?"

"Just normal and in the company of my children," Daniel answered.

"Where are they?" Sonja asked.

"At the hotel, safe and sound."

"Are they coming to the performances?" Sonja pushed a strand of hair behind her ear.

Daniel tried to smile. "Only if I can tempt them." He turned to the other musicians. "See you on stage ready to go." He needed to walk away.

Why does she annoy me so much? he thought. He couldn't help it, he felt her questions and prodding intrusive. He sighed. What was she expecting from him? Extra attention? Why? He shook his head. *I'm not interested in her, period. Back to my job. I'll make them work.*

❧❧❧

First rehearsals after three months were usually interrupted with corrections. At lunchtime Daniel still needed to go through Mozart's dances. He called Mia. To his surprise, she answered right away.

"I knew you would phone, Papa. We're fine here. We went to the shop downstairs and now we're watching a show."

Daniel breathed a sigh of relief. He still hated to leave his kids alone. He could only hope that they didn't forget the safety rules. "I'll be back around three. We can do something then."

During lunch, Daniel was discussing Mozart with the concertmaster when Sonja appeared with a cup of coffee in her hand.

"Can I ask a question, Maestro?"

Not again. "About what, Sonja?"

"Do you know the story connected to Elgar's Romance?"

Daniel thought for a moment. *I have no time for this.* "Yes, I do, but we're behind time already and have to get back to work. You can find it all on the internet."

Sonja smiled. "It just sounds better when someone tells the story."

Daniel got up. "Time's up. Grab your viola, Sonja."

With a laugh, she put down her coffee cup and walked out.

Doesn't she get the message? Daniel wondered. What am I going to do to get her out of my hair short of being impolite? He liked her musicianship and talent but nothing more. *I should be flattered by all that attention but she's the wrong person for it.*

☙☙☙

In the afternoon Daniel took Mia and Julian for a walk around downtown. Shops and markets were busy. Mia had a great time looking through boutiques and sighing over elegant dresses. Julian would have rather stayed with toys and video games. After a while, Daniel suggested, "Let's find a café for a treat. I need some coffee."

On the way there he suddenly stopped and spread out his arms to hold back the kids. "Stop and look. Don't point just look. What do you see there by the black door?"

Both children said, "A man with a black beard."

"He's fighting with someone," Mia added. "He's push-ing him."

Daniel tried to get as many details as he could. *Black-beard Rupert? Here?* "This could be his hide-out—if it is really Rupert. Many men have beards."

The man finally walked to a dark-blue car and got in.

"Can you read the license plates?" Daniel saw the num-bers but not the letters.

Julian craned his neck. "I think it's M and P."

Daniel pulled out his cellphone. "I'll call Willows. He's a policeman and can check that for us."

Mia had a worried look. "Good thing he didn't see us, Papa."

"I think he's hiding right now, not looking," Daniel said.

Andy Willows promised to check for the owner of the blue car. "We can also find out if he has a rap sheet."

"Thank you. How lucky could that be." Daniel rubbed his forehead. "Rupert might not be his real name and his beard is rather long."

Willows chuckled. "If he's on the run he has no time for a trim. Hang in there." He clicked off the phone.

Daniel grabbed Mia's and Julian's hands. "Let's go for supper instead of to the café. It's late enough now."

When Daniel entered the restaurant, he saw a few people waiting to be seated. He turned to Mia. "You want to wait a few minutes?"

She looked around. "Sure."

Someone called. "Maestro, come sit with us."

Everyone looked up. "That did it, Papa," Julian whispered. "You're famous."

Two of Daniel's musicians waved at him. He walked over and also noticed two ladies with them. "I don't want to disturb your supper."

But they insisted. "Our wives are thrilled to meet you—finally."

The waitress grabbed another table and pushed it closer.

"Don't forget the other waiting people," Daniel cautioned. *We're not the only ones here.*

"I'll take care of that," the waitress promised.

Between eating and talking the evening went ahead pleasantly. Even Mia and Julian seemed to enjoy themselves with all the adult talk around them. When Daniel's phone rang he looked at the time. *A bit late for that.*

Andy Willow's voice surprised him. "Come by tomorrow, Daniel, tonight is too late."

Daniel's heart skipped a beat. "Give me a hint, please."

"Rupert is quite a piece of work," Willows continued. "That was his car you saw. His real name is Brent Avery. See you tomorrow."

Daniel took a deep breath. *Coincidence? Never. We had to be at that place at that time to see him.* He went back to the table. "We'll say good night. Work tomorrow morning." The musicians nodded. "See you then."

On their way home Daniel related to Mia and Julian what Willows had told him. Mia got thoughtful. "Do you think Mama sent us there to see Rupert?"

"I don't know, Mia, but if you believe that it's just great. We're not smart enough to be sure of it."

"I'll bet it was Mama," Julian said. "She's always there."

Daniel smiled. In his heart, he believed it too.

Chapter 32

Since rehearsals started at ten o'clock the next morning, Daniel had to postpone his visit to Willows until later. He had to admit he could hardly wait to listen to his news.

Daniel was happy with the musicians' work, the performance that night would be good. But he couldn't quite avoid a visit from Sonja who had a question about an entrance of the violas. Daniel had to smile. She hadn't made any mistakes, so why the question? He decided to be nice and praised her concern. That created a big smile on Sonja's face. *As long as she isn't following me around, I'll bear with it.*

On his way to Andy Willows Daniel hoped with all his heart that Rupert—Brent—would be caught before he could disappear again to another of his hide-outs.

Willows was waiting for Daniel in his office at the police station.

"So, that's where you're working." Daniel sat down. "Nice office. How much can you tell me?"

Andy looked through a stack of papers. "Although we didn't catch the Blackbeard—yet, we nabbed the guy he was fighting with. He had to admit that he knew Brent Avery, called Rupert, and that he himself was part of the smugglers. The fight started apparently over a money transfer he didn't do properly. So, if he does it now, Rupert will pick it up where we can trace it and get him."

"If he didn't already skip town," Daniel interrupted. He slid forward. "You mean, this man will actually give up Rupert? Everybody else was too scared to do it, except the policewoman."

Willows smiled. "We convinced him that once the boss is caught, he will be done for and can't hurt anyone anymore."

Daniel felt a glow of hope going through his body. "That would be amazing, Andy."

Willows had a satisfied look on his face. "I informed Inspector Lankin of it. He's trying to get more of his prisoners to talk by telling them that Rupert will be caught."

"Do you think he might go back to San Francisco to rally his troops? He's never in one place for too long." Then Daniel remembered. "What about Portland? We were there when he tried to get to Julian."

"Daniel, calm down. We have all angles covered, both cities, if need be."

Daniel tried to think clearly. "He's just so slippery. He probably changed cars too."

Andy smiled. "You would make a good detective."

Daniel sighed. "That's what Inspector Lankin said. Okay, please, let me know, day or night. I'm glad to have you on my side." They shook hands.

"See you at your podium, Maestro." Daniel heard him call when he closed the door.

When Daniel told Mia and Julian of Willow's discoveries Julian hopped from one foot to the other. "They'll get him for sure."

Mia beamed. "The sooner the better."

"Don't forget," Daniel warned. "He's still at large. Keep your safety rules. Are you going with me tonight?"

"I would like to come to the symphony concert instead," Mia said.

"I'll come," Julian decided.

For his peace of mind, Daniel knew that he needed to keep Julian close and safe, yet not in the audience. "All right, get ready. Eat supper and we'll go."

∽∾∽

At the theater, Daniel told Julian to sit in the left-wing of the stage. "You might not be safe by yourself between all the people."

"But the sound will be so loud," Julian complained.

"That's how the musicians hear it," Daniel explained. "That's why I'm here to keep them together."

"Okay, Papa, never thought of that."

Andy Willows appeared around the corner. "Need a babysitter, Daniel?"

Daniel shook his head. "I don't believe it. You're here for the music, not to take care of my kid."

"He can sit with us, no problem." Andy winked. "I'm still looking after you. Then I can bring him back to the hotel later."

"Shouldn't you chase after Rupert?" Daniel joked.

"Tomorrow. Make music, Maestro."

"Okay, take him along. Thank you." *At least that's one person I can trust.*

∽∾∽

The performance was well received and Daniel was happy. At his dressing room, Willows and Julian were waiting. Andy put two thumbs up.

"Wonderful. We enjoyed every note. I take Julian home if that's okay."

Daniel laughed. "What are you charging per hour? But fine, thanks again."

With a wave, Willows took Julian's hand and joined his wife who was waiting for them.

Who would've known at the first time I met Andy Willows at the hotel's pool that I would find a friend for life, Daniel thought. Now going for the traditional drink. Would I also have a close encounter with Sonja again? But amid so many other musicians he would be far enough from her. As it turned out, he saw her leave early.

Back at the hotel, Daniel needed to sit down and go over the day's events. If seeing Rupert on the street could lead to his arrest that would be the greatest blessing. Knowing the ways of this man Daniel wasn't sure when that would be. But between Willows and Inspector Lankin, it might be achieved. In the meantime, Daniel had to get his mind around the first rehearsal with the symphony orchestra in the morning: Wagner, Schubert, and Richard Strauss.

The next morning Daniel asked Mia and Julian, "What are you going to do today?"

"We'll take a city tour by bus if that's okay with you. Just until noon. And we have lunch included." Mia was ready to go.

"You will be careful, won't you?" Daniel needed to remind them. "Always remember to look around. We're not totally safe yet."

Both children nodded. "I think it's mainly couples who go," Mia said.

"Okay, I'll call you after my rehearsal. Have fun." *They might as well go. They're already so independent. I think I can trust them.*

❧❧❧

Since Daniel had to direct the whole symphony orchestra of eighty plus musicians who didn't know him, he needed all his concentration on the music. Some of the musicians from the Chamber Orchestra were also part of it. Most smaller ensembles worked that way. The manager caught Daniel on his way to the stage.

"We're so happy you could fit us in with this concert," he said. "You must be overwhelmed with work."

"It's a tight schedule," Daniel admitted. "But I'll make them work hard."

The manager laughed. "I should've warned them." He left down the steps.

Daniel saw the musicians walk in chatting and laughing, among them Sonja. She waved to him. Daniel nodded. *It's all I can and will do.* He grabbed the score of *Don Juan* to start with. It probably needed the most work it being filled with Richard Strauss' rich orchestrations. *Let's start.*

Daniel called out, "Good morning, ladies and gentlemen. I don't know if you had a chance to go over our program. I want to start with *Don Juan.* We only have two rehearsals, so let's get to it."

He took the piece in sections and heard that the musicians hadn't played it for a while. But by lunch, they had worked all the way through.

Just to keep himself from worrying Daniel called Mia. "We're having lunch," she told him. "A nice restaurant. Then we're going home. It was fun."

"I'm glad you had a nice time," Daniel said. "I'll see you in a few hours." *At least they saw something of Seattle. Now back to Schubert and Wagner.*

After his second cup of coffee, he heard a familiar voice close by. He looked up. "You have another question, Sonja?"

"No, I don't." She laughed softly. "I'm just so glad to see you direct our symphony orchestra. It's going to be a great performance."

"Thank you." Daniel got up. "Keep up the good work." He gave her a quick smile. The look in her eyes told him what he had tried to ignore, and it scared him. Sonja had fallen in love with him. He could only hope that his absence in London and back in San Francisco would cool her feelings. How would he possibly make it clear to her that he wasn't available? Daniel raked his fingers through his hair. In his earlier life, various ladies had tried to get close to him. But being married to Elvira nothing like Sonja had happened. Since he had become a widower would that start again? *At least let me make up my own mind if there should be someone.* Daniel still hoped that Sonja would back off and it would be safe for him to tell her the truth.

Back at the podium, he brought his mind back to "*The Meistersingers.*" There too he had to run through a few repeats until he could turn to Schubert's Sixth Symphony.

When he finally closed his scores he felt tired. It had been a good work-out for all concerned. He made his way quickly out of the theater. *I need a nap.*

ℝ

The children were back at the hotel when he arrived. After some tea from the restaurant, he flopped down on the bed. "I need to sleep for an hour, okay? I have one more performance tonight." *Oh, the pleasures of a conductor.*

ℝ

The performance that evening went well again. Summer coming up meant Daniel wouldn't work with the orchestra until September when the new season would start. "I'll have to think about a program and will let you know ahead of time," he told them, then added with a twinkle in his eyes, "unless I'm not around for Seattle."

The faces around them fell. "Why not? Are you deserting us?"

Daniel chuckled. "Only if I get a super job somewhere else."

Sonja's face had paled. "Please, squeeze us in, Maestro. We need you here."

I guess you want me around. Daniel waved his hand. "For now have a great summer. See some of you for rehearsal tomorrow."

Daniel headed for the restaurant. He needed something to eat. A few of the musicians followed him but, to his surprise, Sonja did not. *Maybe she got my message?*

With the meal and a glass of wine Daniel relaxed. From now on relaxing will not be easy, he thought. One more rehearsal, two performances, and then London. Which would be a whole new situation. But before that, he needed to know from Andy Willows as well as Inspector Lankin whether Rupert had been captured. If not neither Daniel nor Mia and Julian could feel safe. Smuggling diamonds would not only involve Amsterdam and New York but maybe London as well. Rupert most certainly must have employed people there. With that in mind, Daniel was going to meet Willows tomorrow afternoon.

Chapter 33

The second rehearsal the next morning went better than before. Apart from a few tempo corrections Daniel was pleased. At lunchtime he couldn't wait any longer. He called Willows. "Give me some good news, Andy. I'm on pins and needles." He heard Andy chuckle.

"Some good news but not the best yet. More of Inspector Lankin's inmates have opened up a bit more about one or two of Rupert's hide-outs. But he hasn't been seen anywhere. He hasn't been spotted at any airport either. Come over later. I have some plans and Lankin's people are looking for him too."

Daniel sighed. "I'm just concerned that his business might include other cities like London, England, where I am on Monday."

"A bit far away from him to control," Andy said. "See you later, Daniel." He hung up.

He might be right. Back to work.

At the end of Schubert's Sixth Symphony Daniel reminded the musicians, "Tomorrow morning from beginning to end, then the performance. A long day. So get a good night's sleep."

The concertmaster frowned. "If my newborn will let me."

Daniel had to smile. "Get earplugs." It reminded him of Julian's teething time.

On his way to Andy Willows Daniel wondered about the plan he had mentioned. What kind of plan could anyone have when the culprit is invisible? How many policemen can they send all through Seattle to tail him if he might not even be here anymore?

Andy was waiting for him but with a frown. Daniel held his breath. "Bad news, Andy? Don't frighten me."

Andy's face lit up again. "Not really. Just wish we could present Rupert to you." He put his hand on Daniel's shoulder. "We know now of four hide-outs, two here and two in Portland. We have them under surveillance. One of Lankin's guys told him that the boss never sleeps longer than one night in either of them. Probably the same in San Francisco." He looked at Daniel. "He needs his money, he'll show up."

Daniel nodded. "What about the construction sites in San Francisco? That's where they are, the transporters of the goods."

"Lankin rounded them all up. Of course, some of them are only there for building houses." The phone rang. Andy listened and smiled. He put the phone down and looked at Daniel. "One step closer. Rupert has been seen today here in one of his hideaways. So, he won't be there tonight again. We'll check on the second one later."

Another baby step. "Catching him there would be the greatest gift for me. I'll still have to be on the alert because my kids are by themselves a lot. They wanted to visit a museum tomorrow. I'm sure Rupert knows we're here because of the performances."

"The museums have security officers walking around. The children should be okay. Hey, we're looking forward to the music tomorrow. See you then." Andy clapped Daniel's shoulder again. "I'm sure it will be great."

"I'll do my best. Good thing I have you on my side, Andy. Keep trying." Daniel didn't quite know whether to be happy or disappointed. He knew the police force was doing its best. But Rupert being in this city while Daniel was here made him jittery. *All my worrying doesn't help. He'll make a mistake soon. Hopefully, before we leave for London.*

☙❧

The next morning started out worrisome for Daniel. Mia was coughing and sniffling. "It just started overnight," she mumbled. "It's just a cold but I don't think we're going to the museum today. Do we have any Aspirins?"

That's all we need, sick kids on this trip. "Stay away from Mia, Julian. One sick kid is enough."

"Can he go with you, Papa? Then I can sleep some more."

"That might be a good idea, sleep it off." Daniel looked at his son. "Can you behave at the theater? I mean, not running around, so I can see you?"

"As usual, Papa. It's okay," Julian grabbed his bag.

"Call me if it gets worse," Daniel called to Mia before leaving.

At the theater, Daniel looked into the library. "Can Julian stay here for a while during rehearsal?" he asked the lady in charge.

The librarian smiled. "Certainly, Maestro, we have lots to look at."

On his way out, Daniel bumped into someone who started to giggle. "As usual, in a hurry."

Daniel froze. "Lydia? What are you doing here?" *I don't believe this.*

"I took you up on your invitation to hear your performance." Lydia looked at him a bit doubtful. "Is that all right?"

"Yes, of course, but this is only a rehearsal." Daniel was still so surprised he didn't know what to say.

"I see you brought your son along. You'll need a babysitter." Lydia had an impish glint in her eyes.

Daniel had to laugh. "How did you know? He'll be more than happy. But I'm glad you came. At least I'll have one fan."

"You'll have many after this evening." She turned. "I'll get reacquainted with your son."

"Thank you, Lydia." Daniel had to admit he was happy to see her. She had been in the back of his mind, shoved back because—well, he was secretly afraid that he wouldn't see her again. What a beautiful surprise. Daniel's spirit felt uplifted, he couldn't help but smile. *I can't believe that Lydia actually came.*

The rehearsal went better than before. Daniel was certain that the performance that night would be to the audience's liking.

At lunch, he was discussing some details with the concertmaster when he saw Sonja floating towards his table. Stay polite, he told himself.

"It's going to be a great evening, Maestro." Both hands were wrapped around her coffee cup. *Are they shaking?* She continued. "I have told a lot of my friends to come."

"Great," Daniel said. "We need listeners who contribute to our musical wealth. You're all doing well." *Now leave, please.* Sonja smiled, turned, and wandered off. She's trying so hard to make me see her, Daniel thought. I actually feel sorry for her. He got up. "Let's get to the last piece. At least we have the afternoon to relax." Then he saw Lydia and Julian come into the restaurant. She waved.

"A young boy needs to eat, so that's what we're going to do."

"Yeah, and I'm not having salads," Julian added.

Daniel laughed. "Lydia, don't you spoil him. He gets easily used to that."

"Only for today," she answered.

Daniel opened the door. "See you later after the last piece of music." *How does Lydia do it? She can light up the whole room. I better stop it. This is probably the last day I'll see her. On with the work at hand.*

Don Juan sounded a lot better, and Daniel didn't worry about the performance that night. He wondered where Lydia was staying overnight. She was waiting with Julian at the stage door.

"That music is so interesting," she said. "*Don Juan* at his best and at his worst."

Daniel smiled. "Not quite as graphic as Mozart and not as simple by looking at the score."

Lydia looked at him. "I'll bet you'll need some rest before the evening."

Daniel nodded. "A nap would be nice." *Or not, depending.* "Where are you staying?"

"The same hotel as you." Lydia chuckled. "It should be a good place where the Maestro lives."

Before Daniel could say anything his phone rang. Mia. "Can you bring me some cough drops, Papa?"

"Sure, how are you feeling?"

"Not too bad, still coughing and sniffling. No fever though. Are you coming home?"

"I'm on my way. See you soon." Daniel turned to Lydia. "My daughter caught a cold, father's duty to get cough drops. Are you having supper before the show?"

Lydia nodded. "Yes, I think so."

"I don't eat much before a performance but count me in including my kids." *Might as well use the time.*

Her eyes widened. "I'll meet your daughter."

"If she's well enough," Daniel said. "But usually food will cure some of it." At the hotel, he turned into the small shop. "Cough drops. See you later, Lydia."

She waved and walked to the elevator.

"She's still nice, right, Papa?" Julian looked where she went.

"Yes, she is. Now back to reality, Buddy. I do need a nap." *And get my mind in order.*

Mia was watching TV and nibbled some nuts. Daniel gave her the cough drops. "Are you getting better?"

Mia shrugged. "It's not getting worse. But I need another box of Kleenex."

After a hot cup of tea, Daniel flopped onto the bed. "Give me an hour, okay?" *Let me not think for a while.*

Chapter 34

Daniel woke up hearing Julian's voice, "You said 'one hour,' Papa." He had to close his eyes again to remember where he was and what he had to do for the rest of the day. Performance and, yes, there was Lydia. Daniel was still at odds with his feelings. He liked her, maybe more than *like*. He got up. "Is there any coffee left in the pot? Any cookies to wake me up?"

Mia laughed. "Coffee and sweets? That will spoil your supper."

"You sound like my mother. But these are dire circumstances. And—you're going to meet Lydia at dinner. I'm sure, Julian has told you everything about her."

Mia shook some cookies out of the box. "Okay, she must be something special, at least according to Julian."

"She's sooo nice, Mia." Julian grabbed two cookies.

Daniel drained his coffee cup. "She just happens to stay at this hotel, will listen to the performance, and has proven to be a good babysitter. So, I'm paying for her dinner."

Mia looked up. "Is she coming to London, too?"

"Good Lord, no. She goes back to Portland." *Why would she even ask that?*

Mia coughed. "Okay, when is supper?"

Daniel checked his watch. "In about half an hour."

At the restaurant, Daniel got a table by the window. "Classy," Mia said. "Good to have a famous father."

"Just my good looks," Daniel chuckled. He looked around and saw Lydia coming in. She waved and smiled. "Come join us, meet my daughter Mia, the future opera singer."

"How nice to meet you, Mia," Lydia said. "I'm glad you could come."

Mia nodded. "I feel a bit better."

During dinner, Daniel noticed that Lydia always included the children in the conversation. *Very clever, not treating them like little kids.*

After a while, Daniel got up. "I have to leave to be at the theater earlier." He turned to Mia. "Are you two staying home tonight?"

"Yes, I'll go to the performance tomorrow. I don't want to cough in the middle of a *piano* section."

"Right, have some dessert. See you tomorrow morning."

"We wish you good luck," both children called.

Lydia laughed. "The same from me. I'm sure of success."

Maybe Mia gets to like Lydia too, at least for one evening. The rest is still far away.

∽∾∾

When Daniel arrived at Symphony Hall, he saw Andy Willows waiting at the stage door. "Hey, Andy, you're early. Any news?"

"News, yes, but not the kind we were waiting for." Andy walked along with Daniel. "Someone must have known where Rupert was hiding and took action. He was found in San Francisco near the Golden Gates Bridge, beaten to death."

Daniel stopped. He closed his eyes and swallowed a few times. "My Lord, what a turn of events." He shook his head. "Whoever did this should be congratulated. He did us a favor."

Andy had stopped too. "Unless someone else takes over now and was waiting for this—or helped with it."

Daniel frowned. "That's all we need. But maybe Rupert was so strong that the rest of the gang will fall apart now. A lot of them are already in jail."

Andy nodded. "We are looking for the murderer, no matter whom he has killed. But I think you can feel a bit safer now."

"Which means I have a performance to do. Andy, thank you for telling me." Daniel shook his hand. Andy turned. "Good luck."

While Daniel was changing in his dressing room the news still jumped around in his head. *What a relief, that is if nobody else is continuing the smuggling business. It's too good a money maker to be abandoned, it might go on."* *He* had to force his mind back to the music. Wagner, Schubert, and Strauss.

"We have a good audience," the concertmaster told Daniel fifteen minutes before the start of the concert. "Not sold out but almost."

Daniel smiled. "Sonja told her friends to come and maybe they have friends too. It's appreciated."

"It's your name, Maestro, that brings them," the musician said.

"Then I better not disappoint them." Daniel had to chuckle. "You all have to support me in my fame."

"We'll do our best." The musician winked and wandered off.

⁊⁊⁊

And they did. The applause at the intermission was steady and Daniel considered the performance a success so far. To his surprise, Lydia stood at the library door with a big smile. "Maestro, beautiful. I loved it."

She looks beautiful too in that dress. "I'm happy you enjoyed it. Different from rehearsals, no interruptions." *Should I ask? She's probably gone tomorrow, so why not?* "We're all going for a drink afterward. Would you like to come?"

Lydia beamed. "Sure, I'd love to. I'll wait at the door." She waved and walked back to the lobby.

Good. Admit it, I want to see her as often as possible. Daniel sighed. *Am I too old for this? Back to Don Juan.* Then he spotted Sonja walking towards him with a big smile.

"Are you happy so far, Maestro?"

"Oh yes, I am. Did your friends come to listen?" *What else can I say?*

"Yes, actually five of them turned up and two more tomorrow."

Daniel looked at his watch. "Be the fundraiser for the symphony, Sonja."

Sonja shook her head. "No, but I…never mind, we have to go in again." With a tiny twitch of her mouth, she went back to the stage.

Daniel took a deep breath. *Yes, I'm getting too old for these games.* The oboe sounded, and there was no more space in his mind for anything but Richard Strauss.

As the music engulfed Daniel with all of *Don Juan's* triumphs and downfalls, he couldn't help but wonder: why was *Don Juan* the only one who became famous? There must have been and still would be many more of them. The audience liked his interpretation. The applause lasted for a long time with bravos and whistles. Daniel felt overwhelmed every time by so much appreciation for his and the orchestra's efforts.

When the people finally trickled out of the theater, Daniel changed into his normal clothes and put cold water on his face. Wonderful, he thought, it couldn't have gone better. As usual, many of the musicians went to the restaurant for their well-deserved drink. As promised Lydia stood by the stage door.

"I wanted to make sure you felt like coming." She looked at Daniel. "Watching you conduct is…inspiring."

Daniel stopped. "Really? Why? I just keep the beat and point to whoever needs to come in at the right time."

"No, you're also acting along with the music, joyfully or sadly."

They walked on. "Hm, I guess it comes automatically with me." *What an observer.*

"That's why you're successful," Lydia said. "You deserve a drink."

Daniel laughed. "And something to eat." *She sounds so sincere, not like she wants to flatter me. I'll enjoy this.*

As laughter and chatter of the musicians greeted them Daniel tried to find seats for Lydia and himself. He also found someone watching him. Sonja. He decided to ignore her, Lydia was his guest for tonight. During a lull in the conversations around him he asked her, "Are you flying home tomorrow?"

"No, I'm listening one more time tomorrow evening," Lydia answered. "It's good for me to learn more about music I don't often hear."

Daniel was surprised in a happy way. *One more day to see her. This is weird. I'm really not up for anything serious, but I'm glad she's staying.* "You're a true fan, Lydia. I appreciate your loyalty."

For the first time Lydia's face turned somber. She looked at Daniel. "You're such an important artist with such a musical life behind you already. I feel as if you treat me special. I don't know why. Is it because I drove you around in Portland?"

Daniel had to look away from those quiet blue eyes. *What am I going to tell her?* He drank some of his wine. "Lydia, you're a special lady. You're competent, pretty, and caring, different from many women I meet. Except my wife, of course. I like talking to you. I'm glad you're staying for another day."

A small smile came back into Lydia's eyes. "Thank you, you're different from a lot of other conductors too. Most of them don't see me."

Daniel nodded. "That's the fate of the workers in the background. I told you before, you're as important to the orchestra as anyone else in it."

Lydia smiled then got up. "Do you mind if I go? I'll see you tomorrow."

"Let me escort you home." Daniel was ready to go. But Lydia shook her head. "No need, Maestro. You stay, it's your success."

Daniel didn't feel he should push her. "Only if you stop calling me Maestro. Call me Daniel."

Lydia laughed. "Okay, Daniel." She made her way out of the door.

Another surprise. Do I need another glass of wine? From across the table Sonja gave him a big smile. Daniel didn't respond. *Enough already. I'm ready to go too. This body needs some rest.*

The next morning at breakfast Daniel was still divided between asking Lydia for a walk or not. He didn't want her to believe that he was asking her for a relationship. Because he didn't know if he could. Memories of years with Elvira were still too vivid. He also knew that a woman didn't want to wait once she knew that he cared for her.

"What are you thinking about, Papa?" Mia asked.

"He's thinking about Lydia," Julian whispered.

"What? Why?" Mia picked some melon pieces from a plate.

I might as well tell her in a funny way. "I'm afraid I'm turning into an old man before I can get a girlfriend again."

Mia's eyes got big. "You like Lydia enough for her to be your girlfriend?"

Daniel sat down with another cup of coffee. "I might but she works in Portland, and I fly around like a gypsy. It's probably not going to work. Don't look so worried, Mia. I'm not marrying Lydia tomorrow, I just want to go for a walk with her."

"Okay, Papa. As long as you don't…Never mind, I'm just surprised." Daniel looked at his daughter. "I'm still thinking a lot about your Mama." He got up. "So, don't worry, okay? One more performance tonight, then London. Now for my walk."

Mia still looked a bit uncertain, but then a small smile appeared. "Well, Lydia isn't too bad. Can we go out too, around the playground?"

"Yes, if you're still careful." Daniel had not told them of Rupert's death. He would do it later.

✑✑✑

Since he hadn't seen Lydia at breakfast, he asked at the desk to ring her room. But the clerk told him that she had gone out. *Darn. I'll try and find her. She might have walked towards the park.* Daniel followed the route he would have taken and caught up with her standing by a fruit stand. "You're an early bird, Lydia," Daniel called. She turned with the purchase in her bag. The surprise showed on her face.

"Good morning, Maestro—I mean Daniel. I thought you would still be sleeping."

Daniel laughed. "Not when you have children. Are you game for a walk?"

"Yes, I wasn't sure yet which way to take. You lead."

"As always, only this time without my stick." *I'm glad she agreed.*

It felt easy to walk beside Lydia, no tension, just conversation and comments about the park and its colors. Daniel finally asked, "How did you decide to become a librarian for an orchestra?"

Lydia looked up. "That's a long story but ended well for me."

"Just wondering," Daniel tried, "I thought you might have a husband and children." *Should I even ask?*

"I might have had but—like I said, it's a long story good for long winter nights." Lydia smiled but Daniel noticed the sadness in her eyes. *Keep it light.*

"Sorry, it sounds ominous. So, we'll wait for a winter's night by the fire."

Lydia bent down and picked a stray piece of grass. "You'll be all over the globe and I'm in Portland."

"Yes, who knows where I am. After London, something might change—or not. But, as you've seen, I'm a guest conductor quite often."

Lydia looked up, then smiled. "You might have to swear to come back to Portland—sometime."

Daniel turned towards a bench. "*Sometime* is such a vague word. Life is unpredictable like all the criminal problems we had to go through." He smirked. "Another story to be told before a fire."

Lydia sat down. "I've heard some things of the trouble you had, but nothing specific. Are you okay now?"

Daniel nodded. "We're going to be. The bad guys all make a mistake sooner or later."

Lydia looked at her watch. "You must need some lunch. I won't keep you any longer."

Daniel was surprised. "You don't keep me, Lydia. We'll walk back together." *Is she afraid of—what? Hopefully not of me. Better make sure of it.* "I told you before, I like talking to you. I don't get many chances to just have a conversation with someone nice like you that doesn't include what music to choose or a timetable."

Lydia looked as if she had more questions, but she got up. Her smile came back. "Don't let your kids wait, Daniel. I'm so glad you caught me this morning."

"Same here. So, you'll endure another concert tonight? Thanks for your support." *Probably for a long time to come.*

At the hotel, Mia and Julian met them. "Good timing," Mia called. "I'm starving, let's have lunch."

Daniel looked at Lydia. But she shook her head. "You go ahead. I'm going upstairs. See you at the theater." With her usual wave, she disappeared inside.

Now there is a switch, Daniel thought. Sonja would have been all over me. Not Lydia. He felt a bit of relief. He had to be realistic: his career, his family, his own still uncertain feelings—he needed to wait. But he would keep in touch with Lydia. *I don't want to lose her out of my life.*

Chapter 35

Daniel decided to call Inspector Lankin before the flight to London. He needed to know more about Rupert's death and if the rest of the gang was still on the loose. After lunch, he reminded Mia and Julian to pack their things.

"You two are coming with me tonight, right? Mia is listening and you, Julian, have no babysitter. Now I'm calling the inspector."

Mia motioned Julian to go with her into the bedroom. "Papa needs quiet," she whispered.

The officer at the station told Daniel that the inspector was on the road to inspect a stabbing.

"I need to speak to him before I fly to London. Will he be back soon?" *I can't wait too much longer.*

"I think so," the officer said. "He always comes back here. I'll let him know."

Daniel paced around. *I would like to be safe now.*

Half an hour later his telephone beeped. "Lankin here," Daniel heard. "Now what's your problem?"

"Hello, Inspector, nice of you to call back. I need to know a few things before I take off again."

"Didn't Willows fill you in?"

Daniel sat down. "Only that Rupert was found dead. What about the rest of the gang? Can we feel safe now?"

Never mind your case of a stabbing, I need facts. Daniel heard the usual sigh over the phone.

"Most of them are in custody for now. Someone has probably made an escape and is thinking of continuing the business. But they know that we know."

Daniel let out a breath. "So I don't have to look over my shoulder anymore?" He heard a snort.

"If you keep your nose out of criminals' business you might be safe."

Daniel had to laugh. "But I'm such a concerned citizen. I'll personally thank you for all your effort when I come home."

"Yeah, yeah. Get back to your music." The inspector hung up.

After a moment of reflection Daniel called, "Okay, kids, you can come and hear some good news."

Mia and Julian appeared wide-eyed. "What, Papa?"

"Sit and listen. Rupert, the Blackbeard, is dead and most of his company is in jail. I think our troubles are over, at least for now."

Both children squealed and hugged Daniel. "Finally! No more worries."

Daniel walked around the room. "I hope so. If the leader is gone the rest will probably scatter. But I'm still not sure if we could be met by some would-be new leader. So, when in London still stay alert for now."

Mia sighed. "Still not quite over but better?"

"Something like that. Now get going for supper, then the concert." *I need some little time in my dressing room.*

೧೨೧

During the walk to the theater, Daniel thought about Lydia again. Would he see her after the performance? Or would she just up and disappear? Hopefully, she would at least say goodbye. For now, Daniel needed to make sure to present a good concert.

"Sit somewhere where I can see you," he told Mia and Julian.

"Maybe we see Lydia again," said Julian. Mia rolled her eyes.

"Tell her hello from me." *Might as well let her know I'm still thinking about her.*

The performance turned out to Daniel's satisfaction. The musicians smiled and enjoyed the long applause. The concertmaster shook Daniel's hand. "I hope we see you more often, Maestro."

Daniel mopped his face with a handkerchief. "We'll see what happens in September. San Francisco first, your Chamber Orchestra too. I also have offers to go back to Munich and Vancouver. Vienna wants me for their New Year's concert which I will accept. So, you see, I'm turning into a gypsy conductor."

The concertmaster laughed. "I would be jumping with joy to have your talent. I wish you success in London."

As Daniel turned to go to his dressing room Lydia walked towards him. "I'm glad to have heard the music again, Daniel. I'm leaving on a late flight back to Portland. Just wanted to wish you a good trip and the biggest success ever."

Daniel swallowed. *I'm almost ready to kiss you.* "Lydia, I want to keep in touch with you, probably by email and phone for now. After London I'll be back in San Francisco, come see me." He could feel Lydia's blue eyes searching his face.

"You really mean that, Daniel? I might just take you up on it." An impish look came into her eyes. "Don't be surprised if you find me in front of your door some time."

Daniel laughed and shook her hand. "I'll be waiting for it. Have a good flight back." *What else can I say? Stay with me one more day? That wouldn't be right for either of us.*

No sooner had he changed into his street clothes when he heard a tap on the door. *Now what?* "I'm out in a second." When he opened the door he found Sonja leaning against the wall.

"Sorry to bother you, Maestro, but you're leaving for I don't know how long. I wanted to wish you good luck in London."

"Thank you, Sonja. But I'll be back in September for the Chamber Orchestra rehearsals."

Sonja looked down at her hands. "Yes, maybe. You don't know this but without you coming back I—" she turned, "I have no life. Sorry." She started to walk away.

Oh, my Lord! "Hold on, Sonja." She stopped. "You can't feel that way," Daniel continued. "I'll always be all over the country and beyond, it's my job. And I'm not ready for a relationship." *She might as well know.*

"I didn't mean it that way. It's just that I love you. I can't help that. I needed you to know. Sorry." This time she turned quickly and kept walking.

Daniel blew out a long breath. *She needed to have it out in the open. Good. Now she knows how I feel, too. I want to get home.* He couldn't help feeling a bit shaky.

At the stage door, he found Mia and Julian waiting with Andy Willows. "Don't tell me you listened again tonight, Andy."

Andy chuckled. "Yes, I did, same great concert. Want to go for a drink?"

"My kids have to get home first, maybe then I'll have one for the road." *Might as well after this kind of a night.*

Later, during conversations with Andy Willows, Daniel's tensions subsided. He realized that there always had been women who had a crush on him because he was a conductor. It had nothing to do with him as a person. Was Sonja one of them? Should he even think about that? He had two children and a wonderful career. *Let me continue my life as well as possible.*

☙❧☙

During the flight to London the next afternoon Daniel told Mia and Julian that it would be nine o'clock in the morning at their arrival. "They are eight hours ahead of us in a different time zone. So, you better get some sleep during the night as usual. At least you don't feel any jetlag."

"What's jetlag, Papa?" Julian asked.

"You feel tired and out of sorts. When you sleep you'll be all right."

Mia looked through the flight magazine. "Are we getting supper?"

"Yes, we do and some extras." Wonderful, Daniel thought, all the comforts of home—well, almost.

☙❧☙

Heathrow Airport bustled with crowds everywhere, passport checks took longer than they had wanted. Finally, they spotted their luggage on the carousel.

"Boy, do you have to go through this every time you go to another country?" Mia asked.

"Yes, I have no way around it."

"But you're someone special, Papa," Julian said. "Can't you just go through?"

Daniel laughed. "Only if I'm a high-ranking politician."

"No fair," Julian declared.

As they walked out of the exit glass doors Daniel heard a voice. "Maestro Abogado!" A tall young man waved his arms.

Daniel stopped. "I don't believe this. Mark Hamel, what are you doing here?"

The man jogged towards them. "I knew you were conducting the summer festival. I thought it would be nice to pick you up—and your family." He looked over to Mia, then to Julian.

"It's been a while, Mark." Daniel introduced the children. "Are you here on business like a concert or on holiday?"

"No, but for a recital, tomorrow night." Mark looked again over to Mia. Daniel noticed that she hadn't taken her eyes off him. "I'll want to hear if you have improved."

Mark smirked. "You're making me nervous, Sir. Let's go, follow me."

"Who is he, Papa?" Mia whispered.

"Mark is a pianist who has made his way to the top. We'll hear him tomorrow." Mia just nodded

Daniel thought that his friend had grown a lot, filled out from the skinny youth he had seen last and had shortened his wavy brown hair. *No mustache, thank God.*

Mark had a car ready to go. Weaving through London's morning traffic, laughing and telling anecdotes they arrived quickly at the hotel.

"Thank you, Mark," Daniel said. "I do appreciate your nice surprise. We'll get settled. Tomorrow morning I'm busy with a meeting first and getting to know the musicians, all eighty of them."

"Which Symphony Hall are you conducting in?" Mark asked.

"The Royal Festival Hall this time. That one has an organ for Saint-Saëns."

Mark winked. "I'd better do some more practicing. See you tomorrow?"

"I wouldn't want to miss it." Daniel gave the luggage to a bellboy, and they walked to the elevator. He noticed that Mia took another look at Mark before the elevator doors closed. *Well, I'll better keep my eyes open. One more thing to think about.*

Up in their hotel suite, Julian asked, "Does Mark play piano really well?"

"Yes, he worked hard and now plays piano concertos and gives recitals. You'll hear him tomorrow."

"Did he play when he was ten like me?"

Aha, comparison. "I think so, probably even earlier."

Julian frowned. "I want to talk to him. He can give me some advice."

Daniel looked at him. "What advice do you need, Julian?"

Julian shrugged. "Just—you know—general."

"You'll get an opportunity, I'm sure." *Maybe a good idea to hear from Mark how much it takes to be a successful pianist.*

During unpacking, Daniel heard a lot of quiet conversations between Mia and Julian about Mark. He had certainly made an impression, Daniel thought. In the late afternoon he could see that the time difference caught up with the children.

"Let's have an early supper and then off to bed with you two." That would also give him an hour to organize the music for tomorrow. He always had a feeling of anticipation in a place where he hadn't conducted before, he needed to know the general feeling inside the building and the acoustics. Daniel hadn't met the president and his group or talked to them on the phone since that was his agent's work. He was curious how the Royal Philharmonic was being run. They didn't know yet what he had planned for the outdoor concerts. Would they make a fuss about his selections? As usual, one brandy would be appropriate, and then a hopefully comfortable hotel bed.

Chapter 36

When Daniel arrived at the Royal Festival Hall the next morning he stood in awe. *My goodness, how modern can a theater be*, he thought. The main building towered over shops and restaurants with wide staircases leading to the upper levels. And everything stood side-by-side with London's Big Eye. Daniel spotted a poster with his picture on it. *Look at that, not too bad.* He smirked at his other self. *Try not to disappoint them.*

"Can I help you, Sir?" a voice interrupted his thoughts. Daniel looked at a friendly face of a man in a business suite.

"I was trying to find the entrance," Daniel said.

The man recognized him. "Ah, our Maestro for the Summer Festival. Welcome." He shook Daniel's hand. "Richard, one of the managers. Follow me. It's a big building to get lost in." He opened a door and let Daniel enter first. Through a long hallway they arrived at a spacious room. Four other gentlemen were already waiting and rose when Daniel came in.

Business suits, some mustaches, hair more or less. Music is after all a business.

After introductions and inquiries as to Daniel's flight and accommodations, he sat down. "I'm sure you want to go over the music I've chosen," he started. "The evening performances are known to you, I think. I have a list of pieces for the outdoor ones." He pushed it over to the person across from him. "I hope you'll agree with them." He saw some nods and a few small frowns.

Finally one of the managers said, "Could you put one more English composer into it?"

Daniel smiled. He had expected that. "How about Delius' 'Over the Hills and Far away?' It shouldn't be too long for an outdoor audience."

"Good choice," all agreed.

"One more thing. I need a lot of rehearsal time considering the amount of music. I would like to start as soon as possible, maybe after lunch?"

The president nodded. "The musicians are standing by right now, Maestro. We'll take you there."

All of them? What an entourage.

The theater inside was amazing, modern but with something, Daniel called a brown, comfortable feeling. The ceiling gave the impression as if covered with comforters. Good acoustics, Daniel thought. The organ looked immense with four keyboards and pipes covering the whole back wall. *Saint-Saëns would have loved it.*

"Quite a place," Daniel said. "I'm impressed."

The president waved at someone. After a few seconds the musicians filed in, went to their places but stayed standing. Daniel turned to them.

"Good morning, ladies and gentlemen. I am looking forward to working with you. How about after lunch starting with the Hungarian Rhapsody?" To his surprise the musicians applauded. "Good, See you then."

To Daniel's second surprise all five managers took him into one of the many restaurants connected to the Royal Symphony Hall. *I wonder how many questions I'll have to answer.*

During a good meal and strong coffee, the questions came…about his career, family, recordings, and places he had conducted. *Like a third degree, only kinder. Do they do this with every conductor being here for the first time?*

After an hour Daniel got up. "Thank you, Gentlemen, you'll have to excuse me. Rehearsals are calling." Everyone rose and shook his hand again.

Daniel knew that he was dealing with a famous orchestra. At the same time, he wouldn't back away from telling them how he wanted the music to be played. This would be work but it was needed to create a success.

On the way back to the theater Daniel called Mia. It took three rings before she answered. "Where are you two?" Daniel asked.

"We're at the restaurant. Can we walk to the building where you are and look around the shops, Papa?"

"All right, but still stay alert promise?" Daniel didn't quite trust the big outdoors yet.

"Promise. See you later."

They sound happy enough. Now to work.

The musicians were practicing when he walked towards the stage. He approached the concertmaster. "Time to get acquainted," Daniel said. The violinist jumped up. They shook hands. "Welcome, Maestro. I'm Robin. We're ready."

At the podium, Daniel turned to the musicians. "Let's start right away with the Rhapsody. Make it sound strong, like an important statement."

It didn't take long for Daniel to find out the orchestra's strengths and weaknesses. He mostly felt it during controlling the sounds from the wind instruments and the timing. Daniel also realized that the musicians had to get used to his gestures. Every conductor worked differently.

After repeating some sections Daniel stopped. "Let's take a breather, then go from the beginning. We leave Saint-Saëns for tomorrow."

Daniel knew he had to watch his usual repeats of certain sections. He was dealing with a well-known, capable orchestra. However, to get the results that had given him his good name, he had to disregard that feeling. He had been asked to conduct and that's what he was going to do to the best of his ability.

After fifteen minutes Daniel signaled Robin, the concertmaster, to get ready again. This time the Rhapsody sounded much better.

"Good," Daniel called out. "Let's switch to Borodin's *Prince Igor*, then call it a day."

There he had to bring out more of a contrast between the moody and lively parts. *Tomorrow*. "Saint-Saëns tomorrow with the organ if possible," he told the musicians. "Thank you."

Daniel felt the time difference now. "I either need coffee or go to bed," he grumbled. "Where are the kids?" *Probably in the shops*. He called Mia.

"We're coming, Papa. I see you already." Both came around the corner. "Don't look so worried, Papa. We're safe."

"It's my job to worry." Daniel walked down to them. "I need coffee. Let's go in here." He saw some of the musicians walking out of the restaurant cradling take-out coffee. They waved.

Both children had a lot of questions about the orchestra. "Can we listen to the rehearsal tomorrow?" Julian asked.

"That would be too boring for you. There're a lot of repeats. Wait 'til the performance."

"Okay." Julian seemed to see the point.

On their way home Daniel, as well as the children, had to admit to an early supper and bedtime. "Eight hours make a lot of difference," Julian commented and yawned.

"We better be chipper tomorrow," Daniel said.

"And we're going to hear Mark play," Mia added.

Daniel chuckled. "You like him, don't you?"

Mia shrugged and blushed.

"Careful, little daughter. Before you know it he'll be gone from one city to the next."

Mia shrugged again and went into her bedroom.

Daniel scratched his head. It had to come sometime, she's almost seventeen after all.

Before going to bed he called Inspector Lankin. It being nine o'clock in the morning in San Francisco he should be at work.

"Don't I ever get you out of my hair?" the inspector grumbled.

Daniel had to laugh. "Let's say, you're never far from my mind, Inspector."

"How flattering. What do you want to know now?"

"Did you catch Rupert's killer? Any idea who he is? Maybe he's the one taking over the business."

Lankin sighed as usual. "The manager of the construction company told us that he knew who that could be. Apparently, another nasty bit of humanity. He gave us a description but we're still looking. I've told Willows as well."

"As long as he's not in London I'm okay," Daniel said. "Thank you, let me know as soon as you have caught him, please."

My eyes are closing, time for some peace and quiet. Saint-Saëns tomorrow.

Chapter 37

The next morning Mia and Julian decided to take a city tour again. "Like the one in Seattle," Mia said. "It's really safe."

"Fine with me, as long as you keep in touch. I'll be up to my ears in music." In a way, Daniel was happy that they didn't stay in the hotel room. All day TV or game playing wasn't healthy. "I'll see you in the afternoon. Keep your eyes open, okay?"

During his walk to the theater, Saint-Saëns' symphony filled his mind. What music! Daniel called it multi-colored and multi-layered. Starting quietly, like a question, it turned lively, although the question came back all through the piece. Through warm and dreamy parts, a feeling of uncertainty stayed behind until finally, the power of the organ brought life and continuation as a resolution. *I'll try to show all that as well as I can.*

The sounds of the musicians practicing cheered Daniel up every time he came to rehearsals. He knew that part of the audience found it grating on their nerves. For Daniel, it belonged to the atmosphere, like the anticipation of what's to come.

Today it gave him an energy boost. Standing on the podium he called out, "I'm happy to hear you all working already," which was answered with low grumbles and chuckles. "Do we have an organist and a pianist?" Daniel asked.

"Yes, Maestro," Robin said, "all is ready."

"Perfect. Let's give it a run-through."

Of course, it took a few tries to switch from the slow beginning to the faster part. With all the emotional changes Daniel had prepared himself for slow, detailed work.

At the lunch break, the librarian handed Daniel an envelope. "This was delivered an hour ago."

Daniel caught his breath. "Did you get a look at the person who delivered it?"

"Just a young man with a red baseball cap, jeans, and red and white runners," the librarian said.

Daniel turned the letter over. He read: To the Maestro, no sender. Ice cubes assembled in his stomach. *This smells like a threat again. I'm not going to open it.* He shook the envelope. It sounded different from just a letter. *I'm so tired of running to police stations. Here I thought I would finally feel safe.* Daniel called down to the office. The president answered. Daniel explained about the past threatening letters and that this was again a new one.

After a shocked pause, the president uttered, "Oh my God, oh my God. I'm calling for an officer to come right now to take this in hand. I'll be there in five minutes."

Daniel called Mia. "We're having lunch," she told him. "The tour is really interesting."

He reminded her to stay alert, not to forget the safety rules. He didn't tell her about the letter. *Later.* Then he took a deep breath. *Even here in London with Blackbeard dead? Is this a note from the next boss?*

The president arrived and Daniel cautioned him to only touch the letter with gloves or a handkerchief. "Fingerprints might solve this," he said. He told the president how the librarian had described the man delivering the letter. "Thank you for looking after it. I need to continue rehearsing." *How am I going to do this now? Am I overreacting? Could it be a letter from a normal person? Then why no name from the sender? Get back to music. I can't worry about this now. I can't let them spoil the work I'm doing. If this should be some kind of a joke I'll wring that person's neck.*

Just when Daniel walked back to the podium, the president waved to him. He came closer and whispered, "The officer wants to talk to you but I told him that he had to wait, that you couldn't be disturbed."

Daniel nodded. "Thank you. I'll get to him later." He closed his eyes for a moment. *Music first, everything else has to wait.*

Continuing with Saint-Saëns he knew that he would have to repeat the whole symphony to make it sound cohesive. Timewise that was not possible. The musicians' union put a limit on the hours they could work. He had to stick to it. Maybe just as well, he thought. *I'll have to talk to the officer waiting for me, whether I like it or not.*

❧❧❧

The officer rose from the chair when he saw Daniel. "Sorry for the wait," Daniel said. "This job comes first."

The policeman smiled. "I know how that feels. Now this letter." He turned it over in his hands. "No idea where it came from?"

"If I knew you wouldn't be here." *Silly question.* Daniel filled him in with some of the history of threats. "I want to make sure that nothing toxic is in there. Take it to your lab. After almost being killed twice I'm getting careful."

The officer nodded. "I have the description of the guy who delivered the letter. We'll be looking for him. Can you make a statement?"

"When? Now? Can I get a ride with you?"

The officer nodded. "Sure. That would be the best." He looked at Daniel. "That music sounded powerful. I might come to the performance."

Daniel had to smile now. "I'm happy with any new fan I can get." He felt easier. Whoever the culprit was he probably wouldn't anticipate the quick reaction to the letter. So he had a bit of time to get home safely to the kids. To make sure he called Mia once more. Yes, they were back at the hotel. *Lord, if I ever needed a drink, it's now.*

Daniel wasn't sure if he should tell Mia and Julian about the letter. It would scare them all over again just when they felt safe. What if it was a hoax? *But I'm barely here, just for the concerts.* No, he had to tell them.

Their reaction was predictable. Mia cried and Julian pounded his fist on the table. "Beasts!" he shouted. "Leave us alone."

Daniel raised his hands. "Calm down, kids. It's only a letter, the police are taking care of it. Maybe by tomorrow, they will have found the person who delivered it."

Mia wiped her eyes. "But what about us, Papa? Can't we go anywhere?"

"I'll do what I have to do. You two can come with me and hang out in the music library if you want to."

Both children nodded.

"For now let's have supper—with extra desserts." Daniel needed to see them smile again. But both of them remained thoughtful through the evening.

Before going to bed Mia asked, "Which one of those people would be in London to do that? How do they know you're here?"

Daniel shook his head. "I'm just as baffled as you, Mia. Let's hope we hear some good news tomorrow. Try not to worry all night. Promise?"

Mia nodded. "Good night, Papa?"

Daniel knew that Mia would worry just like Elvira used to. He looked at his wife's picture. What would she think about all this? "Any ideas, Love? Will it end?" he mumbled. "It has to, put a good word in for us, please."

He needed some sleep to be ready for all the music tomorrow. It would be a long day.

The theater the next morning was humming. Daniel had no idea what speculations the musicians might have seeing him leaving with a policeman.

At the start of the rehearsal, he looked out to them and said, "There was a small incident concerning my safety yesterday. But it's being taken care of by the police. Now we have work to do. I hope you all had a good breakfast." *At least I hear some chuckles.* "Let's get started." Daniel was determined to go through all of the music.

To his surprise, the two first pieces went well. Small corrections could be worked out tomorrow. At lunchtime one of the managers joined Daniel.

"We got confirmation from the police that the letter contained a powdery substance, some drug, with a note saying, 'We're not finished yet.'"

"Didn't I know it," Daniel growled. "What drug?"

The manager shrugged. "Apparently it wouldn't have harmed you unless you had breathed it in." His phone rang. After he had answered it he beamed. "They found the delivery boy. I'm so glad, Maestro."

Daniel let out a breath. "So am I. Thank you for taking over."

"We invited you to make music. We feel responsible for your safety." The manager got up and put his hand on Daniel's shoulder. "Let's hope the boy knows the person who gave him the letter."

Daniel sat quietly with another cup of coffee. *Is my Guardian Angel at work again? This couldn't have happened any faster.*

Mia and Julian walked in. "We're hungry," Julian announced.

"Good, go to it—without too many sweets. I have some good news." Daniel told them what the manager had just found out. He heard two sighs of relief.

"It's not the end of it, but it's the best we have so far. You know the rules." Daniel got up. "I'll have to go on now."

Mia waved from the counter. "See you later."

Good to see them happier again.

Chapter 38

At the end of the rehearsal Daniel was happy with everyone. One more run-through would make it almost perfect. Totally perfect could only be in the composer's mind. Tonight he would listen to Mark Hamel's recital. Daniel was curious about how much he had progressed in the last few years.

Just when Daniel picked up Mia and Julian from the library a policeman came up to him, a different one from yesterday. "Mr. Abogado, we have some news regarding the letter you got yesterday."

"Oh good, tell me." Daniel felt prickly all over.

"The delivery boy showed us the person who gave it to him, a woman." He checked his notebook. "Elizabeth Avery."

Daniel stared at him. "Avery? That's Brent Avery's wife. Blackbeard's wife?"

The officer shrugged. "I don't know…"

"No, you wouldn't. That's my past. I know now why I got the letter. Where is she now?"

"In custody on several charges."

Daniel brushed his hand over his hair. "Thank you. It all makes sense to me now. You have my statement. Let me know if you need me."

Mia and Julian had stood back listening. Now they talked both at the same time. "Who's Brent Avery?" "His wife?" "Why?" "Here in London?"

Daniel had to explain on their way back to the hotel and refresh their memory.

"So, Blackbeard's wife wants to revenge his death?" Mia asked. "But you didn't kill him."

"No, his next-in-line did who wanted to take over. But I was part of exposing the gang. We're getting there. Hey, let's celebrate with a piece of pie."

With a lot of talking and guessing about the events of the two last days, the afternoon went by quickly.

⌘

After supper, Mia and Julian couldn't wait to get ready for the recital. "I'll bet he's sooo good," Julian said.

"After all these years of playing he will be," Mia added.

Daniel looked at her. "You're looking nice with your new skirt."

"Thank you. This is a special occasion." She tried to put her curly hair into a ponytail.

Daniel smiled. *This is the first time she has dressed up for anyone.*

At the recital hall, Daniel said, "I'm not sitting up front. I don't want Mark to get nervous because of me being too close."

"Nice place," Mia said. "Will we meet him afterward?"

Daniel nodded. "You bet. I'll invite him for a drink."

Julian looked at the program. "Great, I'll have questions to ask him."

Poor Mark.

When the light dimmed a lady announced Mark Hamel. Mia whispered, "Break a leg, Mark."

Daniel added, "I agree."

The program consisted of Chopin, Schubert, Mozart, and a Spanish piece by Albeniz. Daniel was impressed.

During a short break, he saw tears in Mia's eyes. "Schubert is so emotional," she breathed.

"Then Mark has managed to touch you," Daniel said.

Julian was quiet. Daniel nudged him. "What do you think?"

Julian's eyes were big. "He's amazing. I wish I could get that good."

Daniel put his arm around Julian's shoulders. "If you want to be then you'll be, with a lot of practice."

"So many different pieces. How can he remember them all?"

"It all comes with years of training. You'll have lots of time to do that."

"Yeah, but I'm almost eleven already," Julian still sounded concerned.

Daniel laughed. "Mark is twelve years older than you. Stop worrying and keep on playing."

The audience showed their approval by a long applause. Mark had to give an encore. He chose a short Bach piece. After that Daniel went to the front and gestured to Mark to meet them.

Mark glowed with pride. "In your wise opinion, Maestro, did I improve?"

Daniel clapped him on the shoulder. "You did great, you grew musically. You deserve a drink or two."

At the restaurant Julian bombarded Mark with questions: how many hours did he practice, how easy was it for him to sight read, did he ever get nervous before playing. Mark tried to smile at Mia in between Julian's talking.

Daniel saw her smiling back. Her eyes lit up when Mark asked her, "Did you like the music I chose?" She explained her reaction to the Schubert piece.

Then Mark asked Daniel, "Can I listen to your performance together with Mia and Julian? I'm still here for a few days."

Daniel looked at him. "I suppose that's all right. But don't forget, she's my daughter."

Mark bowed his head with a humorous glint in his eyes. "I swear, Sir, no harm will come to her—or your son. It's just nicer not to sit there by myself."

Daniel laughed out loud. "What a clever guy you are. Let's drink to that." He didn't have the heart to play the strict father at the first sign of mutual affection. He hadn't been any different at that age. Not different at all.

℘℘℘

Rehearsal the next morning consisted of music scheduled for the outdoor concerts. Daniel thought it would give the orchestra a break from the previous pieces and have fun playing the—what they would call—pop classics of Mozart, Rossini, Bizet, Delius, and Elgar. In Daniel's mind, shorter compositions had to be rehearsed as carefully as the heavier ones. No matter how small, the composer had something in mind that moved him and it had to show. He told the musicians, "Have fun but be precise."

As Daniel knew repeats were unavoidable. At lunchtime he decided to run through it again. After his first cup of coffee, he called the police station. He wanted to know more about this Mrs. Avery. The officer hesitated to give any information, but Daniel convinced him that it was part of keeping him and the children safe.

"Well, Sir, she told us that you were the cause of her husband's death and she wanted to remind you of it."

"Can I hope that this was all she was going to do or did she have other threats in mind?"

"Apparently not, Sir."

Daniel sighed. "Or so she says. Thank you, officer." *Is this now really the end of worrying, waiting, guessing? Hopefully, Inspector Lankin knows that Mrs. Avery has been caught. I'm still not sure if she hasn't already employed someone to continue her revenge.* He looked at his watch. *Time to continue making music.*

At the end of the rehearsal, he called out to the musicians, "Tomorrow is the big day. Let's put everything we've got into it."

"Of course," the concertmaster called back with a grin on his face, "we're number one."

Daniel had to laugh too. "That is encouraging. Maybe I can look around London for a bit now."

Chapter 39

Daniel took Mia and Daniel to the British Museum. Culture had many faces and London had all of them. He loved to watch the wonder in his children's eyes as they looked at the Egyptian exhibition as well as toys, old-fashioned Chinaware and stern-looking busts from history. Mia even took a notebook out of her bag and scribbled into it as both of them moved from place to place. Daniel smiled. *My daughter, the forever student.*

Out of habit, he kept his eyes open looking around. But people moved quite normally among the exhibits. Time passed quickly and, while the kids could have looked around more, Daniel was ready for supper. All this walking and discovering was more tiring than studying scores. *I'm a bit out of shape.* He felt happy that he could spend time with Mia and Julian. It had been a long time since they had done this together.

At bedtime, he could still hear them discussing the things they had seen. *I deserve a brandy tonight.* With the glass in his hand, Daniel walked onto the balcony and relaxed. He looked out over the city. *What a busy place London is and how old.* He heard his cellphone chime. Someone had texted him. Lydia! *My Lord, what a surprise. She's actually thinking of me.* The message wished him good luck for his first engagement in London and ended with "I miss being there and applauding."

Daniel had tried not to think about Lydia too often. He needed to focus on the performances, on eighty-plus musicians who didn't know him. Then there was Mrs. Avery's try for revenge. He was going to text Lydia right back. *What a great ending to this day.*

∾

Before breakfast the next morning Daniel received a call from Inspector Lankin. "I wanted to get you out of bed before you phoned me again," he started. "According to London police, Mrs. Avery is one angry female. But she's not talking about the man who killed her husband as if she isn't interested. She must have known that he wanted to take over the reign. We're still looking for him."

"Could the two of them have planned Rupert's death?" Daniel asked.

Lankin harrumphed. "Why would she go to prison and he gets away? Unless she wants him to disappear."

"She hasn't confessed to her husband's murder, but to threaten me is going to put the emphasis on her and give him time to run," Daniel said. "What a scheming woman. That is *if* they both did it."

The inspector sighed. "Your brain goes on overtime again. But we're working on the case."

"Thank you for letting me know, Inspector. Call me if there is any news." *Where did I get the idea of them both being in the killing together? If that were true why didn't she take off with him? No, something doesn't fit. I need breakfast.*

After Daniel finally had his second cup of coffee the morning continued with one more run-through for the outdoor concerts. It needed two rehearsals consistent with his habits. He would have liked to add a soloist like Mark Hamel but management decided against it.

When Daniel was convinced that the music sounded good enough for two afternoons in the park, he dismissed the musicians. "See you all fired up tonight," he told them.

To make sure that he was also able to do his best he needed some alone time. He let Mia and Julian watch TV in their bedroom and stretched out on his bed. He tried to quieten his mind but the music for tonight vibrated through him as well as thoughts about Lydia. Too bad she was twelve hours flight time away. Where they ever seeing each other again? Maybe after Daniel got back to San Francisco it would be possible. *I'll call her tomorrow. It will be nice to hear her voice. Why Lydia?* Daniel closed his eyes. *Now isn't the time to explain strange attractions, they just are.*

⁀ↄ℮ↄ

After supper, Daniel took Mia and Julian with him to the Symphony Hall. "Stay in the lobby for now. Mark will probably appear pretty soon." He winked at Mia. She blushed. "I have to warn you, sweetheart. You won't see him too often after today. He has quite a few engagements."

Mia nodded. "I hope so, with his talent."

And it's all right with me too. I want Mia around for a long time.

Now his mind had to be on the performance, to live in the music, feel every note, every nuance which he had to convey to the orchestra. But his thoughts drifted over to Lydia again. Eight o'clock would be lunchtime in Oregon. Was she thinking of him? *Enough, time to get real.* He changed into his performance clothes, took out his baton, and said, "Point me in the right direction, okay?" Funny, he thought, how things you work with become like companions. *Now let me wallow in sounds which came from minds I can't even comprehend.*

Musicians were settling in on stage. Far away murmuring drifted from the lobby. *The audience is probably curious if I bring anything new. Let's dazzle them.*

When Daniel strode on stage the applause sounded more enthusiastic than he had expected. After all, he was new here. He showed the musicians two-thumbs-up and *Prince Igor's* overture began.

Applause rose after that and was followed by some bravos. Good start, Daniel thought. Next Liszt's Hungarian Rhapsody. That too got strong approval from the audience. Daniel couldn't help smiling. At the intermission, everyone beamed. Daniel heard one musician saying, "Good audience." "Good conductor," Robin, the concertmaster, added.

Daniel had a drink of water and wondered where Mia, Julian, and Mark were sitting. He paced around, his mind already deeply into Saint-Saëns. *Let's show them what this composer can do.*

From the first quiet bars through the many emotions set to music to the thundering organ at the end Daniel lived in another world. He heard people gasp at the organ's sudden final statement that followed a few seconds of silence.

It seemed that the audience had to take a breath after the last chords, then the applause shook the hall. Daniel just stood there, amazed, and bowed again and again. He finally walked off the stage. The people didn't give up and he had to appear again. *I didn't expect that, this is— unbelievable.* Daniel was sure that London had heard this music before, but maybe not for a while. He headed for the dressing room. His shirt felt damp, and his head still hummed with the orchestra's sounds. *Yes, that was a success. Now to find Mia and Julian.*

Chapter 40

Daniel opened the stage door carefully. He could hear people's voices leaving the theater and wasn't quite ready to give autographs. But a few young women came running up with exactly that request. *One way to get famous.* He smiled and wrote his name on their programs. "We adored your program," one of them said.

Mia, Julian, and Mark waited nearby, Mia giggling and Julian jumping up and down. Daniel could finally hug his kids. Mark stood back.

"All right, Mark, what do you have to say?" Daniel asked him.

Mark shook his head. "I don't know what to say, Maestro. I was blown away."

Daniel chuckled. "I accept your response. Now I need to sit down with some food and a drink. But you, my children, need to get home."

"Oow, no, Papa," came the protest. Mark looked at them. "I'll bring you home if that's okay with your Dad."

"Only if you come back here," Daniel said.

Mark raised his hands. "I'll swear, Sir, I wouldn't miss it."

Mia and Julian still frowned, but then Mia looked at Mark. "Okay, we'll go."

At the restaurant, Daniel met a boisterous crowd of musicians already into their second drinks. They started clapping and cheering him. *That's my reward for the best job in the world.*

Mark came back and got a warm welcome from musicians who had attended his recital. After a quick meal, Daniel sat back and observed the happy crowd. *I think I passed the test.* One hour passed quickly and he started to yawn. Daniel got up. "Time for me to say good night. Thank you all for your great work. See you tomorrow." Outside he took a deep breath. *One amazing evening.*

At the hotel, Daniel could hear Mia and Julian still talking in the bedroom. He knocked on the door. "Time to sleep, kids, see you in the morning."

"Yes, Papa," came two voices.

Daniel wasn't sure if he would sleep, although he couldn't keep his eyes open. "Calm down," he told himself, "One more of the same tomorrow night."

☙❧

When Daniel woke up the next morning, he was surprised that he had overslept. He heard Mia and Julian talking and scrambled out of the blankets. *Time to become human again.* Mia came out of the bedroom.

"Good morning. The music was—wow. Breakfast soon?"

"Five minutes—or ten." *Forever hungry kids.*

After coffee, pancakes, and fruit Daniel wondered how to fill the day. Apart from a few phone calls, he had a lot of time until evening. Unusual for me, he thought. And the children? "Any ideas on what to do today?"

"A hike somewhere," Mia suggested.

"Or a big playground," Julian added.

"Okay, let's go to Hyde Park where we perform tomorrow," Daniel said. "It's not hiking but close to it." Since musical performances had been given before, there would be a platform, hopefully big enough for all the musicians. Mia wanted to jog around and Daniel had to remind her not to go too far. "Remember? Safety rules still exist."

It felt good to just relax for a few hours and breathe quietly. Nevertheless, the music for tonight was not far away from his brain. All sounds around him turned into instruments. *I should call it a privilege.* Out of habit he still observed people around them. *I might do that for the rest of my life.*

∽∾∽

That evening almost as many people filled the theater as the night before. "Maybe the word got around," the concertmaster said, "after our epic performance yesterday."

Daniel chuckled. "Epic? Isn't that a bit heavy?"

Robin shrugged. "Why not? It felt like that to me."

"It was very good, yes," Daniel admitted. "Let's do it again."

When the lights dimmed a quick hush fell over the audience. That's eerie, Daniel thought. But at his entrance, the applause came strong and loud. Again he gave the musicians his thumbs-up sign and the baton came down.

The audience responded again with enthusiasm. Daniel enjoyed himself. *Another great communication between composers and people hundreds of years apart.* During the intermission, his phone rang. *What, the kids?* To his delight, he heard Lydia's voice.

"Congratulations, Daniel. Your name was mentioned in the newspaper. I knew you would convince London of your talent."

Daniel's heart did a flop. "Thank you for calling. I'm right in the intermission. Yes, it's going very well. I wish you were here, you would enjoy it."

Lydia giggled. "If I had a transporter from Star Trek I would do it. I'll send you an email instead."

"Small compensation, but I'm glad we have that. I have to go back for the last big piece. Write soon, okay?"

"I will. Bye for now." Lydia hung up.

What am I doing? Am I really falling for Lydia? Why? What is so different? Daniel shook his head. Just hearing her voice made him happy, even though he knew so little about her. *Slow down, get back to work.*

⌘⌘⌘

The end of the performance turned again into a long session of applause and bravos. Daniel's shirt clung damp on his body as on the night before and he was happy. Yes, he had made his musical footprint in London. A bit late in my life, he thought, but it doesn't matter. To his surprise, Mark was waiting at the stage door.

"Just in case you would be mobbed by pretty girls I wanted to save you," he said with his impish grin.

Daniel laughed. "I might need you tomorrow in the park."

Mark shook his head. "I have to leave tomorrow for Amsterdam with a piano concerto by Chopin." He walked with Daniel to the restaurant. "Promise me to give my greetings to Mia. She is beautiful."

Daniel looked at him. "Don't you ever break her heart. I'll go after you forever."

"No, no, we talked about me being all over the place, but I'll keep in touch. I'll promise."

At the restaurant Mark said goodbye. "I have an early flight. Maestro, I'm grateful to have met you again and being able to listen to your work." They shook hands. Daniel put his hand on his shoulder. "You'll succeed. Don't lose heart when things get tough." He hated to see him go already. *A musician's life: beautiful but restless.* After another wave, Daniel opened the restaurant's door. *Before I faint dead away I'll need food and my usual brandy.*

❧❧❧

Later, on his way back to the hotel, Daniel's thoughts turned already to the next day's music in the park. Hopefully, it wouldn't rain. Some strange feeling made him turn around. A dark figure behind him slowed down. *Someone following me?* Daniel had only a few more steps to the hotel's door. He ran up the stairs. In the lobby, he shouted at the desk clerk. "I've been followed. Call the police." Ice cubes rolled around in his stomach.

The door opened and a masked, dark-clothed man came in and stopped. He stared at Daniel. "Just wanted to meet the person who ruined our lives," he growled.

Daniel's heart thumped. Anger shot up in him. "*Your* lives? What about mine and my children's?" He kept his voice low. "And now what? Kill me? Adding one more to your other victims?"

A piercing clanging of a bell went off and more people joined the desk clerk. But the man walked closer and produced a long knife. "Say your prayers, music man."

Daniel had backed up holding his baton case in front of him. His insides shook. *Is he going to rush me?* He tore the case open and grabbed the baton. He swung it at the man. "You want a fight? I'll slice off your hand." For a second the man stopped.

The front door swung open, and two policemen rushed in. "Drop the knife. Get down on the floor."

Daniel leaned against the counter. The man still grinned at him. "This time you win," he grunted. One of the officers cuffed him while the other one came over to Daniel.

"You just handed us the suspect in the murder of Brent Avery, your Blackbeard. We knew he was here but never thought he would show himself."

Daniel tried to get his breath back. "And there I thought I was safe. Thanks for coming so quickly."

The officer pointed to Daniel's baton and smiled. "What a unique weapon. It would have sliced him."

Daniel started to chuckle. "This is how I defend myself against eighty musicians. I never thought it would be used this way." He turned to the clerk. "The alarm almost killed my eardrums. I need another drink." He turned to the policeman. "Yes, I'll come in tomorrow and make a report. I knew you would ask."

When the police car disappeared, he sank into a seat and closed his eyes. *Is this going to be the last time—finally?*

After a while, Daniel made his way up to his suite. Why didn't that man jump me on the street? he thought. He wanted to see me being afraid. What a mindset.

Mia and Julian slept in their beds. *Amazing. They must have woken up from that infernal bell.* Daniel knew the policy of the hotel was to stay in their rooms unless otherwise advised. Now he needed a shower. Several layers on his body had to be washed away—the sweat of the work and the feeling of evil.

He felt better after that and soon collapsed into bed with a loud groan.

Chapter 41

Daniel's first thought on waking up the next morning was, What do I tell Mia and Julian? Should I tell them that boss number two has been captured? Would it scare them again? By breakfast time he had made up his mind. When Mia asked, "That crazy bell woke us up last night. What was that about, Papa?" he needed to answer but as concise as possible.

"The man that killed Blackbeard came after me in the lobby but the police got him. The desk clerk pushed the button for the bell."

Both children were quiet and stared at him. Then Mia asked, "Did he attack you? Are we safe now, Papa? I mean, really safe?"

Daniel sipped his coffee. "I think so, Mia. Too many of his people are already in jail now. Even if someone starts the smuggling up again, we're out of it. The police will keep an eye on them in various countries."

Julian picked up a piece of toast. "Were you scared when that man came after you? I would've screamed."

"Yes, I admit I was. But…" Daniel smiled. "I threatened him with my baton."

After a pause, both kids broke down laughing. "Like fencing? Your baton, a weapon?"

Daniel sighed with relief. They took it well, maybe because of so many close calls they had experienced. He knew they would have more questions—later. For now, he had to get ready for this afternoon's concert. He also needed to do his report at the police station. He wanted them to let Inspector Lankin know of this incident. "Stay here," Daniel told Mia and Julian. "When I come back we have to get ready for the concert in the park."

❧❧❧

As the concert was announced for three o'clock Daniel arrived at the park early to make sure all was set up properly. Since various bands had played here previously he was sure the workers could be trusted to do a good job. Nevertheless, he had to see it for himself. So far the weather had held off the rain, although clouds covered most of the sky.

To Daniel's surprise, people were already walking into the area where benches and chairs had been set up. Some carried their own seats, even sported umbrellas. The musicians were transported in two buses to forego the parking problem. Daniel remembered Oakland where the buses had been sabotaged. Hopefully, the criminal element had been dealt with this time.

Daniel instructed Mia and Julian to stay close. They had supplied themselves with enough snacks and sodas to—what they called—survive the afternoon.

"We have an audience," the concertmaster commented. "You drew them in again, Maestro."

Daniel smiled. "Just pray for dry weather." He checked his watch. "Let's get ready. You're on." He stepped through the side entrance. On his return, he heard clapping and cheering. *This will be fun.*

The audience seemed to enjoy his choice of music and a few couples were tempted to dance to the waltzes. Fresh air and music, Daniel thought, what a great combination. We should do this more often at home.

After one-and-a-half hours, during the last piece, the first raindrops fell. Umbrellas went up and some people left. But that did not stop the cheering and clapping. Later Daniel could not avoid some young ladies asking for his autograph. *I should be flattered.* Mia and Julian stood at the side giggling. He shot them a stern look. *Let me have some fun, kids.*

On their way home Julian said, "I'll bet they all wanted to marry you, Papa."

Daniel chuckled. "Whew! How fortunate I don't stay for too long. Otherwise, I might create a riot." Both children giggled and chatted until suppertime.

෬෬෬

During the rest of the evening, Daniel's thoughts turned to concerts he had been asked to give in Vancouver, Canada, in Munich, Germany, and back in San Francisco. Vancouver was slated for August as a special concert, purely Berlioz: his *Symphony Fantastique* and *Overture to Le Corsaire.* In September the regular season started in San Francisco, also in Seattle. Munich wanted winter music after Christmas. In the meantime, Daniel knew there would be an extra guest appearance somewhere. He was going to get as much leisure time as possible during the rest of July.

He also wanted to see Lydia again. How to do that? He wasn't sure if he wanted to wait until September at the Seattle Chamber Concert. Would she be willing to come to Vancouver? He wouldn't have her feel like she was "Running after him." Daniel grabbed his cell phone. *Time to write her an e-mail. I want to keep in touch as much as possible.*

❧

Before breakfast the next morning Daniel got a phone call from the president of the London Symphony. "I wanted to catch you before you disappear," he said. "You have done great work, Daniel. We would like you to come back as a guest conductor very soon."

Oh nice. But do I have time for that? "Thank you, Sir. What did you have in mind time-wise?"

"November? Any chance at all?"

Daniel took a minute to think. "November is a busy time before Christmas concerts. How about October?" He told him about his other engagements.

"That would work," came the answer. "I have to consult with our Maestro and the rest of the group." The president sounded excited. "Can you come over on Monday morning to confirm this?"

"We leave at three o'clock in the afternoon so, yes, make it ten in the morning."

"Great, see you then."

They ended the conversation. Yes, Daniel was happy. London was an important step in his success. The next time he would have to leave the children at home. They had school and needed continuity. Mrs. Gantrey would have to help as a babysitter again.

"Mia and Julian let's go for breakfast. Time to refuel my artistic endeavors." Of course, they had been waiting by the door already.

❧

The last concert that afternoon took place in another park. The weather had cleared up. People were coming in early and brought picnic hampers. It's one way to get classical music to people who can't pay for theater seats, Daniel thought.

Just before the start of the concert Daniel heard a gasp in the audience and saw people pointing fingers. What he saw made him laugh out loud. "A streaker! Can you imagine? On a Sunday afternoon?" The nude figure of a man sprinted across the grassy area near the bandshell. "He's fast," the concertmaster said. "He could win a real race." The sound of police sirens came nearer and the man disappeared into some bushes.

After the musicians had settled down again and stopped laughing, Daniel got up on the podium and called, "Let's start with our march in the program to give him a proper send-off." That brought on another bout of chuckles.

The audience clapped and cheered after each piece of music. Daniel was glad he had agreed to the two outdoor presentations. At the end of the concert, the musicians stayed seated and the concertmaster came up to Daniel.

"Since you're leaving tomorrow we all would like to thank you for the great performances you were able to conduct. Some of us would like to invite you for a dinner at the restaurant. Would that be agreeable with you?"

Daniel was surprised. He had been ready to just thank the musicians, wave goodbye, and go on his way. "Yes, wonderful. But I have to bring my two kids along if that's all right. There they are." He pointed to Mia and Julian coming up the steps.

"No problem, they can join us."

Daniel motioned to the children to wait. Some of the musicians came up to him and shook his hand. "Lead on," he told them. "We'll follow."

With a meal, some wine, and lively conversation Daniel enjoyed the evening. Even Mia and Julian laughed hearing tales of mishaps during various performances. At the end, the concertmaster raised his glass and said, "Hopefully we'll see the maestro again soon."

"Probably, Robin. The president already called me about it. In the meantime thank you for your good work."

After the toasting Daniel was ready to go somewhere quiet so they could get their belongings packed for tomorrow. With a lot of waves, he closed the door of the restaurant and took a deep breath.

"Really nice people," Mia said. "Will you come back here, Papa?"

Daniel nodded. "Most likely in October. But you have to stay home. Now let's go and get organized for the flight tomorrow." He looked at his watch. Could he give Inspector Lankin one last call? Then he remembered it being Sunday. He would have to wait until Monday. To his joy, he got another email from Lydia. She always puts a smile on my face, he thought. I really have to check my feelings. How would I feel if I never saw her again? I have to be one hundred percent sure before I go any further. Daniel knew this was the first woman he felt comfortable with—and a bit more—since Elvira's death. But it had only been two years. Her memory was still too fresh. Give it time, he told himself.

Chapter 42

After an early breakfast—at least in Daniel's mind—he called a taxi to get to the theater. He didn't feel like carrying everyone's luggage through the streets. While Mia and Julian stayed at a bookshop he made his way to the president's office.

The managers already sat around the table with their steaming coffee mugs. "Would you like a cup, Maestro?" one of the men asked.

"Yes, thank you." Daniel sat down. *They look rather serious.*

"You did some great performances. Even the outdoor ones sounded fresh." The president smiled. "I was there listening."

Daniel sipped his coffee. "Your musicians are very good to work with, as I knew they would be."

The president continued. "Are you still all right with October?"

Daniel nodded. "As far as I can see, yes. What music did you have in mind?"

The managers looked at each other. "My suggestion is one long one and two shorter pieces like we had this time," said one of them.

"Yes, I agree." The president poured another cup of coffee. "How about Beethoven's Triple Concerto?"

"If we can afford three soloists," the finance director interrupted.

"We'll have to," another manager answered. "It's too great a piece to miss. Would you agree with that, Maestro?"

"I certainly would." *I'll listen to Karajan's famous tape again.* "I also would suggest Mark Hamel as the pianist. He's a special guy of mine." *Mark would be thrilled.* "Is there a date in October?"

"We can work that out with our Maestro and let you know as soon as possible." The president rose and everyone shook hands with Daniel.

After more good wishes and thank-you's Daniel made his way back into the bookstore to pick up Mia and Julian. He felt elated by the outcome of the Philharmonic's decisions music-wise and time-wise. "All right, kids, let's get to the airport."

"I'm glad to go home," Mia said.

"Yes, me too," Julian added. "I miss my piano."

Daniel's phone chirped. *Now what?* He heard Lydia's voice. "Just wanted to wish you a good flight. Let me know when you get home, please."

"I certainly will, Lydia. You couldn't be there to open the front door, could you?" Daniel thought that it would make her laugh. Yes, she giggled.

"Sorry, maybe another time. Be safe up in the air, Daniel. I'm waiting for your email. Bye for now."

Daniel felt a small tug at his heart. *I need to know all I can about her and soon.*

During the eight-hour flight, Daniel partly dozed and read magazines while Mia and Julian enjoyed films and music. But at nine o'clock both fell asleep. "Two more hours," Daniel mumbled. He would have two weeks until it was time to select the music for his first performance in September. Maybe for a change something spooky like *On*

Bald Mountain by Mussorgsky and something exotic like *Scheherazade* by Rimsky Korsakov? Of course, Seattle's Chamber Orchestra was waiting for their program. And what about Munich in January? That still needed clarification about the music. Hopefully a concert with a soloist.

❧❧❧

At the San Francisco airport the line-ups for Customs checks were long. When they finally emerged at the exit Daniel stopped. *No way, that couldn't be. Lydia?* There she stood with a big smile on her face.

"What are you doing all the way down here?" Daniel almost stuttered.

Lydia laughed. "Do you remember Portland where I picked you up at the airport? So, why not here?"

Daniel shook her hand. "You fooled me again but I'm happy about it."

"Let's go then. You need to get home." Lydia went ahead of them to the car park. Daniel still couldn't believe this turn of events. And it made him excited and happy.

During the ride home, Daniel answered her many questions about his London performances. Julian interrupted at one point. "Papa almost sliced a guy with his baton."

"That story needs to wait, Julian," Daniel said. "Not everything all at once." He was glad Lydia didn't press for it.

At his house, she stayed in the car. "You need to relax, get some rest. I'll call you tomorrow."

"Promise? Don't fly home already." Daniel needed to talk to her a lot more.

"I wouldn't come all the way down here for only a few hours." Lydia waved and drove away. Daniel just stood and looked after her disappearing car.

"She loves you, Papa," Julian announced with an impish grin.

Mia frowned. "Isn't she a bit pushy, Papa?"

Daniel laughed. "I told her as a joke to open the front door for us. I just didn't think she would almost do it. I'm glad about it. She'll be a good friend, also for you."

"Hope so. Right now I'm hungry." In the house, Mia pulled a can of spaghetti and meatballs out of the cupboard. Her phone rang. After checking her face lit up. "It's Mark! He emailed me. His concert went really well and he will keep in touch."

"Well, well, so he keeps his promises." Daniel enjoyed Mia's beaming face. But he was restless. "I'm going for a quick walk to get my legs going again after eight hours of sitting." He needed to jog and clear his mind.

Before he realized it, Daniel had reached the small park in the neighborhood. He knew that he had to be honest with himself about Lydia. He wanted her as a friend. Yes, he was also sure it might turn into more. He had been too happy to see her at the airport. *What made her do that? She took my joke seriously. What about Mia? Could she be friends with Lydia after only two years after losing her mother? Maybe her visit will help.*

He also needed to work hard to get his assignments in place, write them all down with musical ideas at the side and pin them up on his corkboard. His mind had to be organized before he could enjoy the next two weeks.

Daniel sighed. He was not going to push for any more than friendship with Lydia right now. It could only be one between miles apart and emails. He was sure, she was aware of it. Just now he was happy to be home again and to let the next weeks lead him into the next part of his life. Hopefully without any more criminal interference. For that Daniel was going to talk to Inspector Lankin once more to make sure.

On his way home he felt as if a weight had lifted off his shoulders for the first time in a long while. He was as sure as anyone could be that he would now be able to properly concentrate on his music, his family, and to be ready for a friendship with a pretty, blue-eyed lady.

About the Author

Gisela Woldenga was born in Oldenburg, Germany, on July 21, 1934. As soon as she could read she started to write: little poems and fairy tales. She still has some of them. When she finished high school, she started working in a lawyer's office, mostly disputes over last wills and testaments and property. Then she moved on to the main taxation office. She met her husband through pen paling—he was already in Canada—and she joined him in 1954 in Ontario. She had her first baby in 1956, her second one in 1957, then moved to Vancouver, BC, and added another baby in 1961.

Woldenga picked up music (piano) again in 1964, started teaching shortly after, and taught for a time. In the meantime, she wrote articles, poems, children's stories. She also took up acting after her kids were safely gone from home, in 1998. Lots of fun! She's still doing it whenever possible. After some courses in writing for children, she started publishing. From there, on into short stories for adults and finally five books.